Chiesa Russa
VIALE LAVAGNINI
58
59
VIA S. REPARATA
VIA S. GALLO
VIA CAVOUR
VIALE GIACOMO MATTEOTTI
FIESOL
VIA 27 APRILE
GUELFA
Piazza S.Marco
60
61
Via Gino Capponi
English Cemetery
64
65
Via Giuseppe Giusti
Mercato
VIA RICASOLI
VIA DEI SERVI
VIA DEGLI ALFANI
VIA DELLA COLONNA
BORGO PINTI
VIALE ANTONIO GRAMSCI
28
29
68
69
Via Calimala
Via dei Calzaiuoli
Via del Corso
Borgo degli Albizi
32
33
72
73
Borgo la Croce
70
71
Via Ghibellina
Via por S. Maria
Via del Proconsolo
34
35
Piazza S. Croce
Viale della Giovine Italia
L. Medici
76
77
Lungarno d. Grazie
Lungarno d. Zecca Vecchia
Ponte alle Grazie
Lungarno Serristori
Lungarno Cellini
Ponte S. Niccolò
80
81
Forte di Belvedere
82
83
Viale G. Poggi
Piazzale Michelangelo
VIALE MICHELANGELO
VIALE GALILEO
S. Miniato

John Kent's

FLORENCE & SIENA

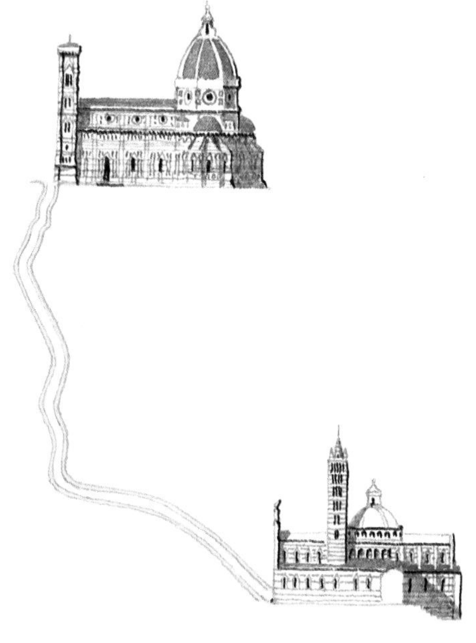

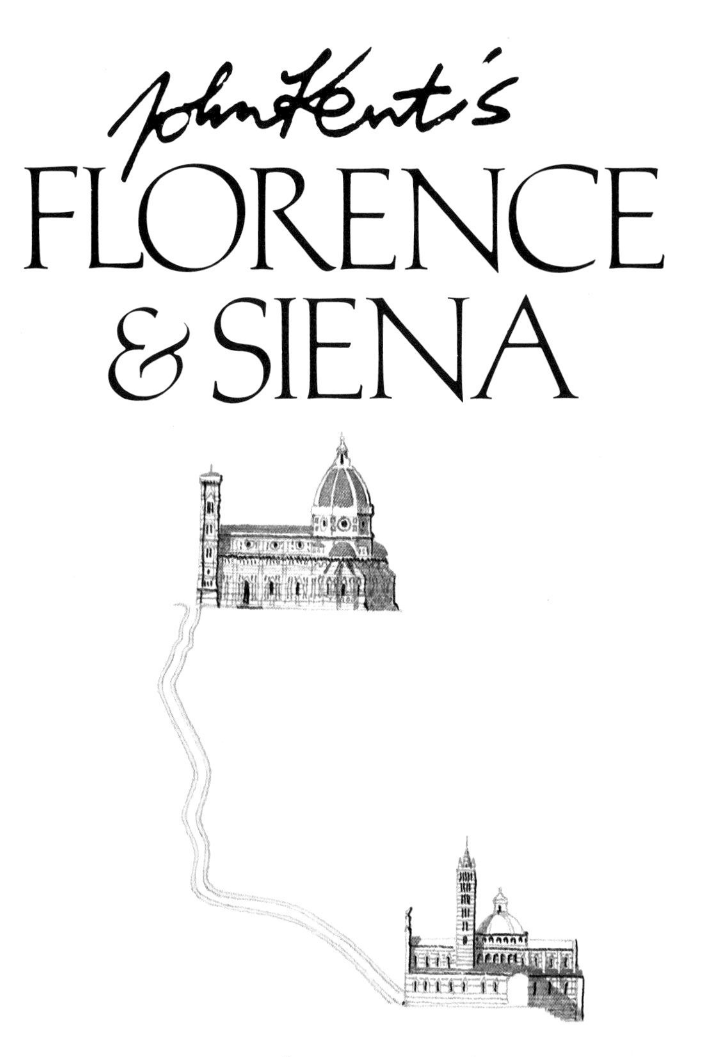

A Colour Guide to the Cities

VIKING

To Nina
who loves Florence but
never has time to get there,
and with special thanks to
Linda Martelli
for her help and her cucina

VIKING

Published by the Penguin Group
27 Wrights Lane, London W8 5TZ, England
Viking Penguin Inc., 40 West 23rd Street, New York, New York 10010, USA
Penguin Books Australia Ltd, Ringwood, Victoria, Australia
Penguin Books Canada Ltd. 2801 John Street, Markham, Ontario, Canada L3R 1B4
Penguin Books (NZ) Ltd, 182–190 Wairau Road, Auckland 10, New Zealand

Penguin Books Ltd, Registered Offices: Harmondsworth, Middlesex, England

First published 1989

1 3 5 7 9 10 8 6 4 2

Filmset in 10/11 Linotron 202 Bembo by
Wyvern Typesetting Ltd, Bristol

Printed in Italy

A CIP catalogue record for this book is available from the British Library

ISBN 0-670-81797 X

Library of Congress Catalog Number
88-82383

Contents

FLORENCE

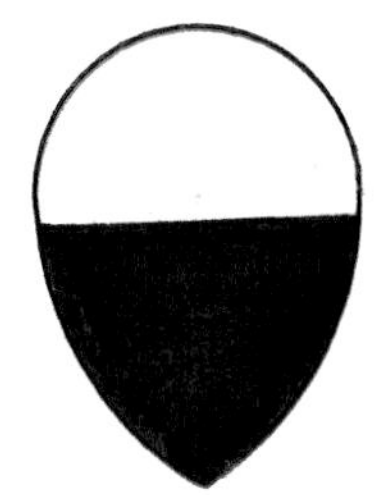

SIENA

NOTE. Opening hours of museums and art galleries may vary from the times given; also, galleries are sometimes temporarily closed for restoration.

LA STORIA

The Florentines have tried most forms of government. Julius Caesar introduced the first when he founded *Florentia* (flourishing) on the narrowest point of the Arno during the Floral Games of 59BC. A government of rape and pillage followed the arrival of the Lombards. It was replaced by Charlemagne with a hereditary margravate of Tuscany, but after the last margrave died without an heir in 1115, Florence became a free city. It elected four consuls on the ancient Roman model, but factionalism amongst the nobles caused consular government to be abandoned in 1207. It was replaced by the rule of a single executive, a *Podestà*, a supposedly impartial foreigner, elected for one year.

In 1198 a distant conflict between two German families for the throne of the empire had provided all northern Italy with badges of war. The nobles called themselves Ghibellines after Weiblingen, the home of the Hohenstaufen emperors, while the merchants and the Pope supported the Welf (Guelph) family. In 1248 the Florentine Ghibellines staged a coup and banished the Guelphs, destroying their houses, but their government was soon overthrown by the common people, who invited the Guelphs back. Together they created the *Primo Popolo* in 1215. This government was dominated by the merchants' guilds, which were to control the city for the next 200 years. The principal exceptions were in 1342, when the Duke of Athens was elected *signore* for life and then thrown out a year later, and in 1378, when the Ciompi revolt brought workers' control for six weeks. By 1434 however, the oligarchy came to be dominated by the party of the Medici. Cosimo, who seldom held any office, was able to rule from his home for 30 years by pulling strings. His son Piero and grandson Lorenzo Il Magnifico followed suit. In 1494 Savonarola introduced a constitution based on the Venetian model. The Medici returned in 1513, eventually becoming grand-dukes of Tuscany. Absolutism prevailed until Tuscany became part of Italy in 1860.

When Giovanni di Bicci de' Medici became banker to the Pope in 1413, his wealth was assured. To protect it he formed an undercover political party. When he died in 1429, he was the richest private citizen in the world. His son, Cosimo (Il Vecchio) used that wealth and the party to make himself *de facto* ruler of Florence for 30 years, although he scrupulously maintained the appearance of a private citizen. His patronage of the arts and artists (he was one of the first to observe that an artist always draws himself) and his love of the Latin classics helped to create the intellectual climate in the city. Cosimo was instrumental in bringing to Florence the Ecumenical Council of 1438, which attempted to heal the division of the Latin and Greek churches. It failed, but it was good business and flooded the city with Greek scholars and their manuscripts. He passed away in 1464, listening, it is said, to a dialogue of Plato. The *Signoria* conferred on him the title once granted to Cicero, *Pater Patriae*, 'Father of his country'. By education and example, Cosimo had prepared his son Piero (the Gouty) and grandson Lorenzo (Il Magnifico) for power. Piero's rule lasted five years and Lorenzo was only 20 when the Medici party invited him to take control of the city. He accepted, observing that, 'It is ill living in Florence for the rich unless they rule the state.' He was a man of great charm and intellect. His poems, the finest of his age, can be found in any anthology of Italian verse. Under his influence Florence became the intellectual capital of Europe. His only failing was in business. In his time the assets of the family bank declined, preventing him from commissioning works of art, yet he constantly recommended artists to friends and other rulers. When Lorenzo died in 1492, humanism in Florence died with him. His incompetent son Piero was driven from the city, but the Medici eventually returned as dukes. Catherine de' Medici is said to have transformed French cuisine and Francesco I founded the world's first systematic art collection in the Uffizi.

THE RENAISSANCE

The Renaissance, the rebirth of man's interest in man, ended a thousand years during which art had been created for the Glory of God. Man, as he appeared in the morality plays and in Byzantine art, had been a cipher. In Florence, Giotto was to begin the change. He painted real people with a depth and naturalism that struck a popular chord. Dante, in his *Divine Comedy*, was the first to write of man's free will and he wrote it not in the clumsy church Latin, but in Italian, the language of the common man. It was the ribald reality of the stories in the *Decameron*, the first prose classic in Italian, that brought Boccaccio fame. He was a friend and admirer of Petrarch, the popular poet whose greatest love was the classical Latin of Virgil and Cicero. Petrarch was the first to look back and see an 'age of darkness' between his own time and antiquity. He was so successful at popularizing the classics that he created a vogue in Florence for the study of ancient texts. From these studies, many wealthy merchants came to see education as not simply a prelude to a career, but for the creation of the whole man, the Renaissance man. They called it the 'new learning' and one of the first to acquire it was Cosimo de' Medici. It was he who commissioned Donatello in 1430 to sculpt his sensuous David, the first free-standing, life-sized nude since antiquity. This glorification of the human form was designed to be seen from any

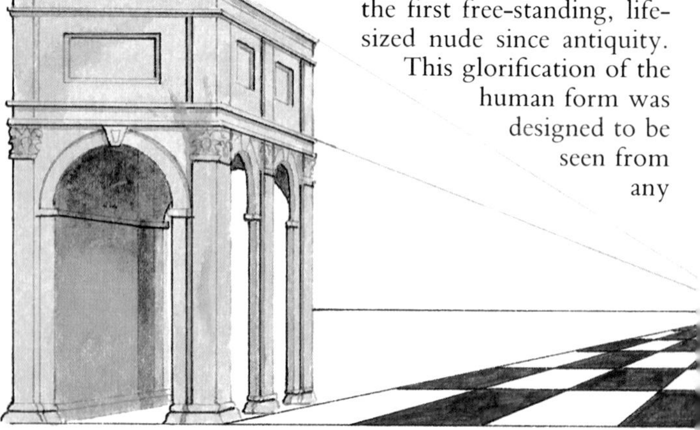

perspective. This new science of optics is said to have been invented by Brunelleschi, the goldsmith, sculptor, painter, and architect. His discovery was first exploited by Masaccio, who created in the Carmine and in S. Maria Novella frescos of such form and depth that they became an object of wonder and study for every artist of the age. Cosimo was one of the first to treat artists with respect. 'They are not journeymen,' he would say and he always found work for Donatello, Filippo Lippi and others. He spoke several languages and was knowledgeable on all subjects. 'What he does not know', wrote Pius II, 'is outside the range of human knowledge.' His passion was philosophy, particularly Plato, and he engaged Marsilio Ficino to translate Plato into Latin. From their nocturnal discussions grew the Platonic Academy. His father had owned three books. Cosimo's collection was to number 10,000. Lorenzo shared Cosimo's passion for Plato, whose birthday was celebrated each 7 November with a banquet. Lorenzo had a good sense of humour and once wrote a poem about the ravenous appetite of his friend 'Old Barrel-belly' (Botticelli) who shared his household, as did Leonardo and the young Michelangelo, who spent two years there. It is ironic that Michelangelo's giant *David* was commissioned to celebrate the fall of that house. The Renaissance (*Rinascita*) was named by Giorgio Vasari, who supposed himself to be living at its zenith, but as he named it, it faded.

Cosimo il Vecchio

When Catherine de' Medici departed for France with her train of chefs in 1533, the Medici kitchens were the finest in Europe. Today the best Tuscan kitchens are in the home, but many restaurants serve the classic dishes. The basic ingredient of Tuscan food is olive oil. It is even used in some sweet cakes. The rarest and most expensive is the old-fashioned stone-pressed *Olio di Prima Spremitura* from Lucca. The finest machine-pressed oils come in four grades:
1. *Extravergine*, 2. *Sopraffino Vergine*, 3. *Fino Vergine* and 4. *Vergine*.

Antipasti

Crostini
These are small slices of toast served hot and spread with chicken-liver pâté, or sometimes with a tomato and chilli paste.
Fagiolo con Tonno
The Tuscans are known as *mangiafagioli*, bean-eaters, for their love of haricot beans, which were first made fashionable by Duke Alessandro de' Medici. Here they are mixed with tuna fish and served with chopped onion, parsley and oil, and seasoned with freshly ground black pepper.
Antipasti Misto
A plate of *salame toscano, salumi* and ham (*prosciutto*) with perhaps, one or two *crostini*.
Prosciutto di Cinghiale
A strong-flavoured ham made from wild boar. (*Prosciutto* is normally served with melon or fresh figs.)

Primi Piatti

Minestrone di Verdura
The famous vegetable soup.
Zuppa di Verdura
Traditionally the Tuscan staple diet was not pasta, rice or polenta, but bread. In this dish, minestrone is served on a slice of toasted bread rubbed with garlic.
Minestra di Fagioli
Haricot-bean soup.
Tortino di Carciofi
A baked omelette of hearts of artichoke.
Porcini alla Griglia
There are over 200 varieties of mushroom (*funghi*) in the region, the largest being the *porcini*, here brushed with olive oil and grilled.
Frittura di Spinaci
A spinach-flavoured omelette.
Risotto alla Fiorentina

The meat and rice come in almost equal quantities.

Panzanella
A delicious bread salad of tomatoes, onion, basil, olive oil, salt and pepper.

Pasta
There are not many pastas, but *bavette* is like spaghetti and *pappardelle* is similar to tagliatelle.

Secondi Piatti

Bistecca alla Fiorentina
The Florentine T-bone steaks come from an ancient breed of snow-white oxen, the Chianina cattle from the Val di Chiana. A two-year-old bull may weigh a ton and the meat is famous for its tenderness. It is cooked over a scented wood fire and then garnished with salt, pepper and olive oil.

Vitello Arrosto
Roast veal, the Chianina baby beef.

Arista Fiorentina
Roast saddle of pork, which bishops of the Greek Orthodox Church visiting Florence in 1438 judged to be *'aristos'* (excellent).

Costata alla Fiorentina
Entrecôte or rib-steak.

Trippa alla Fiorentina
Tripe braised with onions and celery in a tomato sauce.

Pollo alla Brace
Chicken cooked with sage and garlic over an open fire.

Trote alla Griglia
Grilled trout.

Stracotto
A beef stew. The name means overcooked, so it is quite tender.

Anguilla alla Fiorentina
An eel casserole with peas and tomatoes.

Cinghiale
Wild boar; once only seasonal, many are now reared for the table.

Contorni

Spinaci
Cooked and served with olive oil, lemon juice and pepper.

Fagioli Bianchi
Haricot beans with oil and lemon.

Fagioli all'Uccelletto
Beans cooked with tomatoes, sage and garlic.

Piselli con Prosciutto
Peas and ham.

Dolci (Sweets)

Panforte di Siena
A marvellous medieval cake made of candied fruits, almonds and honey.

Biscotti di Siena
Hard almond biscuits for dunking in a dessert wine.

WINES OF

A 13thC border dispute between Siena and Florence was settled by each city agreeing to send forth a rider at cockcrow. Where the riders met would mark the new boundary. The Florentine bird was a half-starved black cock that crowed much earlier than its pampered Sienese counterpart, so that the Florentines had covered threequarters of the distance before they met. This included the towns of Castellina, Radda and Gaiole, which formed the 13thC League of Chianti (the first recorded use of the word) under Florentine protection. Their emblem was a black cock, *gallo nero*.

Baron Ricasoli is credited with the development of the Chianti blend which is now, by law, 75–90% Sangiovese grapes mixed with Canaiolo and two white grapes, Malvasia and Trebbiano. Young Chiantis used to be sold in the famous straw *fiaschi*, now too expensive to make. A *vecchio* must be aged for two years and a *riserva* for three. The *governo* system of secondary fermentation is what makes young wines so 'prickly' – *frizzante*.

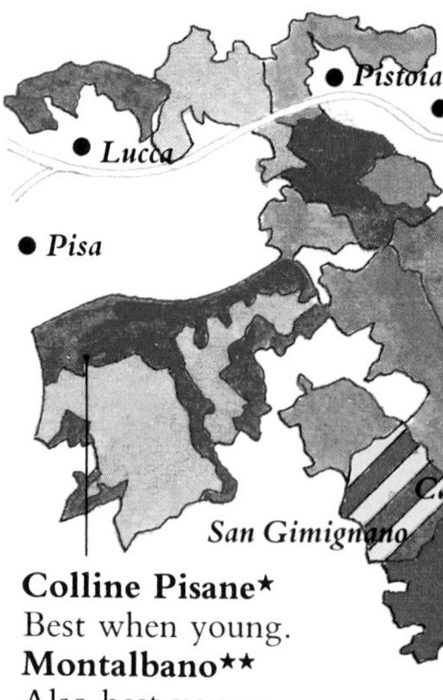

Colline Pisane★
Best when young.

Montalbano★★
Also best young.

PRODUCERS:
Artimino — *Il Poggiolo*
Baccherato — *Tenuta di Capezzana*

Vernaccia di S. Gimignano★★★
A white wine which Michelangelo said 'kisses, licks, bites, tingles and stings'.

Pietrafitta — *La Torre*
Monte Oliveto — *Il Palagio*

Chianti Classico★★★
Most but not all producers belong to the Gallo Nero consortium.

PRODUCERS:
Monsanto — *Badia a Coltibuono*
Capannelle — *Montagliari*
Ruffino — *Villa Caffagio*
Villa Antinori — *Brolio*
Castelgreve — *Castellare*
Melini — *Castello di Ama*
Cispiano — *Villa Cerna*

TUSCANY

Rufina (Chianti)★★★
This area produces wines of the highest quality.
PRODUCERS:
Frescobaldi *Nippozzano*
Montesodi *Selvapiana di Vetrice*
Poggio Reale *Le Coste*
Villa di Monte *Spalletti*
Tenuta di Poggio *Remole*

Colli Fiorentini (Chianti)★★
Best after 4 or 5 years.
PRODUCERS:
Castello del Trebbio *Il Corno*
Giannozzi *Lilliano*

Colli Senesi (Chianti)★★
A fuller and stronger Chianti than the northern wines, it is best young.
PRODUCERS:
Ficomantanino *Felsina del Cerro*
Castel Pietraio *Villa Cusona*
Chigi-Saracini di Pietrafitta
Constanti Emiglio

Vino Nobile di Montepulciano★★★★
Here the Sangiovese is blended with 25% of white grapes. It is best after 5 years.
PRODUCERS:
Bologna Buonsignori *Casalte*
Avignonesi *Saiagricola*
Poliziano *Boscarelli*
Contucci *Fanetti*
Pantano *Valdipiatta*

Putto
A rival consortium to the Gallo Nero, with members in all zones but Classico.

Brunello di Montalcino★★★★
Made only from the Brunello variety of the Sangiovese grape, it is best after 10 years.

Rosso di Montalcino★★
Made for early drinking.
PRODUCERS:
Altesino *Costanti*
Franceschi *Case Basse*
Tenuta Caparzo *La Gerla*
Biondi-Santi *Lisini*

IL DUOMO

S. MARIA DEL FIORE

The Duomo, or *Domus Dei* (House of God) was begun in 1296 by Arnolfo di Cambio. His brief was simple. The cathedral was to be of the 'greatest lavishness and magnificence possible'. When Pope Eugene IV consecrated it in 1436 it was mostly complete but for the facade, one third finished. A competition for a new facade was announced in 1491. Botticelli, Verrocchio, Filippino Lippi and others all submitted designs, but the judges were embarrassed by an entry from Lorenzo de' Medici. Diplomatically, they deferred the decision to him. It was Lorenzo's turn to be embarrassed and the matter was shelved. For the visit of his son, Giovanni, as Pope Leo X in 1515, a temporary, painted facade excited much admiration but nothing developed until the 19thC when

after 92 projects had been considered, the design of Emilio di Fabris was selected. The work was completed in 1887.

Tower of Giotto

He only built the base, which would have fallen over if his successor, Andrea Pisano, had not doubled the thickness of the walls. The green marble on the facade comes from Prato, the white from Carrara and the pink from the Maremma. At the rear, a door opens on to a climb of 414 steps to the top (272 ft).

S. Reparata

The Duomo was built around an earlier church dedicated to the obscure Palestinian saint Reparata, on whose day a Gothic army was defeated in Tuscany. It was demolished in 1375. The crypt is now a museum.

Gallery

It was left unfinished after Michelangelo branded it a cricket's cage.

Sculptures

These are copies. The originals by Andrea Pisano and Luca della Robbia can be seen in the Duomo museum.

THE DUOMO

New Sacristy
Luca della Robbia made the bronze doors and the enamelled terracotta lunettes above.

Michelangelo's Pietà
He had intended it for his own tomb in Rome and carved a self-portrait on the figure of Nicodemus, but broke it in anger when he found the marble was flawed. The original is in the Duomo museum.

Ascent to the Dome
A climb of 463 steps to the 353 ft high gallery.

Dante and his Poem
Frescoed by Domenico di Michelino in 1465.

Sir John Hawkwood
The most successful general of his day, his army of mercenaries was called the 'White Company' for their dazzling armour, and was the inspiration of Conan Doyle's book of that name. The Italians called him Giovanni Acuto for the sharpness of his wit (and, no doubt, his sword). Rather than have him march against them, the Florentines gave him citizenship and made him chief of the army with a tax-free pension for life. When he died in 1394 he was given this memorial. It was completely repainted in 1436 by Paolo Uccello.

Niccolò da Tolentino
Painted by Andrea del Castagno in 1456.

Paolo Uccello's Clock
Painted in 1443.

Brunelleschi's Tomb
Crypt of S. Reparata
Cupolo Fresco

'Without the fresco, it seemed higher and greater,' lamented Lapini on seeing Vasari's and Zuccari's work.

Murder in the Cathedral

All eyes were lowered as the sanctuary bell sounded for the celebration of High Mass on Sunday, 26 April 1478. It was the signal for the assassins of Giuliano de' Medici to strike and he died instantly, but his brother Lorenzo the Magnificent, on the other side of the church, leapt forward as two 'embittered priests' lunged at him. He escaped into the new sacristy with a neck wound. The bell was also the signal for the Archbishop of Pisa, with a body of mercenaries disguised as his retinue together with members of the Pazzi family who had hatched the plot, to enter the Palazzo della Signoria and seize control of the government. They were left in various rooms while they waited for the *Gonfaloniere* (titular head of state), for whom they had an 'urgent message from the Pope' (also a party to the plot). The *Gonfaloniere* was suspicious; he had recently fitted all the doors with catches that could not be opened from the inside. As news arrived of the murder, the conspirators were trapped.

THE DOME OF

No dome of this size had been attempted since antiquity. Nobody knew how. By 1418 however, when a competition was announced to solve the problem, one man had discovered the secret: Filippo Brunelleschi. After losing the competition to sculpt the doors of the Baptistery to Lorenzo Ghiberti, Brunelleschi went to Rome, where he spent several years studying the architecture of the ancients and, in particular, the dome of the Pantheon. He proposed to build a double dome, one inside the other, which he explained would need the support of neither arches nor piers and could be raised with very little scaffolding. His scheme was met, at first, with disbelief and then laughter and derision. Amid uproar he was twice removed bodily from the hall. At a later meeting, he demolished all other schemes, but when he was asked to produce a model of his own ideas, he flatly refused, knowing that his ideas would soon be stolen. Instead he suggested that the commission go to whoever could stand an egg on a flat marble surface. This odd challenge was accepted. Everyone failed except Brunelleschi who, to the outrage of his competitors, simply cracked the egg on its base and it stood upright. 'Anyone could do that,' they said. To this he replied, 'With my plans anyone could raise the cupola.'

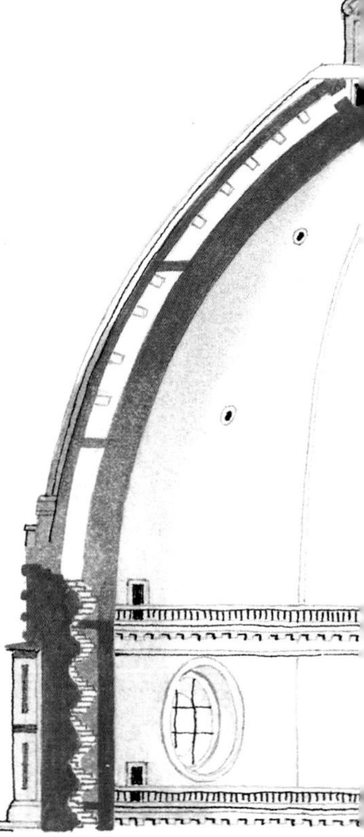

BRUNELLESCHI

Impressed by his confidence, the wardens gave him the commission, but his enemies had him thrown into jail on the technicality that he was not a mason. On his release the wardens were then persuaded that the work was too important to be entrusted to one man and his old rival Ghiberti was made his partner. Brunelleschi still refused to reveal his plans and work started but stopped at a height of 24 ft when he retired to bed feigning an illness. 'Ask Lorenzo,' he croaked to the masons when they came for their instructions. Being ignorant of what should be done, Lorenzo countered by saying, 'I will do nothing without Filippo.' He was restored to health when the wardens agreed to his plan for Ghiberti to design and build some stone ties. These were demonstrably unsuitable and Ghiberti was dismissed. Brunelleschi was then made superintendent for life; he finally revealed his model and his genius became apparent. He had designed windows to light the stairs and had even planned the provision of canteens with kitchens inside the dome, so that the workers need not descend for lunch. It was completed in 1461, fifteen years after his death, when he was laid to rest inside the cathedral. Michelangelo, speaking of the sister dome he was building at St Peter's in Rome, said, 'It will be larger, but not more beautiful.'

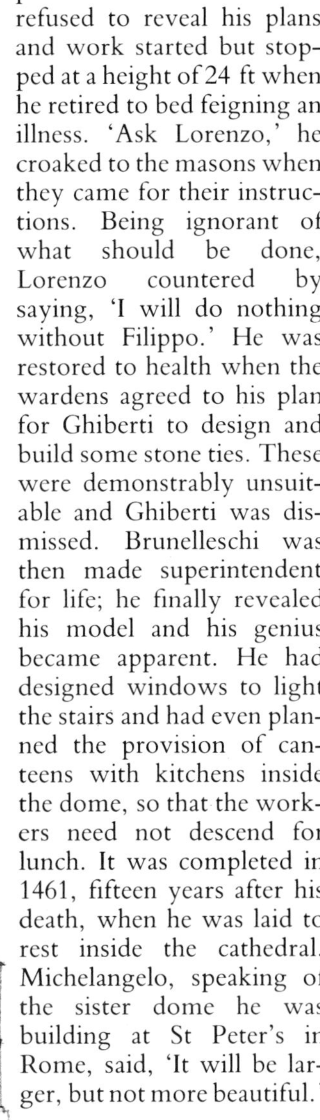

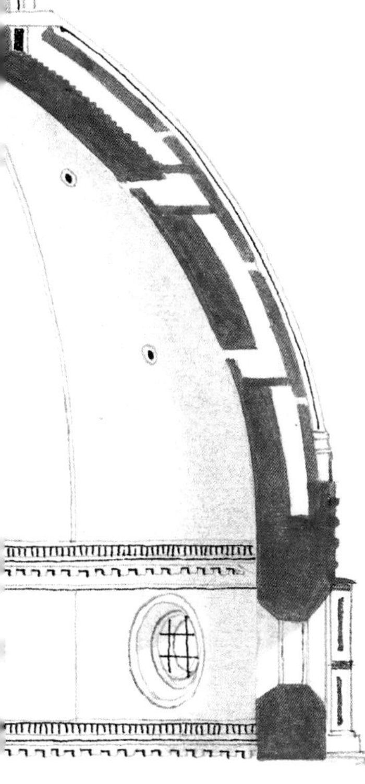

BAPTISTERY

Once a year all the children born over the previous twelve months were baptized *en masse* in a large pool that stood inside. Amongst the babes in 1266 was Dante Alighieri. In his time it was believed that the temple had once been dedicated to Mars. In fact, it is a 7thC building, re-roofed and clad in white and green marble in the 11th and 12thC.

South Door Sculpture
The Beheading of the Baptist, by Vincenzo Danti.

East Door
Above it is Sansovino's Baptism of Christ with an added 18thC angel. The twin porphyry columns on either side of the door were gifts of the Pisans in 1135.

North Door
The Sermon of the Baptist, by Francesco Rustici.

Pillar of St Zenobius
It marks the site of an elm tree that miraculously burst into leaf in midwinter when it was brushed by the coffin of the 5thC Bishop Zenobius.

Tomb of Anti-Pope John XXIII

In 1410 the Great Schism between the Popes of Rome and Avignon was further complicated by the election of a third pontiff, Baldassarre Coscia. A libertine Neapolitan, he was rumoured to have seduced some 200 women while he was papal legate in Bologna. He took the name John XXIII and enjoyed wide support until the Council of Constance was convened in 1414 to resolve the problem. To his surprise, it called for the abdication of all the claimants. He absconded, but was captured and put on trial. Gibbon writes, 'The more scandalous charges were suppressed; the vicar of Christ was only accused of piracy, murder, rape, sodomy and incest.' After four years he bought his liberty and retired to Florence, where he died in the home of his former banker, Cosimo de' Medici, who employed Michelozzo and Donatello to build his tomb.

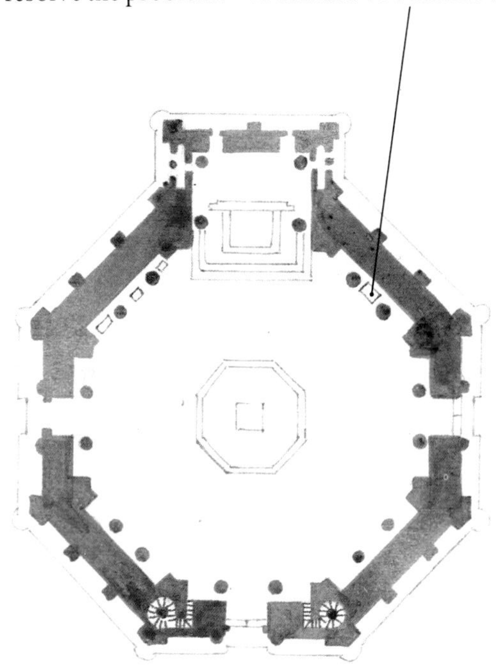

THE BAPTISTERY DOORS

SOUTH DOORS

Andrea Pisano

The guild of the wool merchants commissioned Pisano to start work on Florence's first monument in bronze. This was modelled in wax and then cast by Venetian craftsmen in 1332. The chasing and polishing took four years. The doors were finally hung in 1336. They depict 20 scenes from the life of St John the Baptist.

NORTH DOORS

Lorenzo Ghiberti

Ghiberti said of the competition to sculpt these doors in 1401, 'The palm of victory was conceded to me by all the experts.' His contemporary, Manetti, says the commission was awarded jointly to Brunelleschi and Ghiberti, but Brunelleschi refused to share the work and quit. Their trial pieces can be seen in the Bargello.

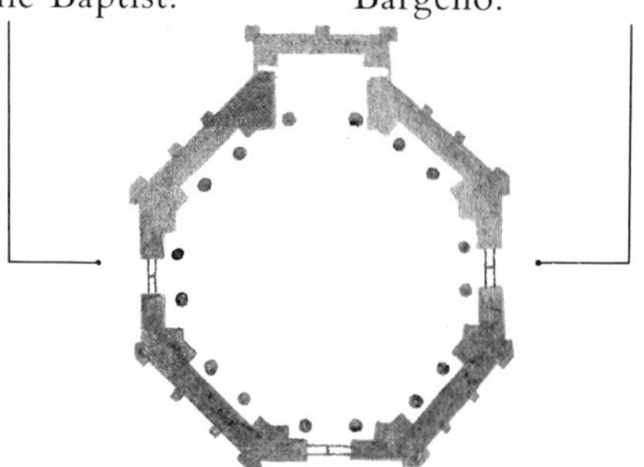

EAST DOORS

Lorenzo Ghiberti

Ghiberti began work on these in 1425, as soon as he finished the north doors, which had cost 22,000 gold florins (the same as the annual defence budget). There were to have been twenty narrative panels, but Ghiberti reduced them to ten, putting several incidents into each relief. They were hung in 1452. Michelangelo judged them to be 'worthy of gracing the entrance to Paradise'.

The creation of Adam and Eve

The story of Noah and his sons

The story of Jacob and Esau

The story of Moses

Stories from the lives of Saul and David

The story of Cain and Abel

Abraham: the sacrifice of Isaac

The story of Joseph

The story of Joshua

The meeting of Solomon and the Queen of Sheba

SOUTH DOORS

Andrea Pisano

1. The Angel and Zacharias	*2. Zacharius is struck dumb*	*11. John before Herod*	*12. John is imprisoned*
3. The Visitation	*4. The birth of the Baptist*	*13. John's disciples visit him in prison*	*14. Christ and John's disciples*
5. The naming of John the Baptist	*6. John goes into the wilderness*	*15. Salome dances before Herod*	*16. The beheading of John*
7. John preaches to the people	*8. Behold the Lamb*	*17. The head of John is brought before Herod*	*18. Salome offers Herodias the head of John*
9. John baptizes the people	*10. John baptizes Christ*	*19. John's body is removed*	*20. The burial of John the Baptist*
21. Hope	*22. Faith*	*25. Charity*	*26. Humility*
23. Fortitude	*24. Temperance*	*27. Justice*	*28. Prudence*

NORTH DOORS
Lorenzo Ghiberti

25. The Way to Calvary	*26. The Crucifixion*	*27. The Resurrection*	*28. Pentecost*
21. The Agony in the Garden	*22. Christ is arrested*	*23. The Flagellation*	*24. Christ before Pilate*
17. The Transfiguration	*18. The raising of Lazarus*	*19. The Entry into Jerusalem*	*20. The Last Supper*
13. Christ is baptized by John	*14. The Temptation*	*15. Christ expels the money changers*	*16. Christ walks on the water*
9. Annunciation	*10. Nativity*	*11. Adoration of the Magi*	*12. Christ among the doctors*
5. St John	*6. St Matthew*	*7. St Luke*	*8. St Mark*
1. St Augustine	*2. St Jerome*	*3. St Gregory the Great*	*4. St Ambrose*

MOSAICS OF

Some of the 13thC mosaics have been attributed to Cimabue, notably some panels illustrating the life of the Baptist.

The Life of St John the Baptist

1. *Annunciation of his birth*
2. *The naming of St John*
3. *St John in the wilderness*
4. *The preaching of St John*
5. *St John baptizes*
6. *The arrival of Christ*
7. *The baptism of Christ*
8. *St John accuses Herod*
9. *The imprisonment of St John*
10. *St John sends disciples*
11. *Christ and the disciples*
12. *The dance of Salome*
13. *The beheading of St John*
14. *Herodias receives the head of the Baptist*
15. *The burial of St John*

The Life of Christ

1. *The Annunciation*
2. *The Visitation*
3. *The Nativity*
4. *The Adoration of the Magi*
5. *The Magi are warned in a dream*
6. *The Journey of the Magi*
7. *Presentation at the Temple*
8. *Joseph is warned in a dream*
9. *The Flight into Egypt*
10. *The Slaughter of the Innocents*
11. *The Last Supper*
12. *The Road to Calvary*
13. *The Crucifixion*
14. *The Deposition*
15. *The Resurrection*

The Life of Joseph

1. *The dream of Joseph*
2. *The telling of the dream*
3. *The conspiracy of his brothers*

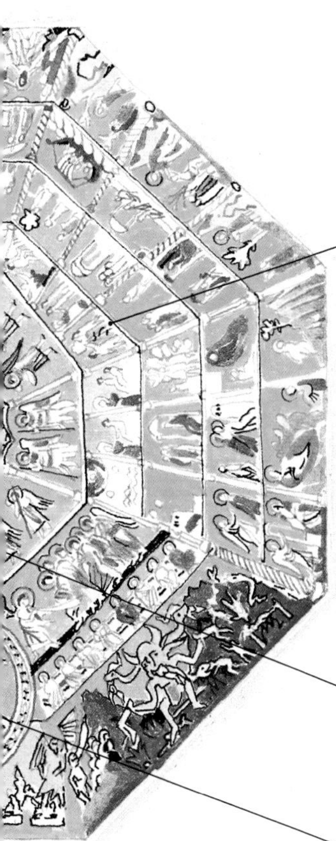

4. Joseph is delivered to the Midianites
5. Israel is told of the death of Joseph
6. Joseph is sold to the Ishmaelites
7. Joseph before Pharaoh
8. Joseph and Potiphar
9. Joseph in prison
10. The dream of Pharaoh
11. The telling of the dream
12. Joseph interprets the dream
13. The storing of grain
14. The distribution of grain
15. Joseph with his chariot and his brothers

Episodes from Genesis
1. The Creation
2. The creation of Adam
3. The creation of Eve
4. The Temptation
5. The covering of nakedness
6. Banishment from Paradise
7. Cain and Abel
8. Their offerings to God
9. Cain slays Abel
10. The mark of Cain
11. Noah and his three sons
12. The building of the ark
13. The loading of the ark
14. The flood

The Angelic Host
Cherubim, Seraphim, Dominations, Powers, Archangels, Angels, Principalities, Virtues, Thrones. The nine orders of heavenly beings described by Dionysius (5thC) are shown more clearly here than elsewhere in Christian art.

The Last Judgement
Christ as Judge
The elect
The damned
Prophets and Apostles
Angels

Bandinelli Statue

S. Maria Maggiore

Palazzo Arcivescovile
The Archbishop's residence was rebuilt in 1895.

S. Lorenzo
See pp. 30–31.

S. Giovannino d. Scolopi
Duke Alessandro de' Medici lay in state here after being murdered in the bed of a good woman he had hoped to seduce. His assassin was a cousin who saw himself as a second Brutus. Ammannati is buried in the church he rebuilt.

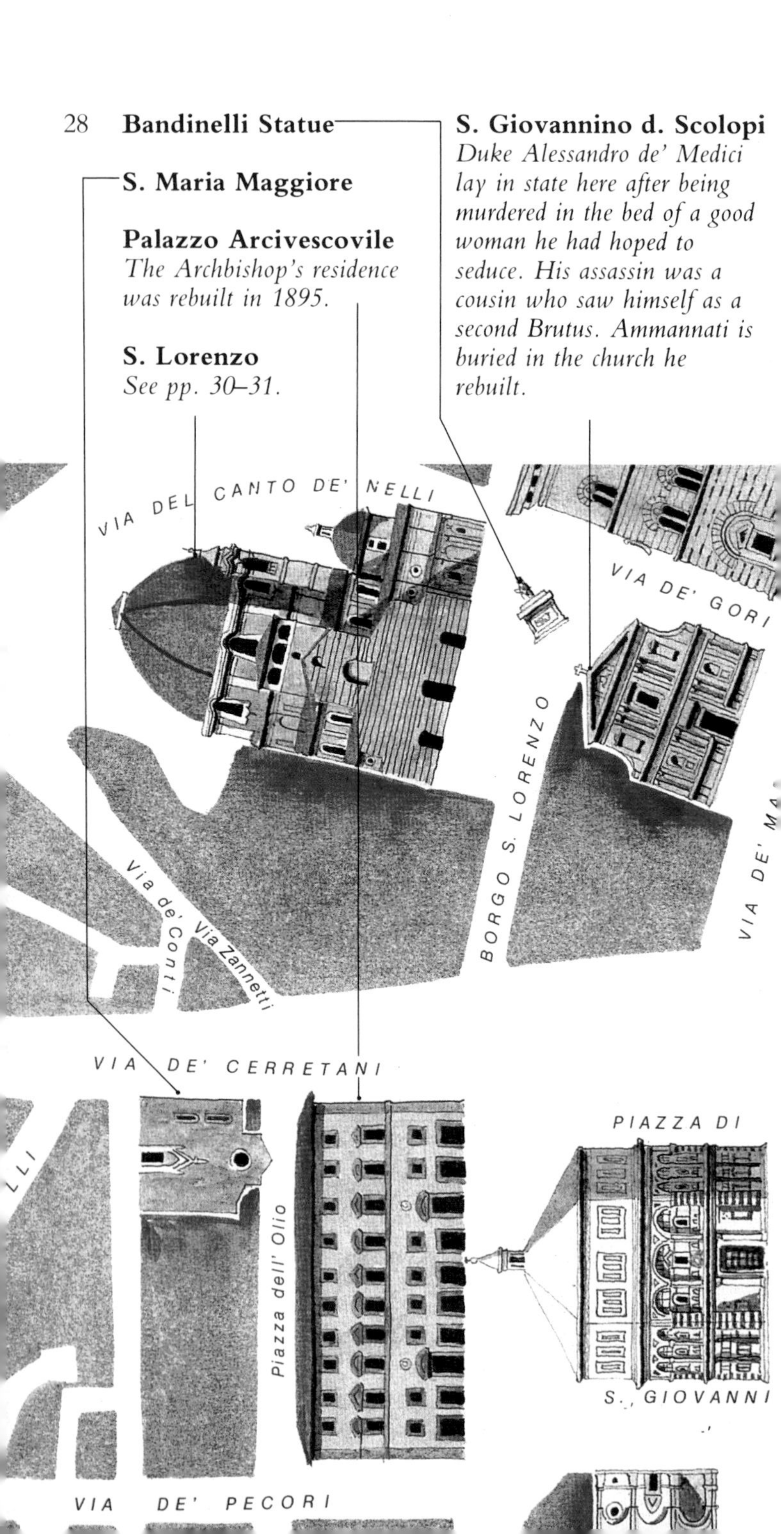

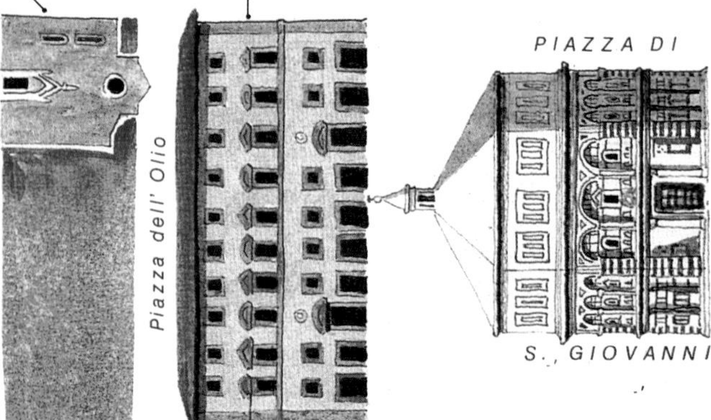

S. Michele Visdomini
Pontormo painted the Holy Family inside in 1518.

Museo dell'Opera del Duomo
Michelangelo sculpted his David in the courtyard of this, the cathedral works department. It now houses his Pietà and many other originals brought here for conservation. Hours: 9.00–13.00 and 15.00–18.00 (winter 16.00); Sunday 10.00–13.00.

Palazzo Pucci
Attributed to Ammannati.

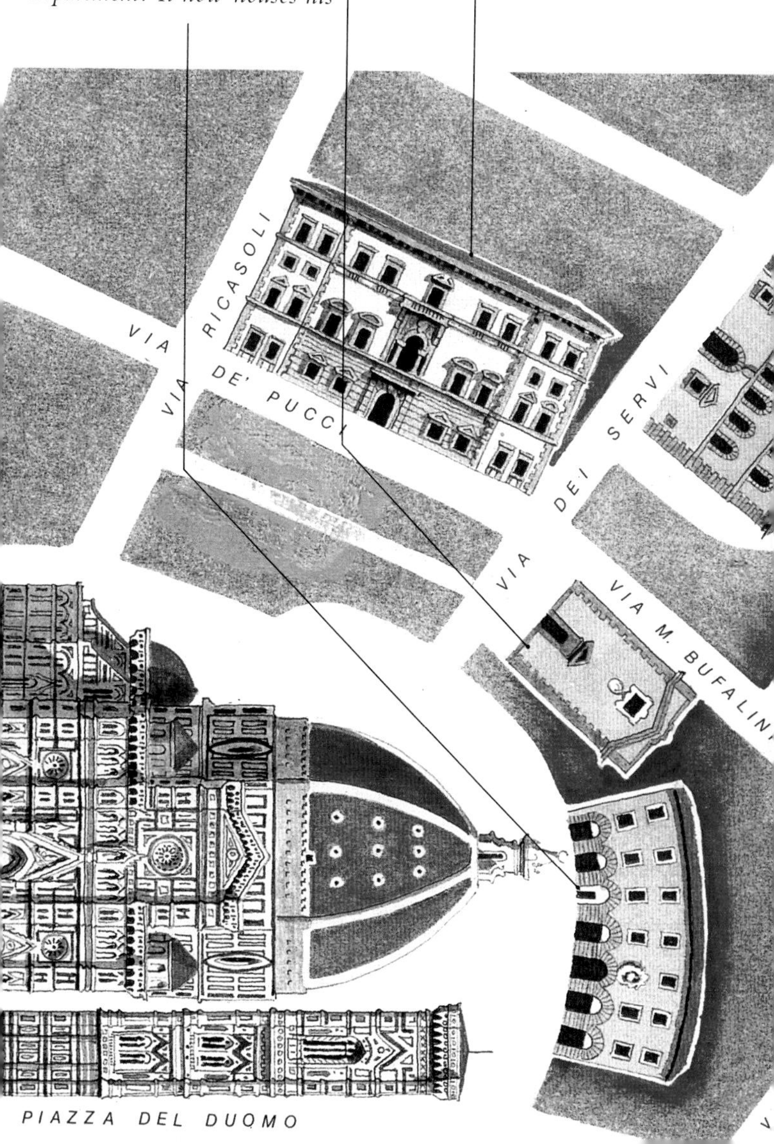

S. LORENZO

Not counting the two Popes and the two Queens of France, all the leading members of the Medici family are buried here. The earliest church was consecrated by Bishop Ambrose of Milan in 393. Brunelleschi began the present building in 1421. Michelangelo was asked to design a facade, but nothing developed beyond his model, which can be seen at Casa Buonarroti.

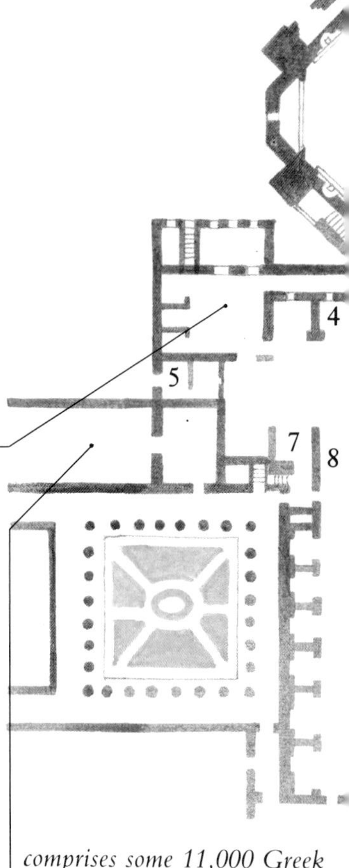

Old Sacristy
The earliest part of the building, it contains:
Sarcophagus of Giovanni di Bicci de' Medici and his Wife
by Andrea Cavalcanti, called Buggiano
Bronze Sarcophagus of Giovanni and Piero de' Medici
by Verrocchio
Triptych
School of Taddeo Gaddi
Donatello
Tondi of the Four Evangelists
The bronze doors
School of Ghirlandaio
St Anthony Abbot, St Julian and S. Leonardo
Biblioteca Laurenziana
Founded by Cosimo de' Medici and enlarged by his grandson Lorenzo, the library comprises some 11,000 Greek and Latin manuscripts and 4,000 of the earliest printed books. There is a 5thC Virgil, Cellini's manuscript of his Autobiography *and a Book of Hours that belonged to Lorenzo. The rooms were designed by Michelangelo in 1524.*

S. LORENZO

Medici Chapels
Hours: 9.00–14.00; festivals 9.00–13.00; closed Monday.

Chapel of the Princes
A grandiose memorial to the Medici dukes, designed by Don Giovanni de' Medici and Buontalenti and begun in 1602.

New Sacristy of Michelangelo
Begun in 1520; he left Florence with it unfinished.

LEFT:

The Tomb of Lorenzo, Duke of Urbino,
the dedicatee of Machiavelli's The Prince, *with figures of Dusk and Dawn*

RIGHT:

The Tomb of Giuliano, Duke of Nemours,
with Night and Day

Madonna and Child
The unfinished monument to Lorenzo il Magnifico and his murdered brother Giuliano.

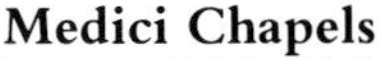

1. Donatello
Two pulpits raised on columns, his last works (1460)

2. Tabernacle
by Desiderio da Settignano

3. Rosso Fiorentino
Marriage of the Virgin

4. Madonna and Child
attributed to Alberto Arnoldi

5. Lavabo
by Donatello workshop

High Altar Crucifix
by Baccio da Montelupo

6. Burial Place of Cosimo de' Medici,

7. Filippo Lippi
Annunciation

7. Donatello Monument
1896. He is buried beneath.

8. Bronzino
Martyrdom of S. Lorenzo

Piazza della Repubblica
Originally the Roman Forum, it was the Mercato Vecchio until 1888, when many medieval buildings surrounding the square were demolished.

Column of Abundance
A copy of Foggini's work.

Orsanmichele
First it was a convent, then an open grain market, but the portals were closed in 1380 when it became a church and two upper floors were added as an emergency grain store. The 14 niches on the outside contain statues (some copies) commissioned by city guilds.

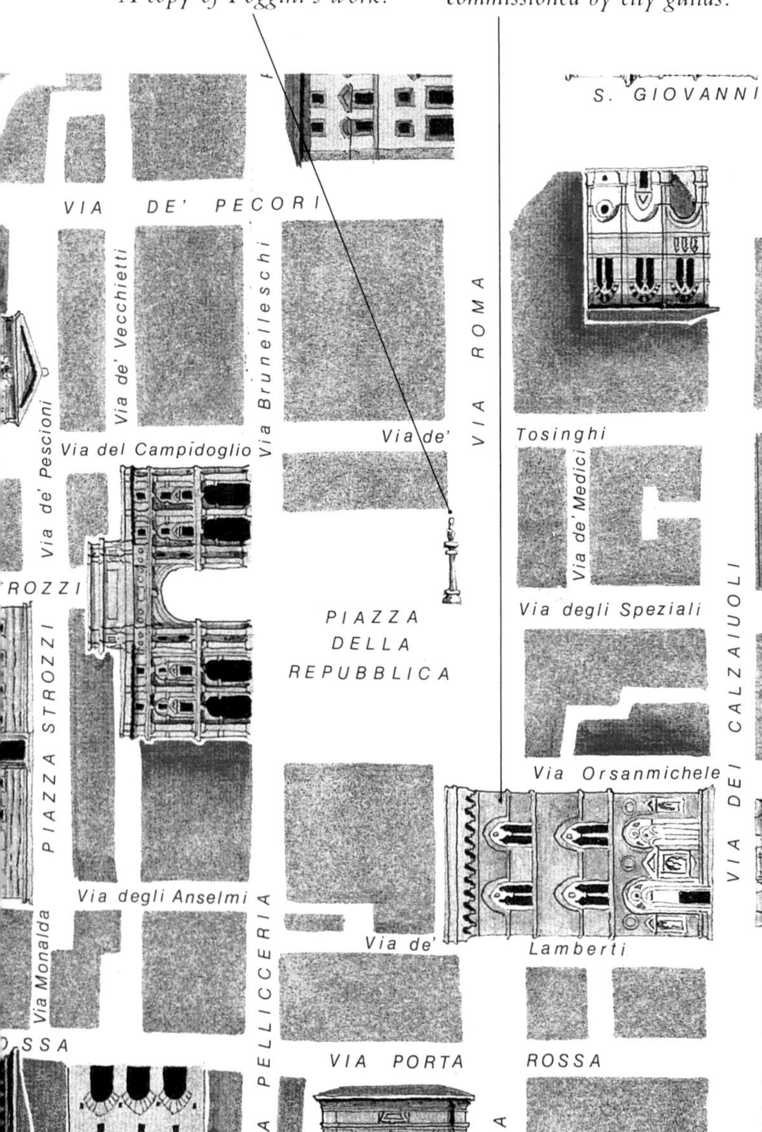

Casa di Dante
Reconstructed as a museum in 1865. Hours: 9.00–12.30 and 15.30–18.00; Sunday 9.30–12.30; closed Wednesday.

S. Margherita in S. Maria de' Ricci
The portico dates from 1611.

Palazzo Salviati
The birthplace of Duke Cosimo I. His frightened nurse was ordered to drop him from an upper window so that his proud father could catch him in his arms.

S. Margherita de' Cerchi
Dante was married here.

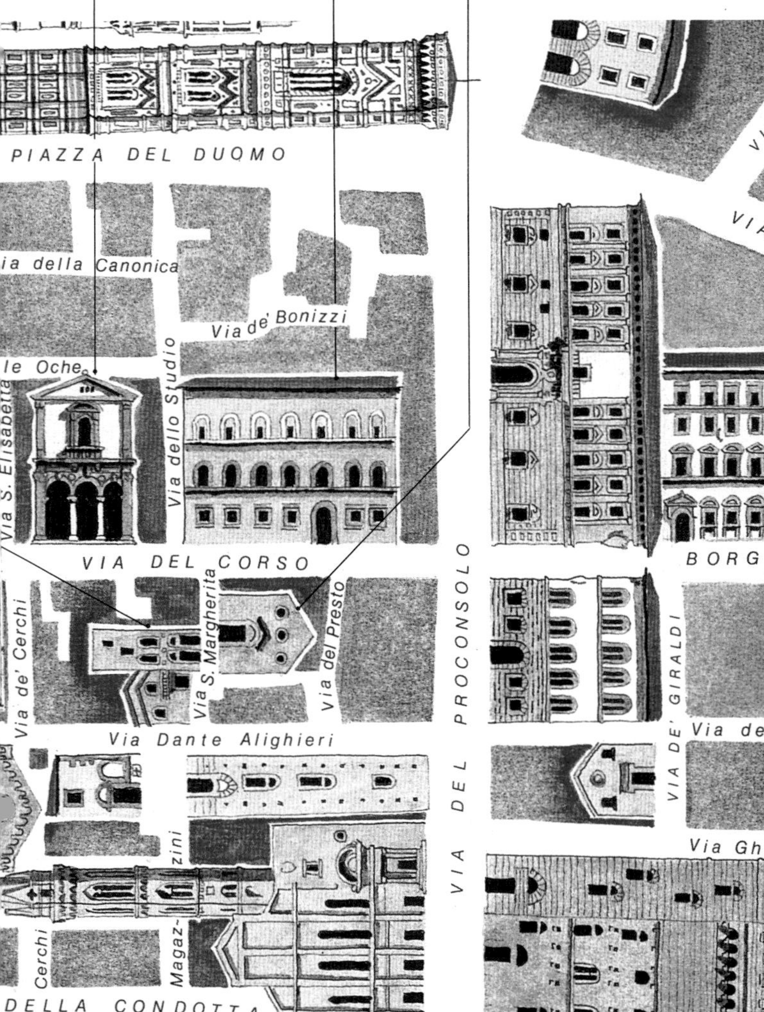

Palazzo Davanzati
A marvellous museum of a medieval nobleman's house built c. 1330. Hours: 9.00–14.00 (13.00 Sunday); closed Monday.

Palazzo di Parte Guelfa
The residence of the captains of the Guelph party that ruled Florence from 1267 to 1376. It is only open for exhibitions.

Mercato Nuovo
It was new when Cellini worked here in 1551.

S. Stefano al Ponte

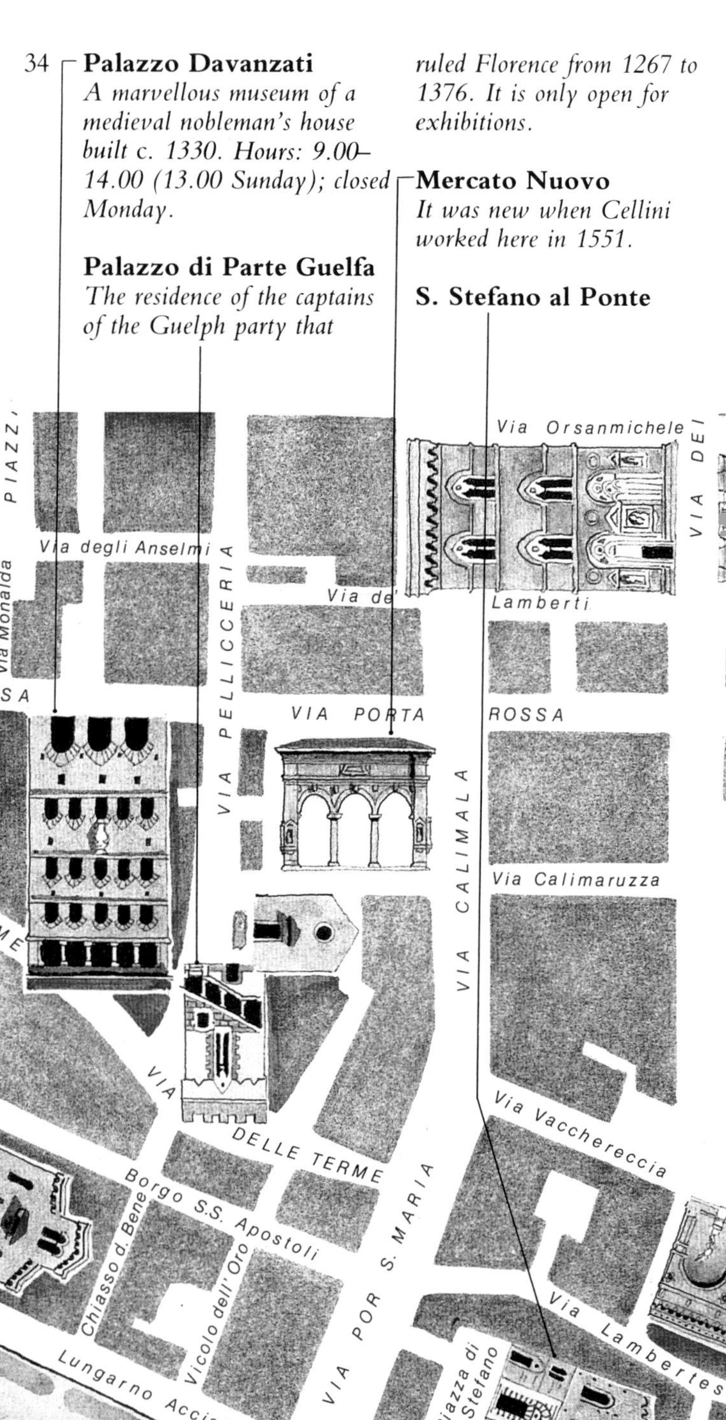

Uffizi Gallery
Details on pp. 104–15.

Torre della Castagna
The residence of the nine elected Priors before the Palazzo Vecchio was built.

S. Martino del Vescovo
Founded 986. Rebuilt 1479.

Badia Fiorentina
A Benedictine abbey was founded here in 978. Boccaccio lectured here on Dante. Inside is a panel by Filippino Lippi of St Bernard's vision of the Virgin and Mino da Fiesole's monument to Ugo, Margrave of Tuscany and son of the founder.

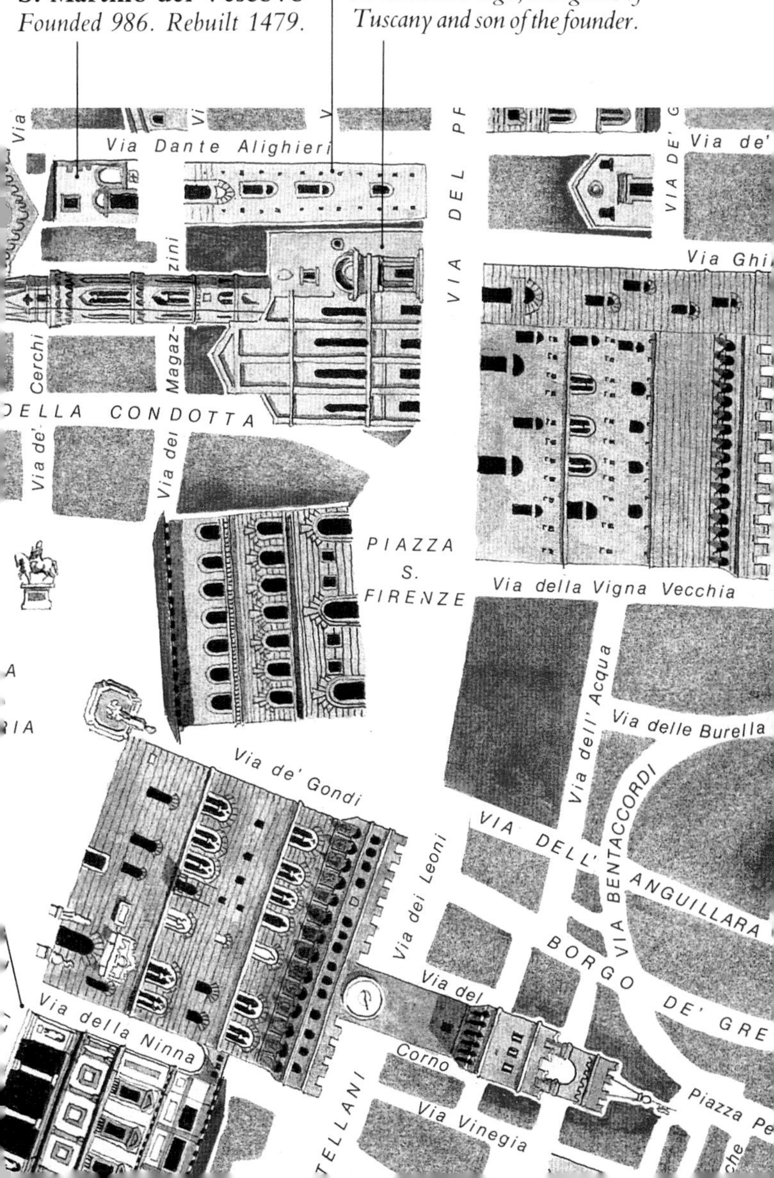

When the houses of the defeated Ghibellines were razed to the ground by the victorious Guelphs in 1268, the piazza emerged for the first time.

Palazzo Vecchio

It was built between 1299 and 1307 as the Palazzo del Popolo, to accommodate and protect the nine elected Priors, who were obliged to live here as virtual prisoners during their two-month term of office. Collectively they were *signori*, so it became the Palazzo della Signoria and then the Palazzo Ducale until the dukes abandoned it and it became the Palazzo Vecchio.

The Vacca

A great bell, 'the cow', was used to summon citizens to an open-air *parlamento*. The bell was destroyed by Duke Alessandro in 1530.

Aranghiera

The origin of the word harangue, this was a platform from which citizens were incited to war or vendetta.

Barberia

A small cell in the bell tower where Cosimo de' Medici was incarcerated for two weeks in 1433 prior to exile.

The Statuary

These were mostly conceived as political statements, the earliest being:

Donatello's Judith and Holofernes

It was commissioned in 1455 for the household of Piero de' Medici.

Michelangelo's David

This represented the victory of republicanism over the tyrannical Medici Goliath.

Neptune Fountain

The sculptor Ammannati later admitted failure in this work, a view made popular in a rhyme, *'O Ammannato, Ammannato, che bel marmo ha rovinato'* (What a fine marble you have ruined).

Savonarola

The fanatical friar persuaded Florentines to rid themselves of worldly goods in an enormous 'bonfire of vanities' in the piazza in 1495. Three years later, he himself was deemed a luxury and he was hung and then burnt on the spot marked by a porphyry disc.

Cellini's Perseus

His masterpiece was commissioned by Duke Cosimo I to celebrate the victory of his tyranny over republicanism.

Loggia
It was built as a covered *aranghiera* in 1376–82.

Bandinelli's Hercules and Cacus
Hercules was another symbol of Florentine republicanism. The work was first promised to Michelangelo but after he left the city it passed to Bandinelli. The sculptor was horrified to hear Cellini regale Duke Cosimo and his friends with the many faults of the work, including, as Cellini maintained, 'muscles that had been copied from a sack full of melons'.

Giambologna's Rape of the Sabines and Hercules and the Centaur

The Rape of Polyxena
by Pio Fedi (1886)

Ajax with the Body of Patroclus
A Roman copy of a Greek work.

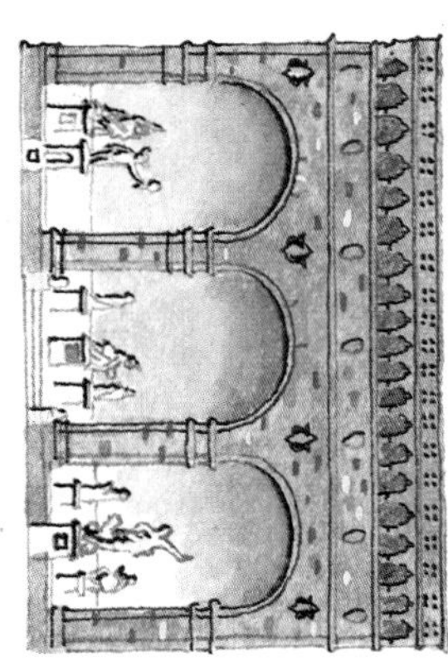

PALAZZO

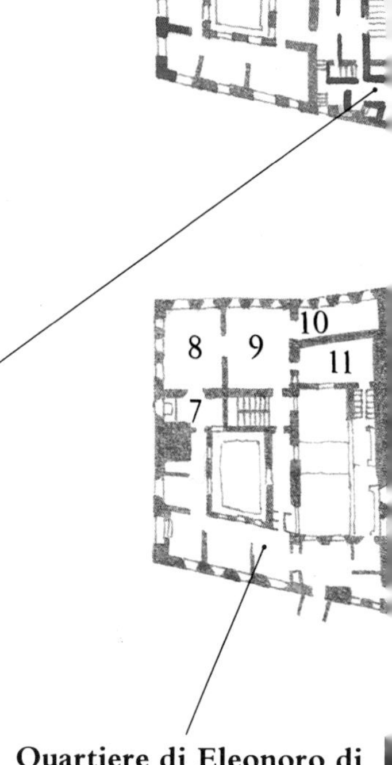

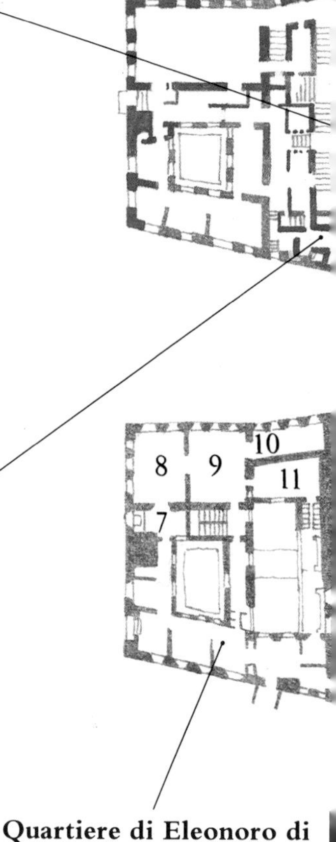

SALONE DEI CINQUECENTO

The room of the Five Hundred was built to hold the Great Council of the Republic under a constitution based on the Venetian model which was introduced by Savonarola in 1494. Michelangelo and Leonardo da Vinci were engaged to decorate the two long walls, but both left the city with only their cartoons prepared. The present decoration was carried out by Vasari, Vincenzo Borghini and others. The walls illustrate victories over Pisa and Siena. The 39 panels in the ceiling represent the cities of Tuscany and the apotheosis of Cosimo I.

Michelangelo
Victory. It was intended for the tomb of Pope Julius II.

Giambologna
Virtue Triumphs over Vice

Vincenzo de' Rossi
Six Labours of Hercules

STUDIOLO DI FRANCESCO I

The decoration reflects the duke's interest in science. The four walls represent the Four Elements.

Quartiere di Eleonoro di Toledo
Decorated by Ridolfo del Ghirlandaio.

Galleria Siviero
A collection of 141 works including a Masaccio and a Rubens rescued by Rudolfo Siviero after they had been stolen by the Nazis.

V E C C H I O

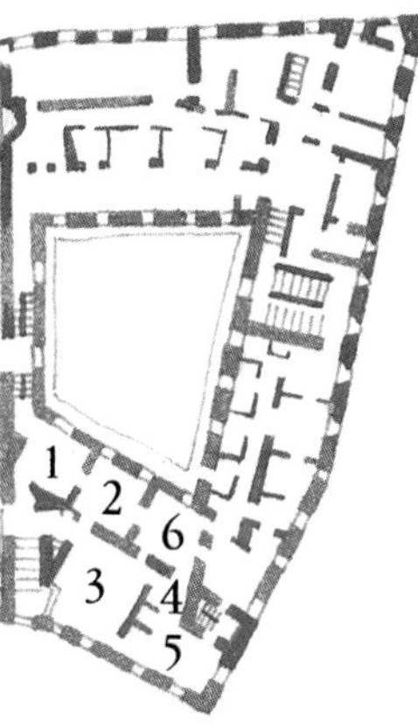

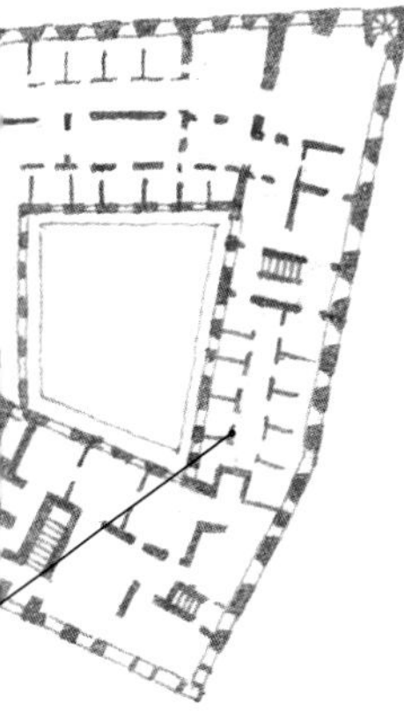

Chapel
Decorated by Bronzino.

QUARTIERE DI LEONE X

The rooms of the Medici Pope Leo were decorated by Vasari and others.

1. Sala di Cosimo il Vecchio
Ceiling: Cosimo's return

2. Sala di Lorenzo il Magnifico
Ambassadors before Lorenzo

3. Sala di Leone X
Life of Giovanni de' Medici

4. The Chapel

5. Sala di Clemente VII
Vasari's(?) famous panorama of the siege of Florence

6. Sala di Cosimo I
Prisoners before Cosimo I

7. Cappella della Signoria
Decorated by Ridolfo del Ghirlandaio.

8. Sala d'Udienza
The ceiling and doorway of the audience hall are by the Maiano brothers; the frescos of the Roman hero, Marcus Camillus, are by Salviati. Donatello's Judith and Holofernes is here (removed from the piazza for safekeeping).

9. Sala dei Gigli
The Room of the Lilies

10. Cancelleria
Once the office of Niccolò Machiavelli.

11. Guardaroba
Fifty-three painted maps of Tuscan territories.

Quartiere degli Elementi
Five rooms decorated by Vasari with allegories of the elements.

S. Felice
A Gothic church with a facade by Michelozzo (1457).

Casa Guidi
After their secret marriage in 1846, Robert and Elizabeth Browning lived and wrote here until her death in 1861.

Pitti Palace
The ambitious Luca Pitti specified that the windows of his house be as big as the front door of the Medici palace. His impoverished descendants sold it to the wife of Cosimo I who found it much more agreeable than the Palazzo Vecchio. The 7-bay

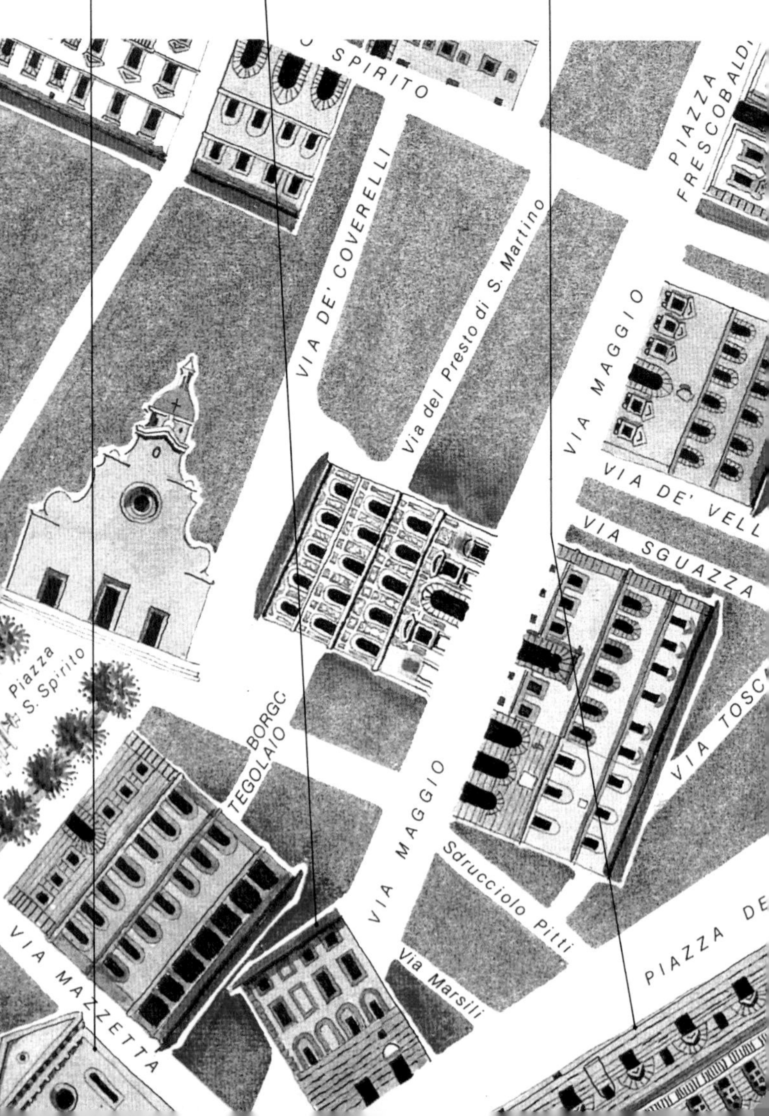

building was subsequently enlarged to the 20-bay palace that we see today. It now comprises six museums:

Galleria Palatina
Galleria d'Arte Moderna
Museo degli Argenti
Appartamenti Monumentali
Palazzina d. Meridiana
Coach Museum

Hours (all): 9.00–13.00; closed Monday.

S. Felicita

Grand-dukes used to attend services by peering in from a window in the Corridoio.

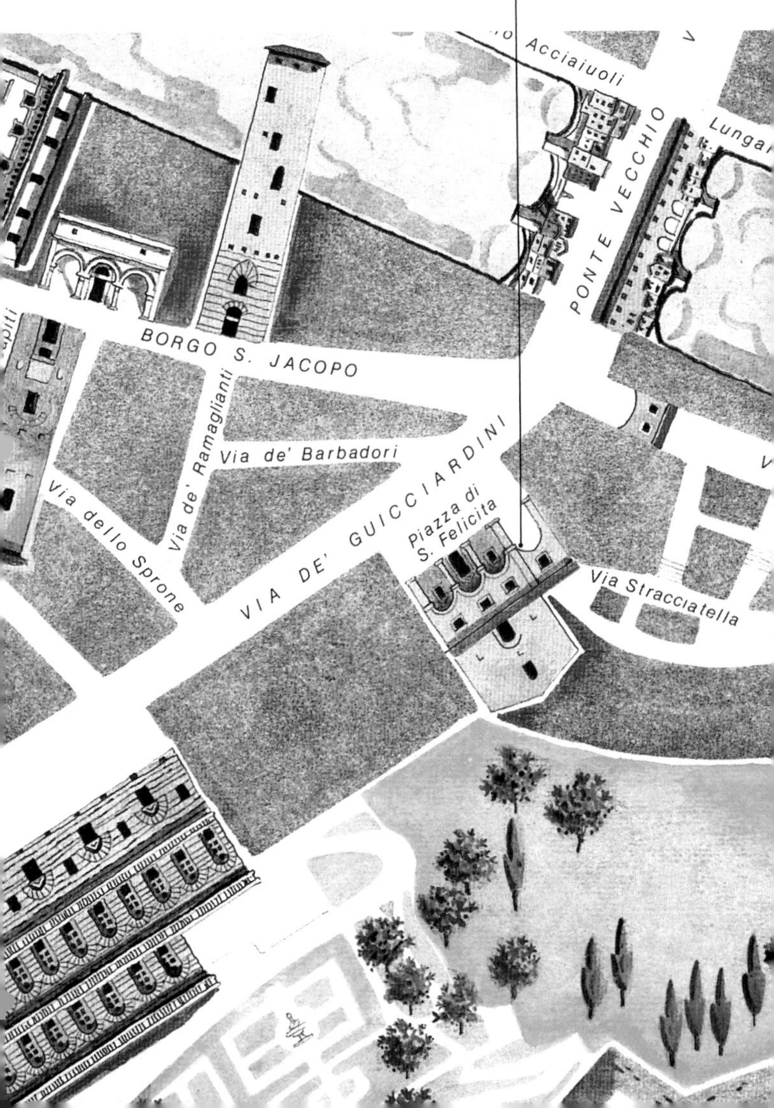

PALAZZO

GALLERIA PALATINA

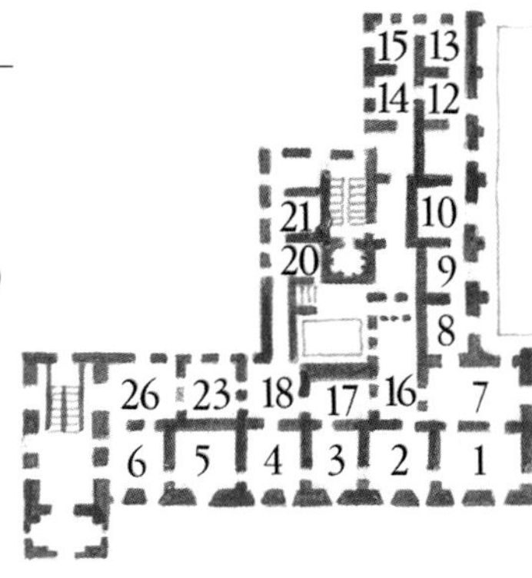

ROOM 1

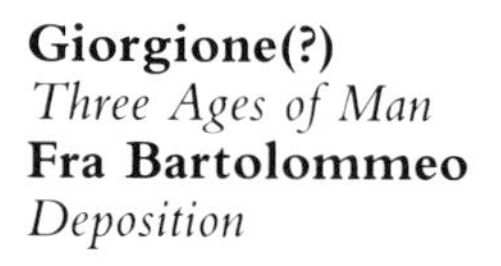

Titian
Portrait of Piero Aretino
Julius II (a copy of Raphael)
The Concert
Portrait of a Lady (la Bella)
Canova
Venus Italica

ROOM 2

Titian
Portrait of a Gentleman
Mary Magdalen
Van Dyck
Charles I and Henrietta-Maria
Andrea del Sarto
Holy Family
Deposition
Rosso Fiorentino
Madonna

ROOM 3

Rubens
Four Philosophers
Consequences of War
Van Dyck
Cardinal Bentivoglio
Titian
Cardinal Ippolito de' Medici

ROOM 4

Raphael
Portrait of a Lady
Giorgione(?)
Three Ages of Man
Fra Bartolommeo
Deposition

ROOM 5

Raphael
Madonna della Seggiola
Maddalena Doni
Madonna del Granduca
Perugino
Deposition

ROOM 6

Andrea del Sarto
Assumption (two works)
Titian
Philip II of Spain
Diego de Mendoza
Raphael
Portrait of an Expectant Mother

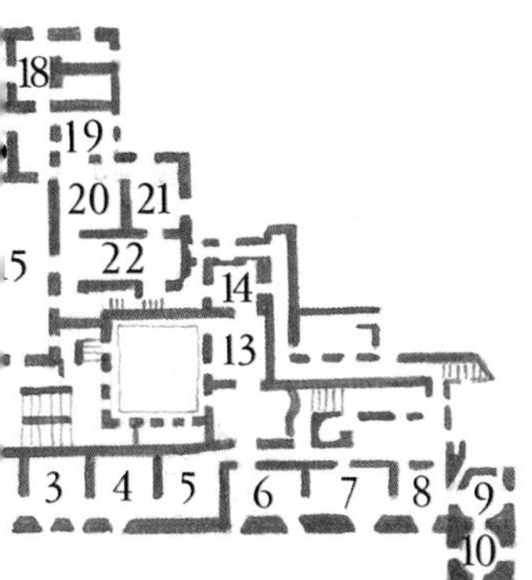

ROOMS 7–17

Various works

ROOM 18

Filippo Lippi
Madonna and Child (tondo)

ROOM 22

Rubens
The Three Graces

ROOM 23

Filippino Lippi
Death of Lucretia
Raphael
Madonna dell'Impannata

ROOM 25

Caravaggio
Sleeping Cupid
Cristoforo Allori
Judith with Head of Holofernes

ROOM 26

Matteo Rosselli
Fame and Virtues (ceiling)
Benedetto Bocchi
Majolica pavement of Bacchus

STATE APARTMENTS

Lavishly decorated in the 19thC by the House of Savoy, they contain many portraits of the Medici by Sustermans.

GALLERIA D'ARTE MODERNA

Sited on the floor above the Galleria Palatina, the collection is mostly of Tuscan artists in 41 rooms.

MUSEO DEGLI ARGENTI

Housed in the summer apartments are the Medici collections of crystal, cameo, jewellery, ivory and the silver treasure of the Archbishops of Salzburg brought here by the House of Lorraine.

PALAZZINA DELLA MERIDIANA

Contains historical costumes and a collection of paintings, furniture and majolica.

Boboli Gardens
The private gardens of the grand-dukes were first opened to the public in 1766. Hours: 9.00–16.30 (17.30 March, April, September, October; 18.30 in summer).

Isolotto
This was laid out by Alfonso Parigi in 1618.

Giardino dei Cavalieri
It is laid on a bastion built by Michelangelo in 1529.

Abundance
by Giambologna and Pietro Tacca

Porcelain Museum
A collection of Italian, French and German ware. Hours: 9.00–13.00; closed Monday.

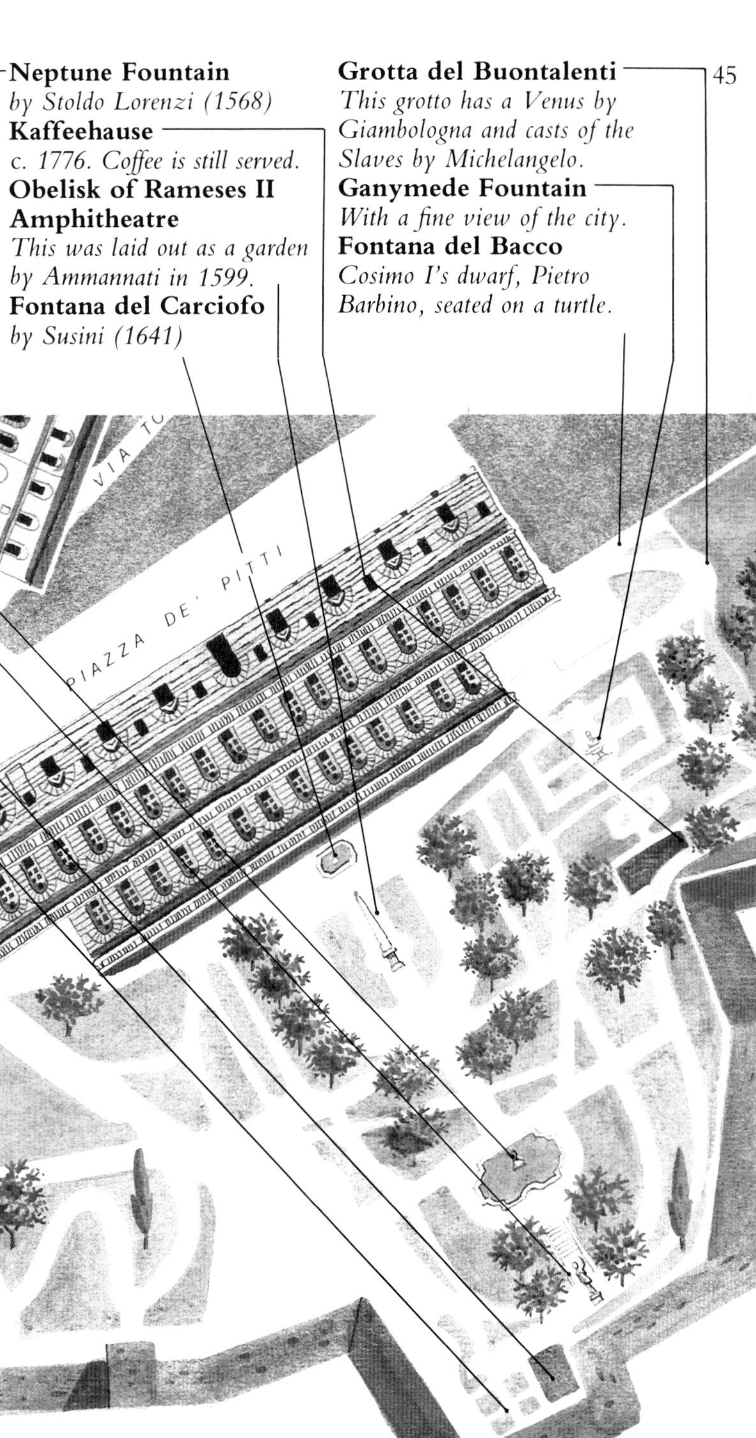

Neptune Fountain
by Stoldo Lorenzi (1568)
Kaffeehause
c. *1776. Coffee is still served.*
Obelisk of Rameses II
Amphitheatre
This was laid out as a garden by Ammannati in 1599.
Fontana del Carciofo
by Susini (1641)

Grotta del Buontalenti
This grotto has a Venus by Giambologna and casts of the Slaves by Michelangelo.
Ganymede Fountain
With a fine view of the city.
Fontana del Bacco
Cosimo I's dwarf, Pietro Barbino, seated on a turtle.

S. Maria del Carmine
The frescos of Masaccio in the Brancacci chapel were at once recognized as masterpieces and were studied by all aspiring artists, including the young Michelangelo, who had his nose broken here for insulting the work of a fellow student, Pietro Torrigiano.

Palazzo Manetti
This 15thC house was the home of Sir Horace Mann, the British envoy, 1740–86.

S. Spirito
Floor plan on the next page.

Palazzo Guadagni
Built by Cronaca c. *1505.*

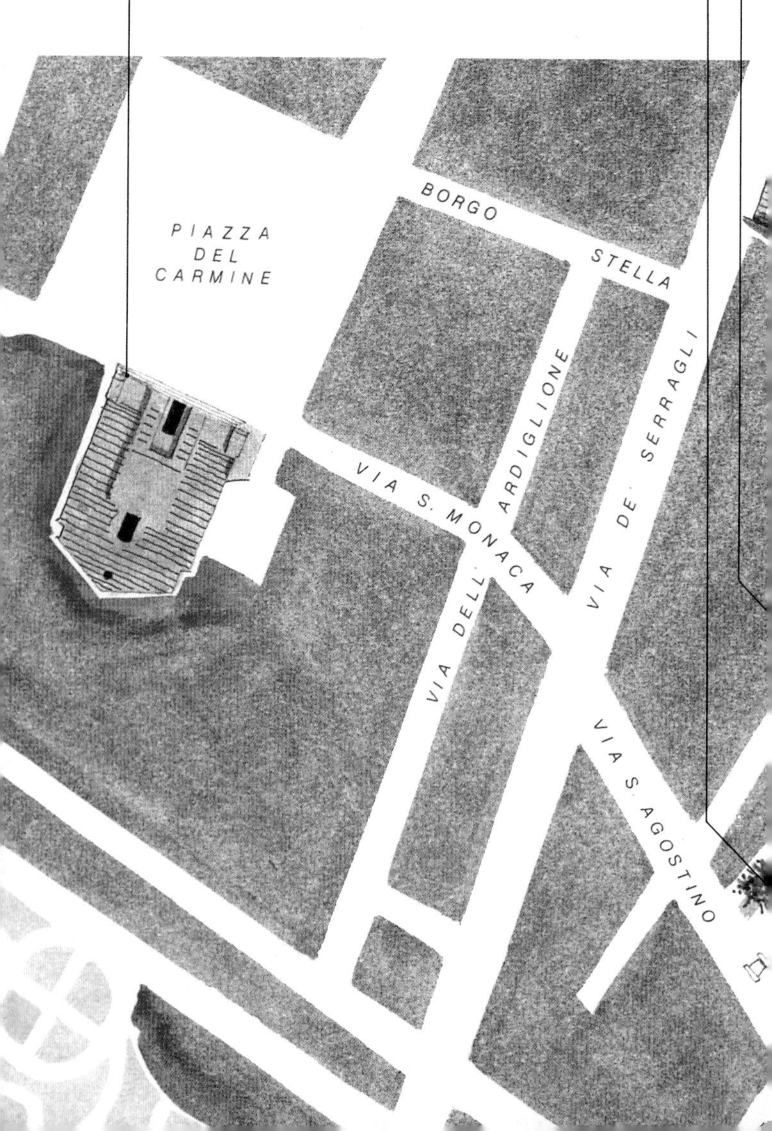

Palazzo Bianca Cappello
Archduke Francesco fell in love with the noble Venetian Bianca Cappello and built this house for her. She became his grand-duchess two months after the death of his first wife. Florentines thought her a witch who dealt in poison, especially when they both died of malarial fever on the same day.

Palazzo Ricasoli
Horace Walpole complained of a cold winter here in 1740.

Palazzo Ridolfi
Two palaces of 15–16thC.

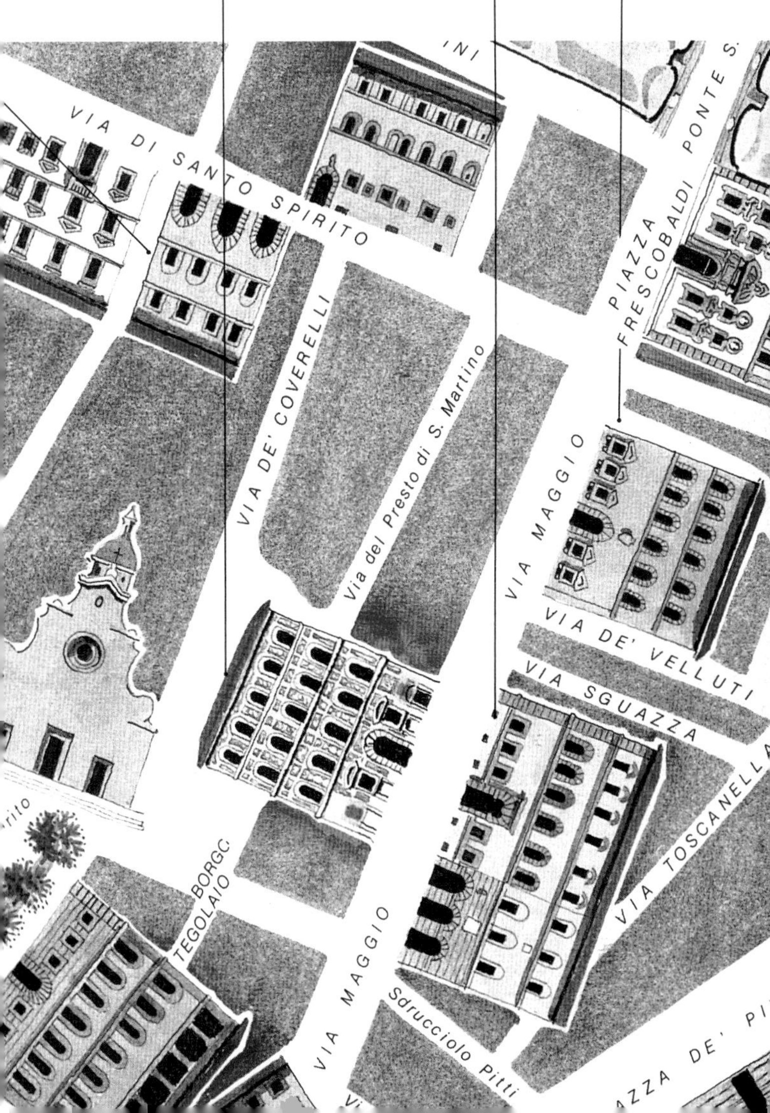

S. SPIRITO

The Augustinian monks of S. Spirito gave up a meal every day for fifty years to help finance their church. Vasari said it would have been the most perfect temple of Christianity if Brunelleschi's plans had not been altered after his death. The inside walls are divided into 38 chapels.

1. Pier Francesco Foschi
Disputa
2. Nanni di Baccio Bigio
Copy of Michelangelo's Pietà
3. Nanni Unghero
St Nicholas of Tolentino
4. Giovanni Stradano
Christ and the Moneychangers
5. Gherardini
Coronation of the Virgin
6. Passignano
Martyrdom of St Stephen
7. Giovanni Baratta
Tobias and the Angel
8. Curradi
Crucifixion
9. Pier Francesco Foschi
Transfiguration
10. Madonna del Soccorso
11. Buontalenti
Polychrome marble altar
12. Filippino Lippi
Madonna with Saints
13. Copy of Perugino
The Virgin and St Bernard

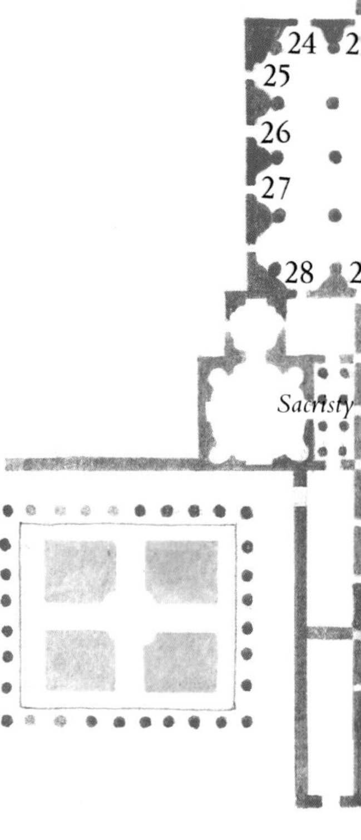

14. Sagrestani
Marriage of the Virgin
Rossellino
Sarcophagus of Neri Capponi
15. Madonna and Saints
16. Maso di Banco
Polyptych: Madonna and

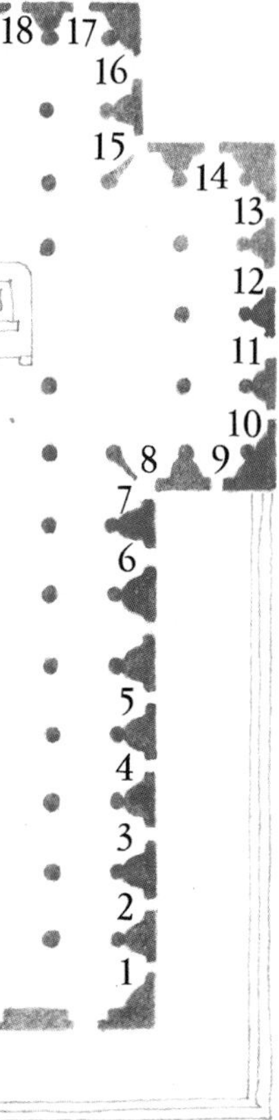

Child and Saints
17. Aurelio Lomi
Epiphany
18. Alessandro Allori
Martyred Saints
19. Alessandro Allori
Christ and the Adultress

20. Jacopo Vignali
Clara of Montefalco
21. Florentine School
Annunciation
22. Nativity *(late 15thC)*
23. Madonna and Saints
24. Verrocchio
S. Monica and Nuns
25. Cosimo Rosselli
Madonna and Saints
26. Sansovino
Corbinelli altarpiece
27. Maestro di S. Spirito
Trinity with Saints
28. Raffaellino dei Carli
Madonna and Saints
29. Michele Ghirlandaio
Way to Calvary
30. Madonna and Saints
31. Petrucci
Pala Dei (a copy)
Vestibule
The coffered vault is by Cronaca.
Sacristy
Inspired by the Baptistery.
33. Ridolfo del Ghirlandaio
Madonna, St Anne and Saints
34. Rutilio Manetti
St Thomas of Villanova
35. Taddeo Landini
Copy of Michelangelo's Risen Christ
36. Pier Francesco Foschi
Resurrection

S. Trinita
The facade is by Buontalenti. Inside Domenico Ghirlandaio frescoed scenes from the life of St Francis with many contemporary portraits, including Lorenzo il Magnifico. Luca della Robbia sculpted the tomb of Bishop Federighi.

Palazzo Minerbetti

Casa Gucci
Fighting broke out in the family boardroom in 1978 and Paolo Gucci left to set up on his own. Family lawsuits however, prevented him from using his family name, so in revenge, he revealed details of

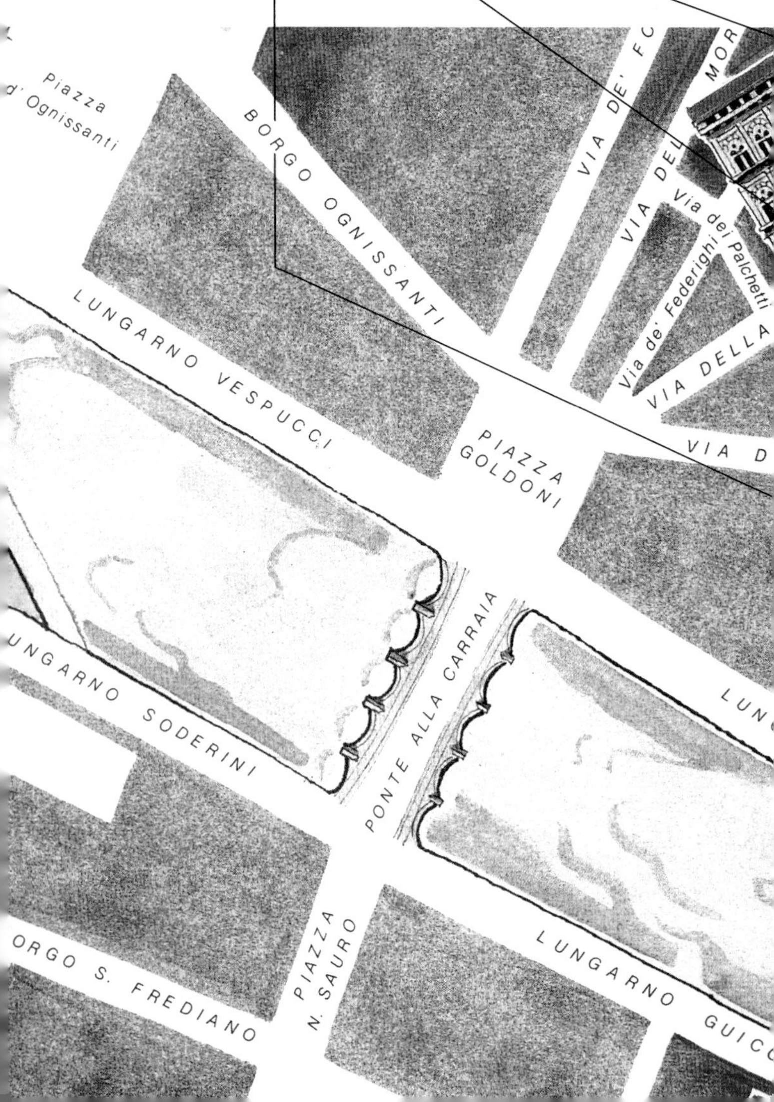

the family's novel accounting methods. His father, Aldo, 88, went to jail in New York. His two brothers were charged in Rome, while his cousin Maurizio fled to Switzerland. The 1987 bill for inter-family lawsuits was £480,000.

Palazzo Strozzi del Poeta

Palazzo Bartolini-Salimbeni
Built 1523.

Column of Justice
From the baths of Caracalla in Rome, a gift of Pius IV.

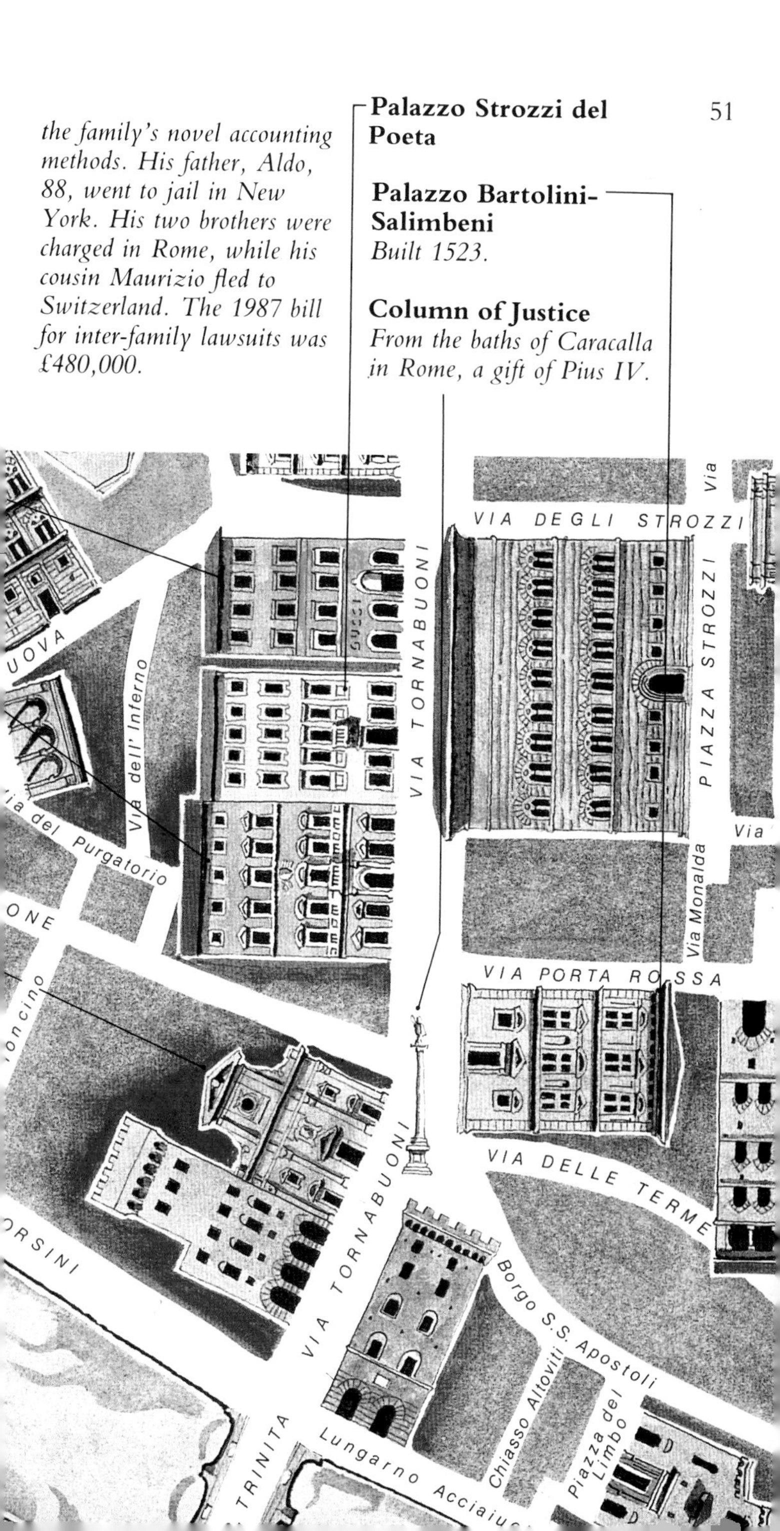

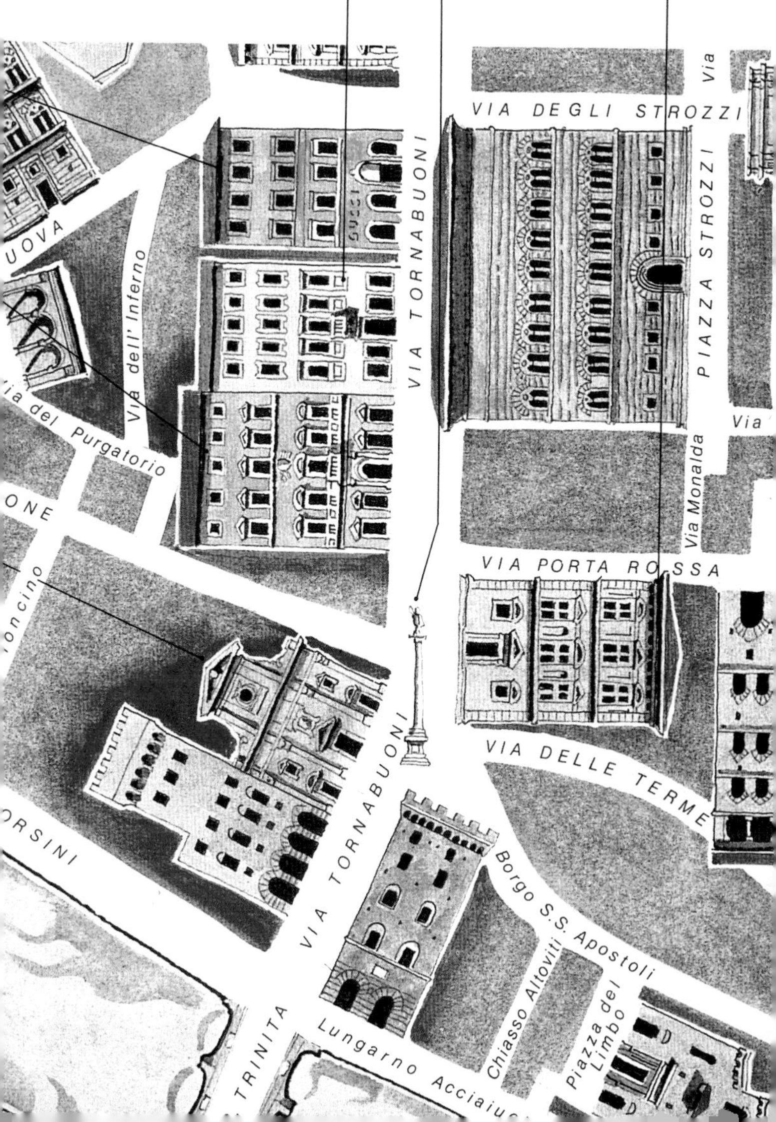

52 **Palazzo Rucellai**

Named after a red dye oricello *that they imported from the east, the Rucellai employed Leon Battista Alberti to design this, the first classical house in Florence (1451) and the Loggia opposite, which was built for the celebrations of the marriage of Bernardo Rucellai to Nannina de' Medici in 1466.*

S. Pancrazio

Now deconsecrated and a sculpture museum. The Rucellai chapel is 18 Via della Spada.

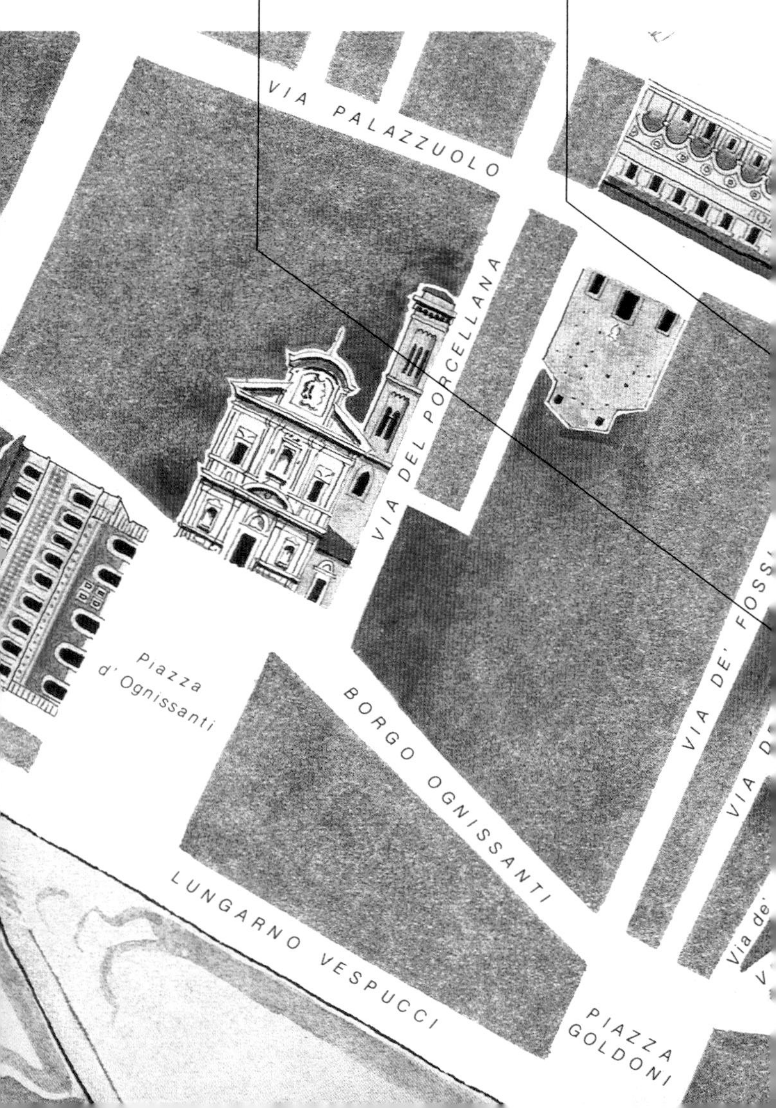

Palazzo Strozzi
Fearing opposition to his plan to have the grandest house in the city, Filippo Strozzi took his drawings to Lorenzo de' Medici, saying 'Look what the architect has done. It is much too grand for a modest man like me.' As expected, Lorenzo disagreed.

S. Gaetano

Palazzo Antinori
(1469) Once the Antinori family, in common with other nobles, sold wine outside the palace. Now they sell it inside, in a wine bar.

Palazzo Larderel

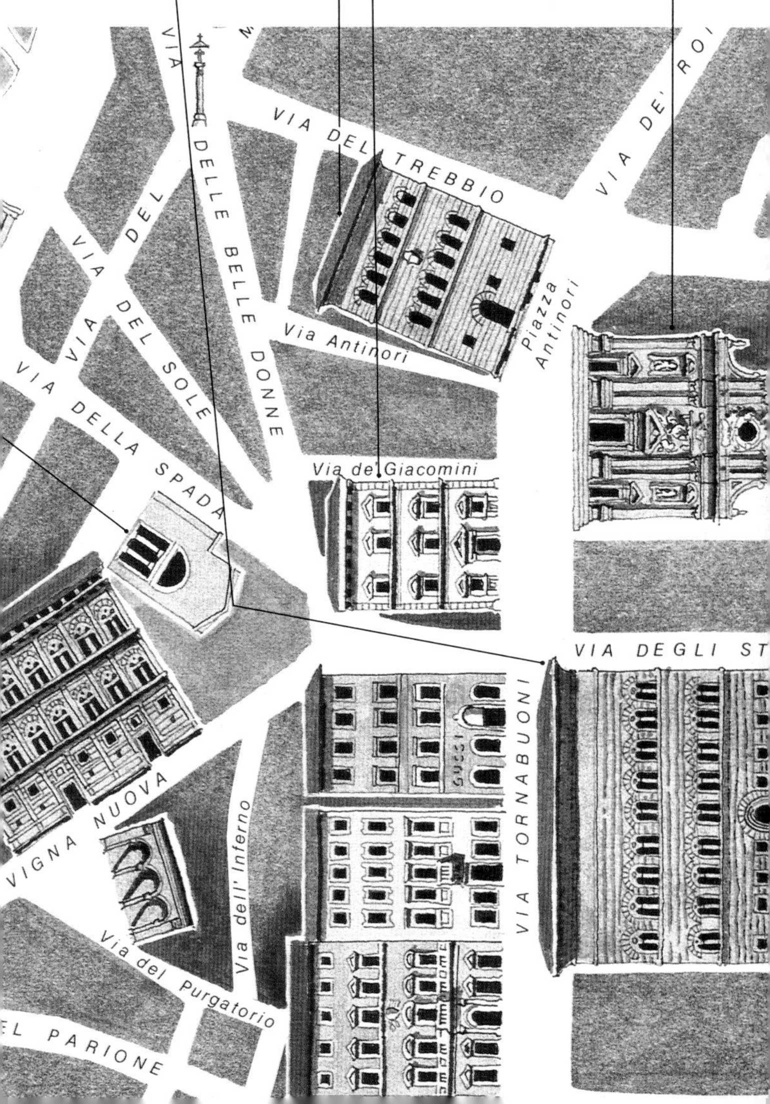

Stazione Centrale
The railway station.

Sita Autobus
For buses to Siena.

Loggia di S. Paolo
A copy of Brunelleschi's Loggia degli Innocenti, completed in 1496.

S. Maria Novella
*The militant order of Dominicans (*Domini Canes*, the Hounds of God) aimed to stamp out heresy. Their idea of pleasure was self-flagellation, which they encouraged, to the singing of psalms, on the 1st and 3rd Sundays of the month.*

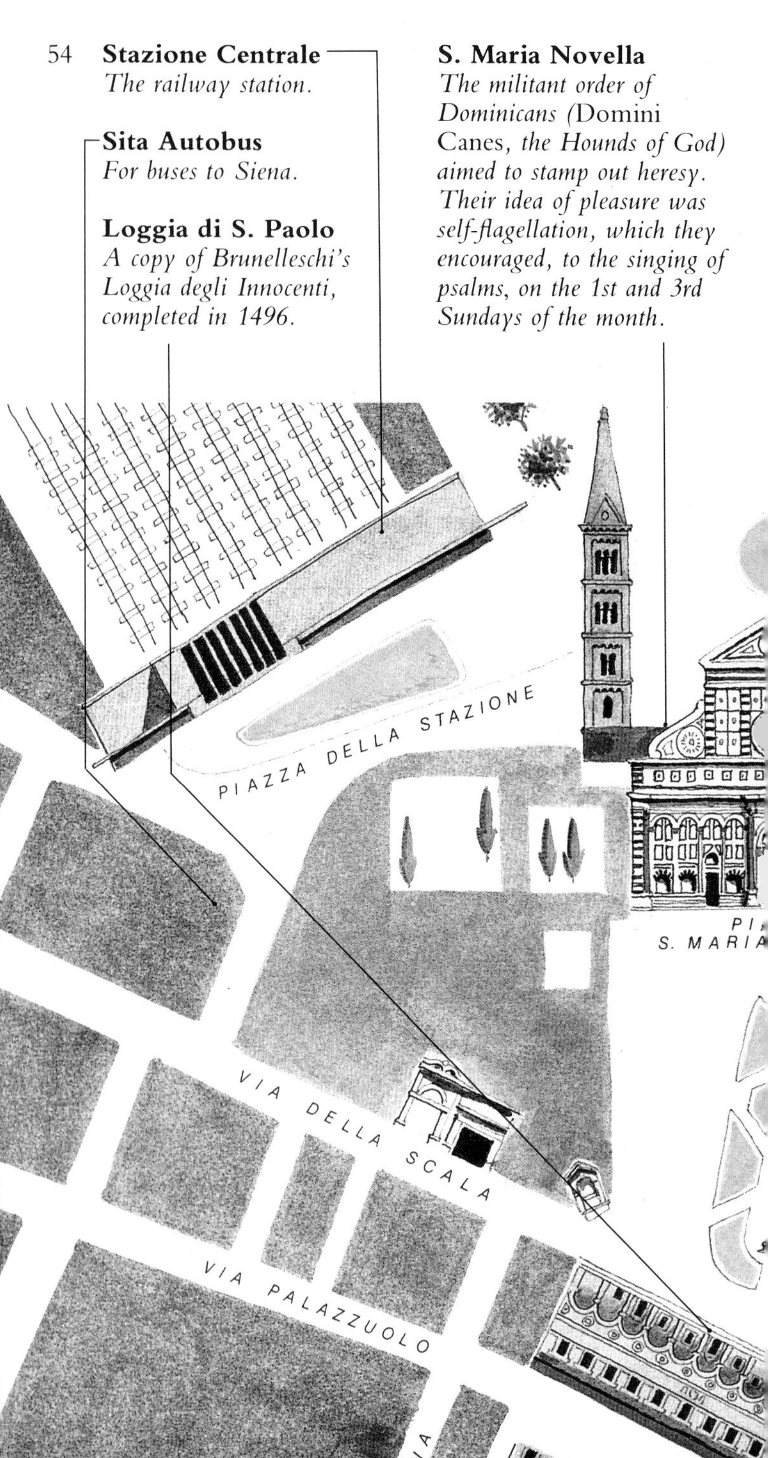

Boccaccio set the beginning of the Decameron *here in the church that had just been finished when the plague struck in 1347–9. The facade, the upper part designed by Alberti, was the first attempt to apply classical Roman ideas to church architecture. The Rucellai family had their name and their device, a billowing sail, prominently displayed in case of doubt as to who had paid for it.*

Croce al Trebbio
The site of a battle between Dominicans and 'heretics'.

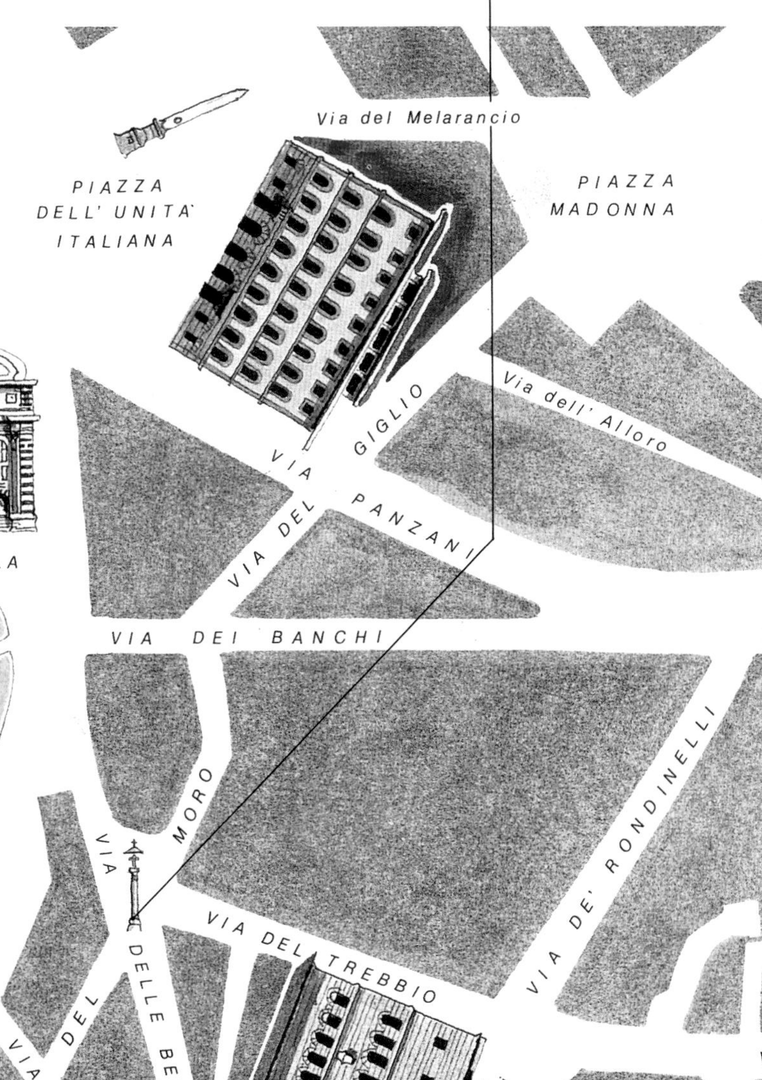

S. MARIA

CLOISTERS

Hours: 9.00–19.00; Sunday, 8.00–14.00; closed Friday.

1. Chapel of St Anne
Frescos of St Anne and Saints

2. Chiostrino dei Morti
The oldest part of the convent (c. 1270).

3. Spanish Chapel
Named for Eleonora of Toledo, it was frescoed by Andrea di Bonaiuto (c. 1365).

4. Museo d'Arte Sacra
Reliquaries, vestments, etc.

5. Green Cloister
Paolo Uccello
*Frescos of stories from Genesis, painted in green earth pigment (*terraverde*).*

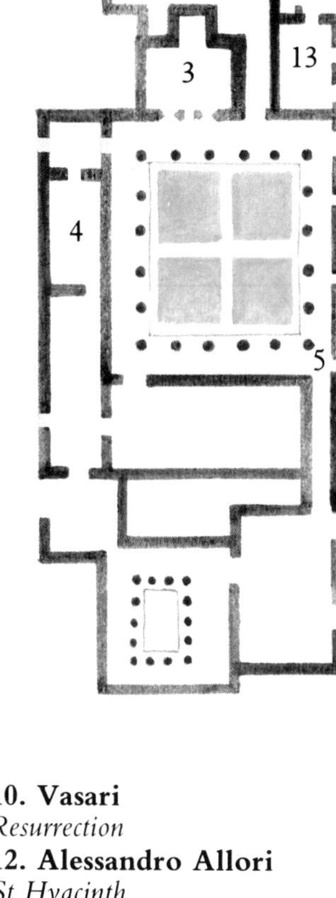

INTERIOR

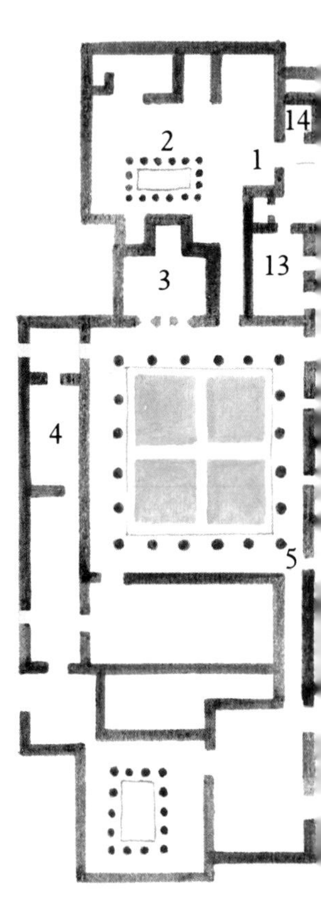

1. Strozzi Chapel
Frescos by Nardo di Cione (c. 1357)
VAULT: *S. Thomas Aquinas and Virtues*
END WALL: *Last Judgement*
RIGHT WALL: *Inferno*

6. Santi di Tito
Resurrection of Lazarus
Annunciation

7. Tomb of Antonio Strozzi

8. Alessandro Allori
Christ at the Well

9. Masaccio
Holy Trinity

10. Vasari
Resurrection

12. Alessandro Allori
St Hyacinth

13. Sacristy
Giotto
Crucifix (above entrance)
Giovanni della Robbia
Lavabo

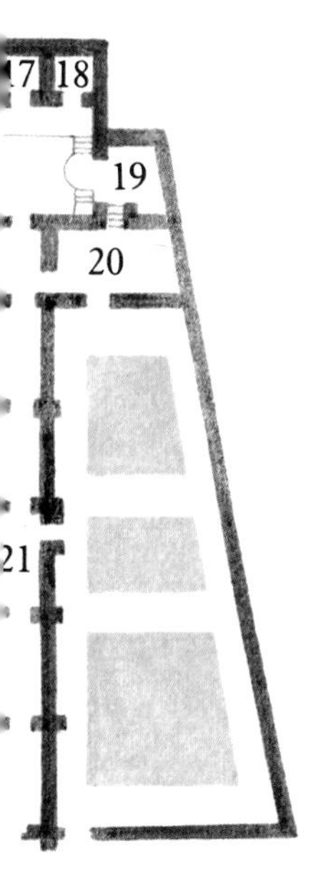

14. Gaddi Chapel
Bronzino
Resurrection of the Daughter of Jairus
15. Gondi Chapel
Brunelleschi
Wooden crucifix. Donatello is said to have dropped an apron full of eggs in astonishment at this work. It had been carved in secret in response to Donatello's crucifix in S. Croce, which Brunelleschi had said looked like a peasant. This was how Christ should look.
16. Main Altar
Crucifix by Giambologna
Domenico Ghirlandaio
Frescos (light fee)
RIGHT WALL: *Scenes from the Life of the Baptist*
LEFT WALL: *Scenes from the Life of the Virgin*
END WALL: *Coronation of the Virgin; Miracle of St Dominic*
VAULT: *The 4 Evangelists*
17. Strozzi Chapel
Filippino Lippi
RIGHT WALL: *Crucifixion and Miracle of St Philip*
LEFT: *Martyrdom of St John The Raising of Drusiana*
VAULT: *Adam, Noah, Abraham and Jacob*
Tomb of Filippo Strozzi
by Benedetto da Maiano
18. Bardi Chapel
Vasari
Madonna of the Rosary
19. Rucellai Chapel
Nino Pisano
Statuette of the Madonna
20. Chapel of the Pura
Jacopo il Meglio
St Vincent Ferrer Preaching
21. Naldini
Purification of the Virgin
Deposition

Fortezza da Basso
It was built after the fall of the republic in 1529 to protect the garrison brought in to prop up the unpopular Duke Alessandro de' Medici. The troops were Spanish, as no Florentines could be trusted for the role. It is only open for exhibitions.

Palazzo dei Congressi
An international conference centre.

Mercato Centrale
The city's main market was built by Giuseppe Mengoni in 1874. Hours: 7.00–13.00 (also Saturday 16.30–19.30 except July and August).

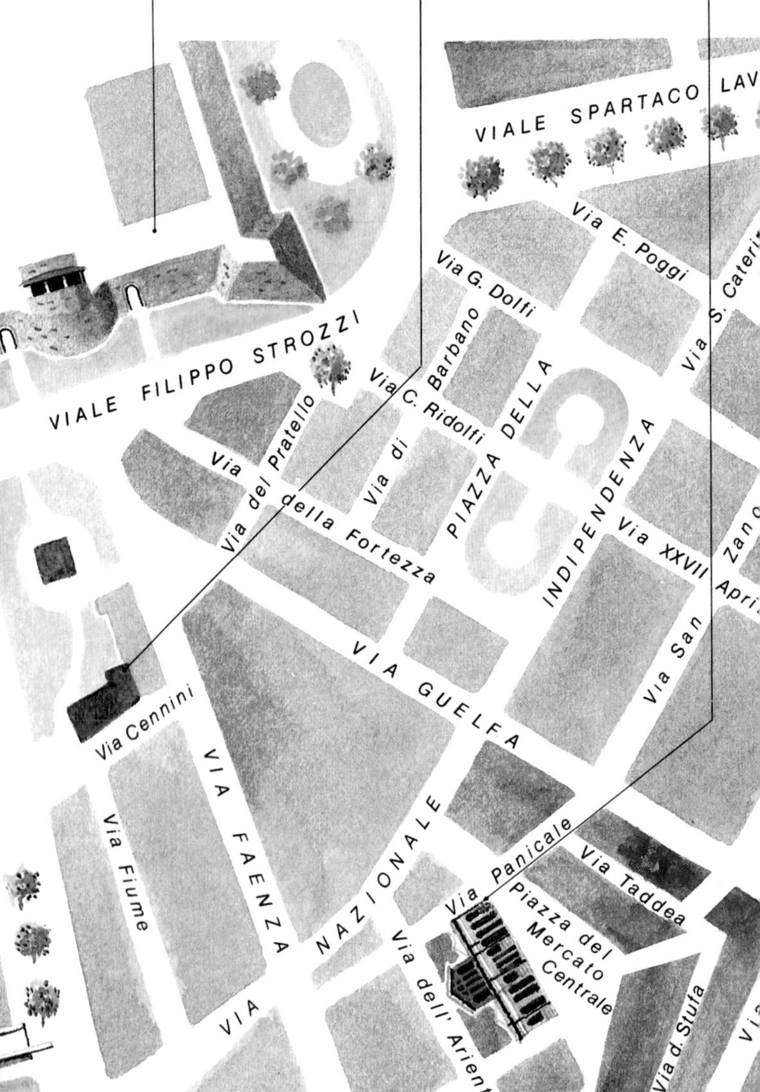

Viale
The avenues mark the line of the old city walls which were demolished in the 19thC when Florence was briefly the capital of the newly united kingdom of Italy (1861–75). Medieval walls, it was felt, were inappropriate for a modern expanding city.

Palazzo Capponi

Museo Archeologico
It houses one of the most important Etruscan collections in Italy. The first floor has an Egyptian museum and an Etrusco-Greco-Roman museum. Hours: 9.00–14.00 (13.00 Sunday); closed Monday.

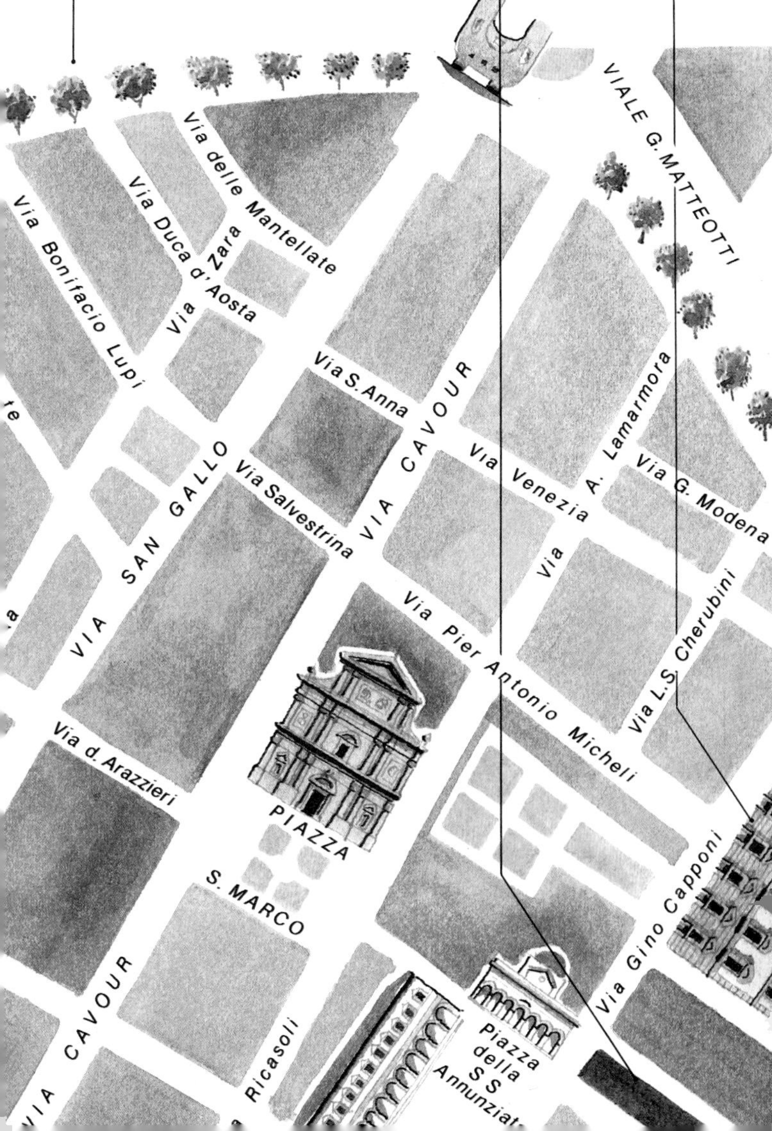

S. Apollonia
Ring the bell for admission to this former convent to see The Last Supper, the masterpiece of Andrea del Castagno (c. 1450).

Palazzo Pandolfini
Built in 1520 to a design of Raphael.

S. Marco
Floor plan on next page.

Palazzo Marucelli

Casino Mediceo
Now the Courts of Assizes and Appeals, it was built for an illegitimate son of Francesco I in 1574.

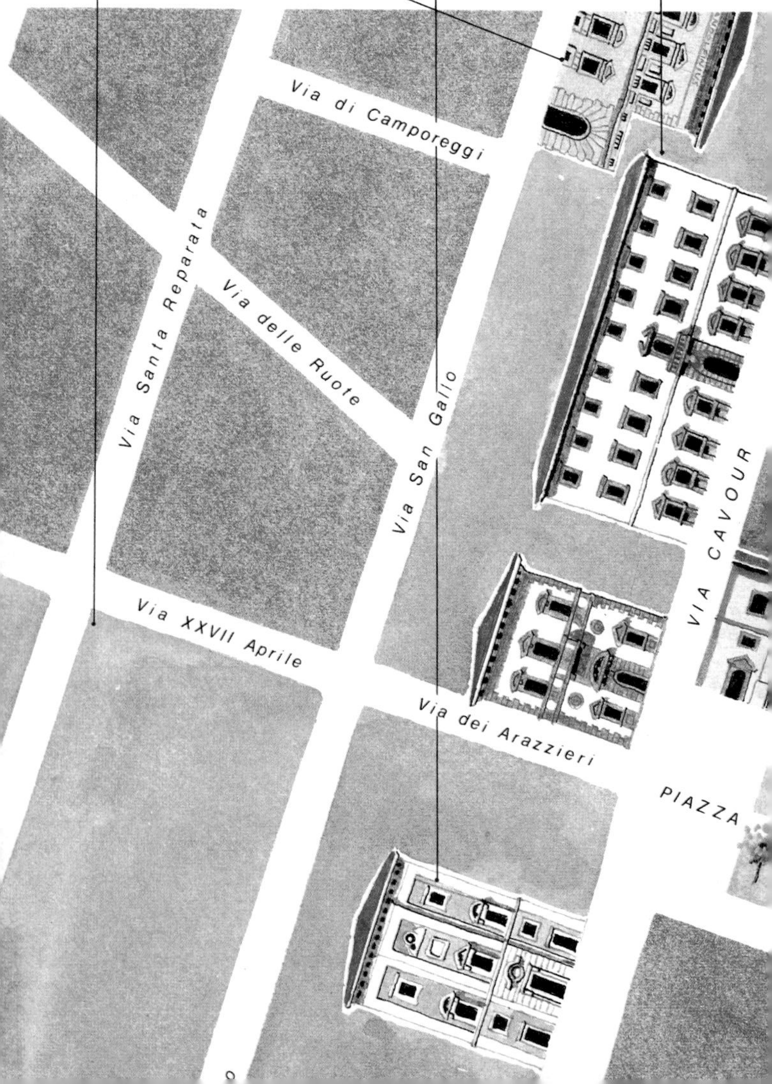

Galleria dell' Accademia
Here can be seen the originals of Michelangelo's David (1501–4), the Four Prisoners intended for the tomb of Julius II, (1521–3), and his Matthew, the only completed apostle for the facade of the Duomo. Also on display are works by Botticelli, Filippino Lippi, Bronzino and many others. Hours: 9.00–14.00 (13.00 Sunday); closed Monday.

University
The Studio Generale was founded by the city in 1321.

MUSEO DI

Cosimo de' Medici founded Europe's first public library in this Dominican convent, built by Michelozzo between 1437 and 1452. It is now the museum of Fra Angelico of Fiesole.

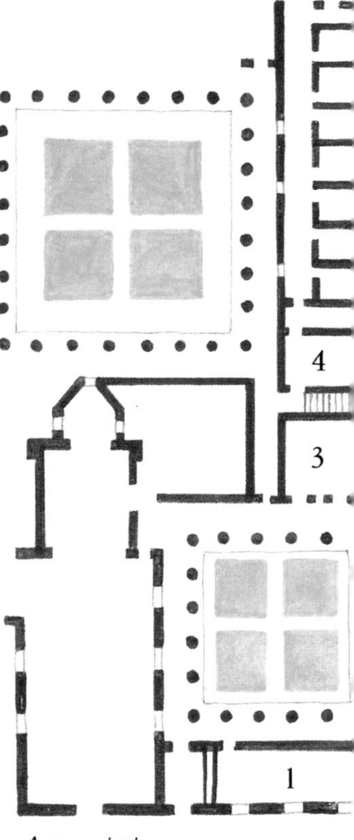

CLOISTER OF S. ANTONIO

Fra Angelico painted the four corner frescos:
St Thomas Aquinas
Christ Welcomed by Dominicans
Pietà
St Dominic at the Cross

1. PILGRIMS' HOSPICE

Fra Angelico
Deposition
Madonna and Child with Saints
The Marriage and Dormition of the Virgin
Last Judgement
Naming of the Baptist
Life of Christ
Madonna della Stella
Madonna and Child
Deposition
Madonna Enthroned (marble frame designed by Ghiberti)
Pala del Bosco ai Frati
Two small roundels
Roundel of the Virgin
Madonna Enthroned
Sts Cosmas and Damian
Annunciation
Adoration of the Magi
Alesso Baldovinetti
Marriage at Cana
Baptism of Christ
Transfiguration

2. GREAT REFECTORY

Often closed.
Fra Angelico

S. MARCO

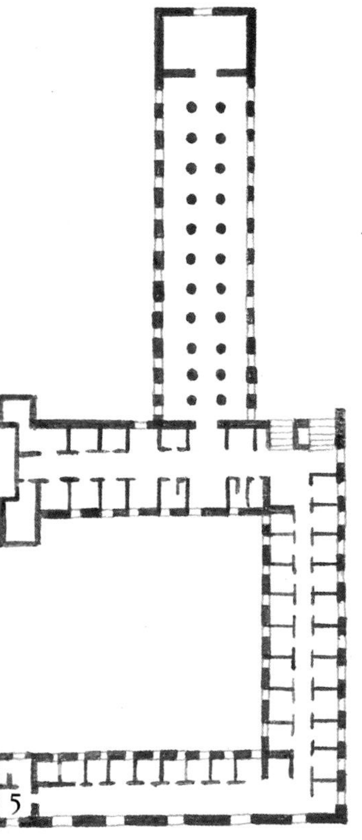

Lunette of St Peter Martyr
Crucifixion with Sts Nicholas and Francis

3. CHAPTER HOUSE

Fra Angelico
Fresco of the Crucifixion and Saints

4. THE SMALL REFECTORY

Domenico Ghirlandaio
Fresco of the Last Supper
Della Robbia
Terracottas

CORRIDOR

A collection of architectural fragments outside the cells of the Foresteria.

FIRST FLOOR

Fra Angelico's well-known Annunciation is at the head of the stairs.
The Dormitory has 44 cells, each decorated with a fresco by Fra Angelico or his assistants.

5. CELL OF SAVONAROLA

The room from which he was taken for torture and execution in 1498.
Fra Bartolommeo
Portrait of Savonarola

LIBRARY

Built by Michelozzo (1441), it contains many illuminated choir books and psalters.

CHURCH OF S. MARCO

Fra Bartolommeo
Madonna and Saints
Byzantine Mosaic
Madonna in Prayer (8thC)
Tomb of Pico della Mirandola

64 **Palazzo Medici-Riccardi**

Cosimo de' Medici's first choice of architect was Brunelleschi, but he rejected his model for being too grand. 'Envy', he used to say, 'was a weed that should not be watered.' On hearing the news Brunelleschi smashed the model into a thousand pieces. Cosimo then turned to Michelozzo who completed the house in 1460. At that time it was cube-shaped like the Palazzo Strozzi, but it was lengthened after it was sold to the Riccardi family in 1659. Inside is the Medici Chapel.

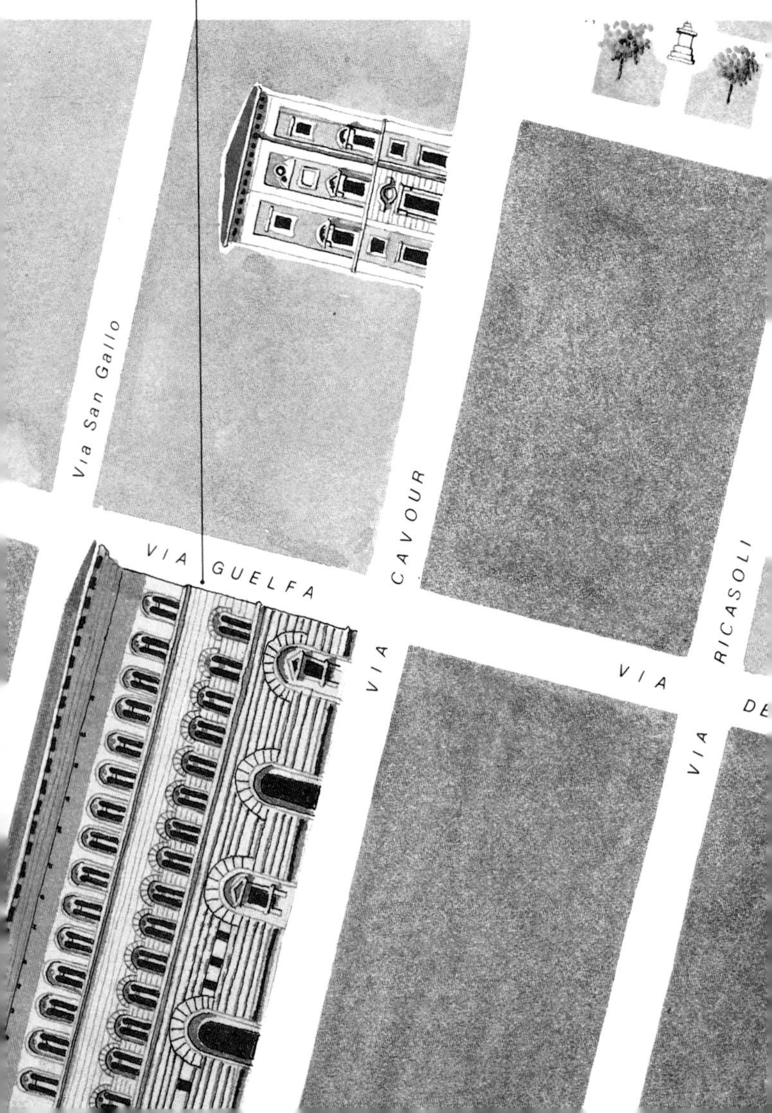

Medici Chapel
The splendid frescos by Benozzo Gozzoli, The Procession of the Magi (1459–60), include members of the Medici family and other Florentines. Hours: 9.00–19.00 (13.00 Sunday); closed Monday.

Ospedale degli Innocenti
Designed by Brunelleschi in 1419, it was built as a hospital for foundlings. The blue and white medallions are by Andrea della Robbia. The Gallery has works by Domenico Ghirlandaio. Hours: 9.00–19.00 (13.00 Sunday and winter); closed Monday.

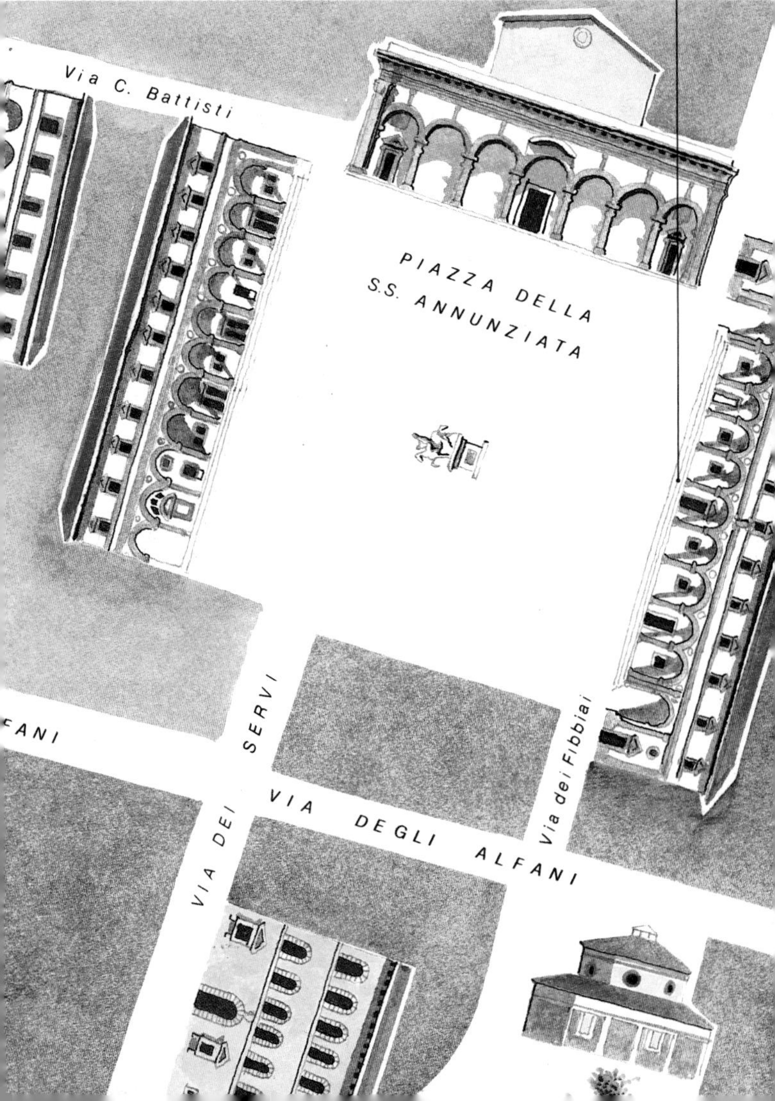

SS. ANNUNZIATA

Founded by the Servite Order in 1250, the church was rebuilt by Michelozzo and others between 1444 and 1481.

Chapel of St Luke
The seat of the artists' confraternity, many are buried here, including Cellini and Pontormo.

Vasari
A self-portrait as St Luke painting the Madonna

Pontormo
Madonna and Saints

Luca Giordano
Ceiling fresco of the Vision of St Bernard

Chiostro dei Voti
Frescos from right to left:

1. Rosso Fiorentino
Assumption

2. Pontormo
Visitation

3. Franciabigio
Marriage of the Virgin

4. Andrea del Sarto
Birth of the Virgin

5. *Coming of the Magi (with a self-portrait)*

6. Alesso Baldovinetti
Nativity

7. Cosimo Rosselli
S. Filippo Benizzi

8. Andrea del Sarto
4 scenes from the life of S. Filippo Benizzi

Tribune
Begun by Michelozzo and completed by Alberti in 1477.

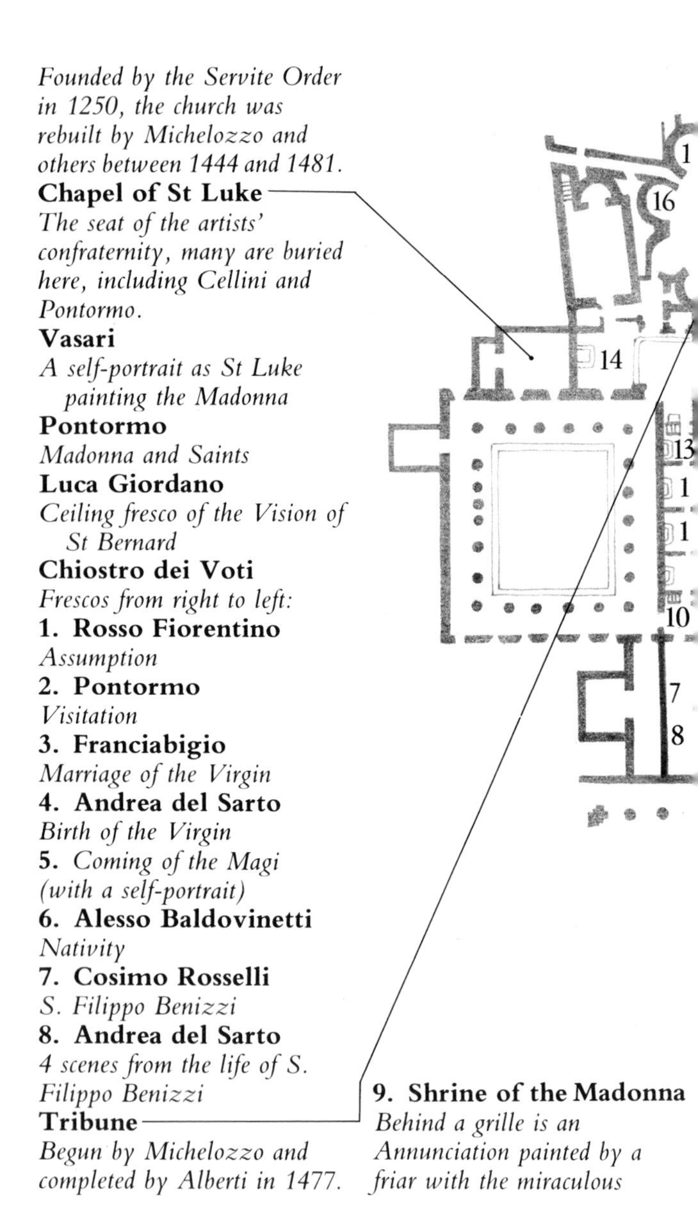

9. Shrine of the Madonna
Behind a grille is an Annunciation painted by a friar with the miraculous

intervention of an angel. For centuries it has been an object of pilgrimage for women seeking a pregnancy.

10. Medici Oratory
Andrea del Sarto
Head of the Redeemer
11. Andrea del Castagno
Trinity with Saints
Vision of St Julian
12. Giovanni Stradano
Crucifixion
13. Perugino
Assumption
14. Michelozzo
Terracotta Baptist
15. Tomb of Bishop Angelo Marzi Medici
by Francesco da Sangallo
16. Bronzino
Resurrection
17. Sarcophagus of Giambologna
18. Bandinelli
The Dead Christ Supported by Nicodemus (a self-portrait)
Behind the monument are reliefs of Bandinelli and his wife. He is buried here.
19. Painted Crucifix
by Alesso Baldovinetti
20. Monument to Orlando de' Medici
by Bernardo Rossellino
21. Colloredo Chapel
Designed by Matteo Nigetti.
22. Wooden Crucifix
by Antonio da Sangallo
23. Empoli
Madonna Altarpiece
23. Matteo Rosselli
Vault frescos

Palazzo Sforza Alimeni
An early 16thC building.

Rotonda S. M. d. Angeli
Begun by Brunelleschi in 1434, he never finished it. Modelled on the Temple of Minerva in Rome it is now used for lectures.

Museo di Firenze com' era
A museum of the city as it was. Hours: 9.00–13.00; closed Thursday.

S. Maria Nuova
A hospital founded in 1286 by Folco Portinari, the father of Dante's Beatrice.

Casa Cellini
Disaster struck as Cellini was casting his Perseus here in 1554. The furnace cracked and some alloy was lost to the fire. 200 pieces of pewter plate were hurled into the mould to try and make up the loss. Cellini retired to bed racked with fever. When he awoke and broke the mould, he was amazed to find a complete statue with not an ounce of metal left over. He attributed this to the work of God.

Teatro della Pergola
A theatre site since 1656.

Casa Buonarroti

Michelangelo never lived here, but bought three houses on the site in 1508 and left them in 1564 to his nephew, Leonardo, with a set of plans for building this house. It has been a public museum since 1858 with a number of the artist's drawings and sculptures, including his wooden model of the facade for S. Lorenzo. Hours: 9.00–13.00; closed Tuesday.

Loggia del Pesce

It once stood by the Ponte Vecchio for the sale of fish. It is now a fleamarket.

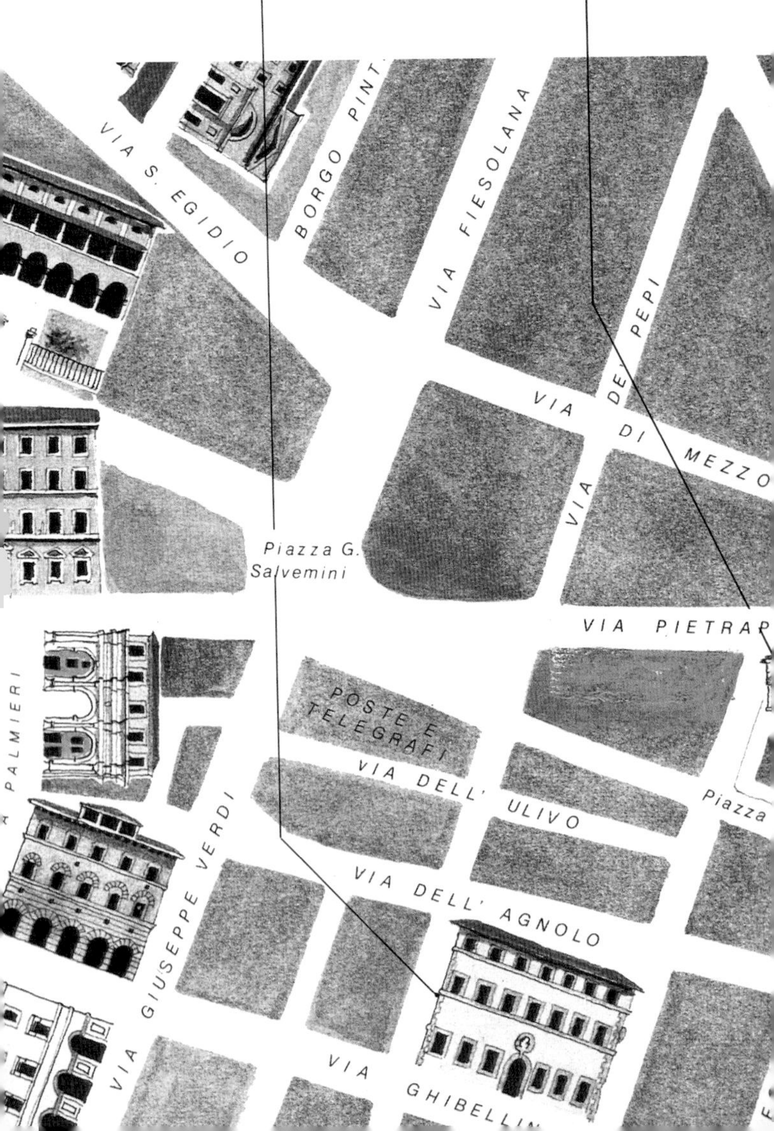

S. Ambrogio
Behind the 19thC facade lies a 13thC church with a fresco of the Madonna and Saints from the school of Orcagna; a tabernacle by Mino da Fiesole, who is buried under the pavement; and a large fresco of a Procession with a Miraculous Chalice by Cosimo Rosselli with many contemporary portraits.

Synagogue
It was built in the Spanish-Moorish manner in 1882.

Porta Beccaria
The gate of the butchers.

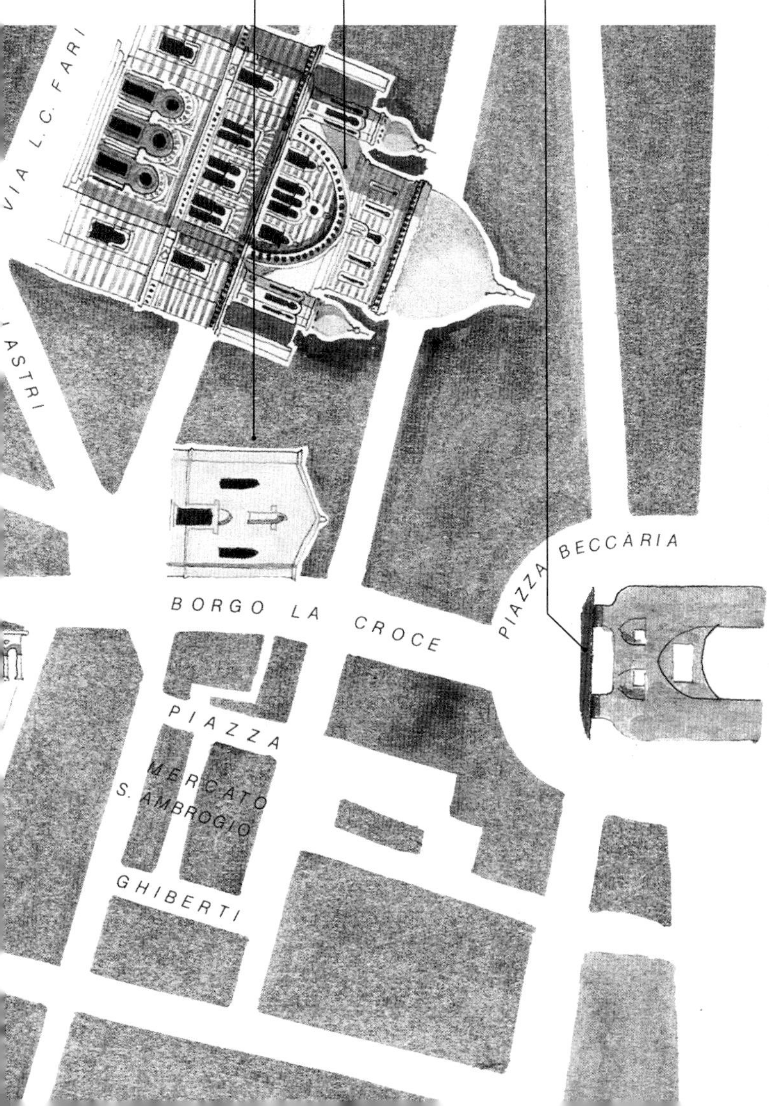

Palazzo Nonfinito
Left unfinished by Buontalenti and others, it is now the Museo Nazionale di Antropologia ed Etnologia.

Palazzo Pazzi
The home of the Pazzi conspiracy to murder the Medici in the cathedral.

Bargello
It was built as the Palazzo del Popolo in 1255, but soon became the residence of the Podestà *(the chief executive – usually a foreigner for his supposed impartiality). In 1574 it became the police headquarters and prisons (*bargello*). It is now the*

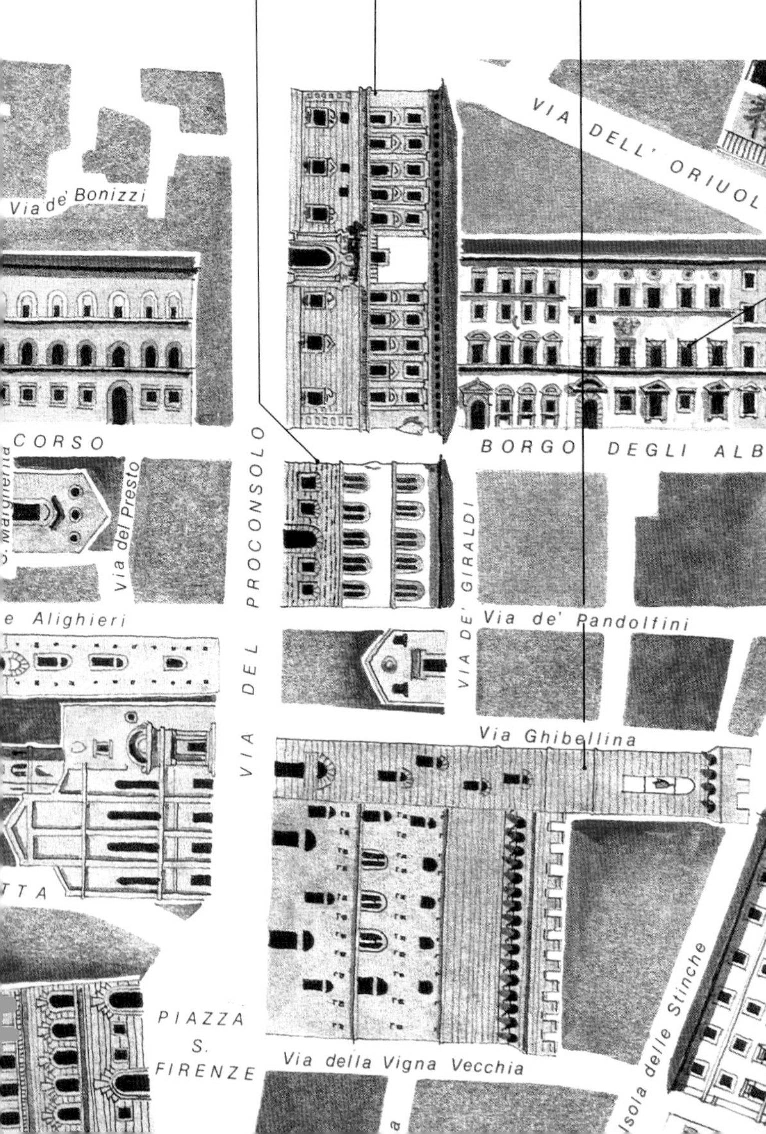

museum of Florentine sculpture. Hours: 9.00–14.00 (13.00 Sun.); closed Monday.

Palazzo Ramirez-Montalvo
Built by Ammannati (1568).

Palazzo Altoviti
Decorated with sculptured heads of famous Florentines.

Palazzo Salviati-Quaratesi

S. Pier Maggiore
The portico is all that remains of the church.

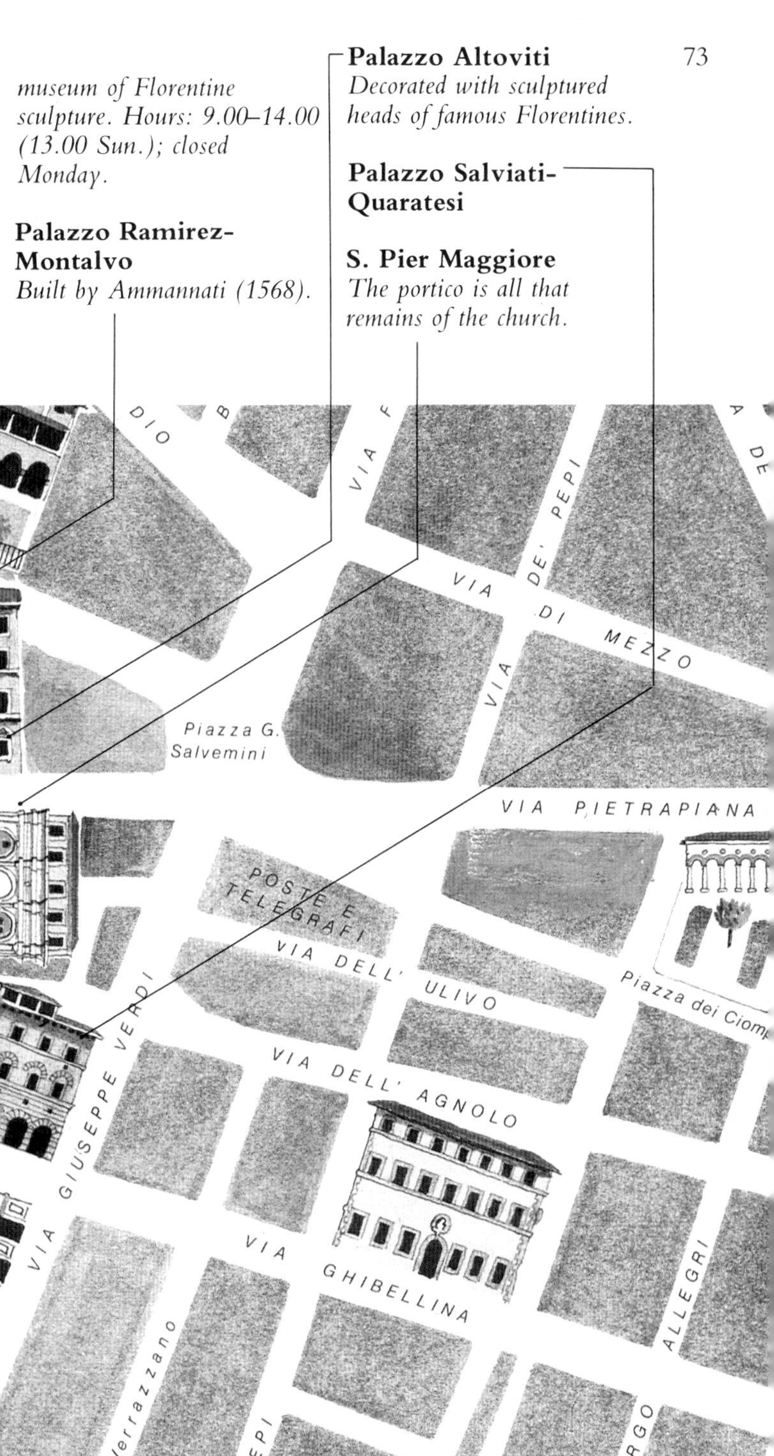

BARGELLO

ROOM 1

Taddeo Gaddi
Fresco of Madonna and Child
Rustici
Terracotta of horsemen in battle
Sansovino
Terracotta Madonna and Child
Michelangelo
Bacchus, his first major work
Tondo of Madonna and Child
Bust of Brutus
Apollo (or David)
Cellini
Bust of Cosimo I
Narcissus
Perseus Freeing Andromeda
Statuettes of Perseus, Mercury, Minerva, Jupiter and Danaë and her son
Ammannati
Two Graces
Vincenzo Danti
Moses and the Serpent
Honour conquering Defeat
A bronze door
Bandinelli
Adam and Eve

CORTILE

Danti
Cosimo I as a Roman
Niccolò di Piero Lamberti
St Luke (from Orsanmichele)
Ammannati
Six statues

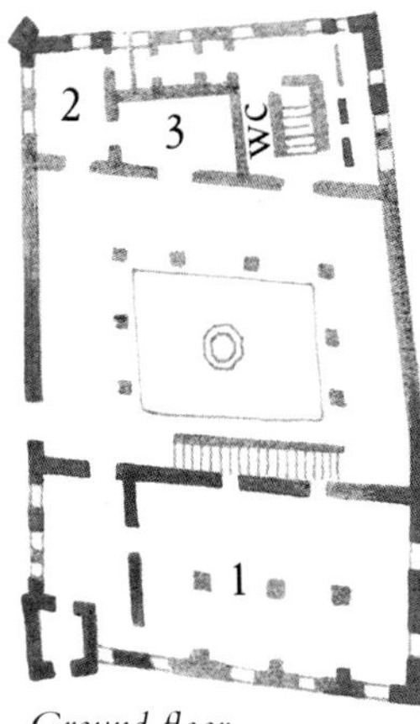

Ground floor

First f

ROOM 2

Paolo di Giovanni
Madonna and Child
Arnolfo di Cambio
Three Acolytes
Tino da Camaino
Madonna and Child

ROOM 3

Special exhibitions

ROOM 4

16thC sculpture

ROOM 5

Donatello
David (1409)
St George (Orsanmichele)
The Marzocco (Lion)

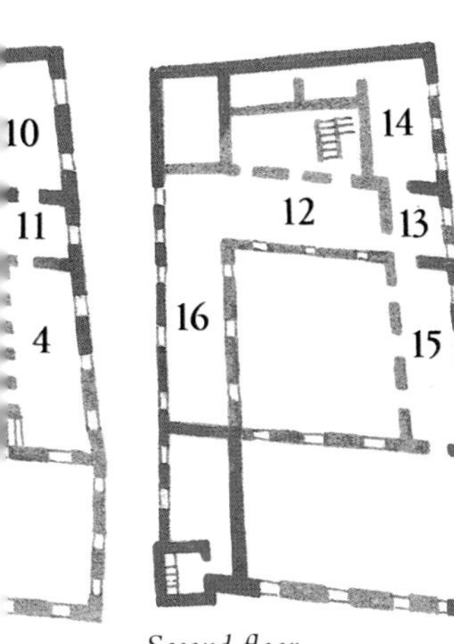

Second floor

Bronze David (1430)
Amor Atys
Michelozzo
Two Madonnas
Luca della Robbia
Madonna with an Apple
Madonna of the Rose Garden
Lunette
Two scenes of St Peter
Agostino di Duccio
Madonna and Child (two)
Desiderio da Settignano
St John the Baptist
The Panciatichi Madonna
Bust of a child
A Young Lady
Vecchietta
S. Bernardino of Siena

Ghiberti and Brunelleschi
Their trial reliefs for the doors of the Baptistery.

ROOM 6

Islamic art

ROOM 7

The Carrand Collection of decorative arts

ROOM 8

Chapel with 14thC frescos

ROOM 9

A collection of ivories

ROOM 10

A collection of majolica

ROOM 11

The Bruzzichelli Gift

ROOM 12

Giovanni della Robbia
Nativity
Bernini
Bust of Constanza Bonarelli

ROOM 13

Andrea della Robbia
Bust of a boy
Portrait of a girl

ROOM 14

Verrocchio
David
Woman with a Posy

Palazzo Cocchi
Built c.1480.

Roman Amphitheatre
The streets still follow the walls of the ancient theatre built in the 2ndC to hold up to 15,000 spectators. The martyrdom of S. Miniato was an attraction in AD *250.*

Piazza S. Croce
This was a popular site of tournaments, games and spectacles, including a 16thC Florentine game of football.

Palazzo Corsini
Now the Heraldic Institute.

Torre Alberti

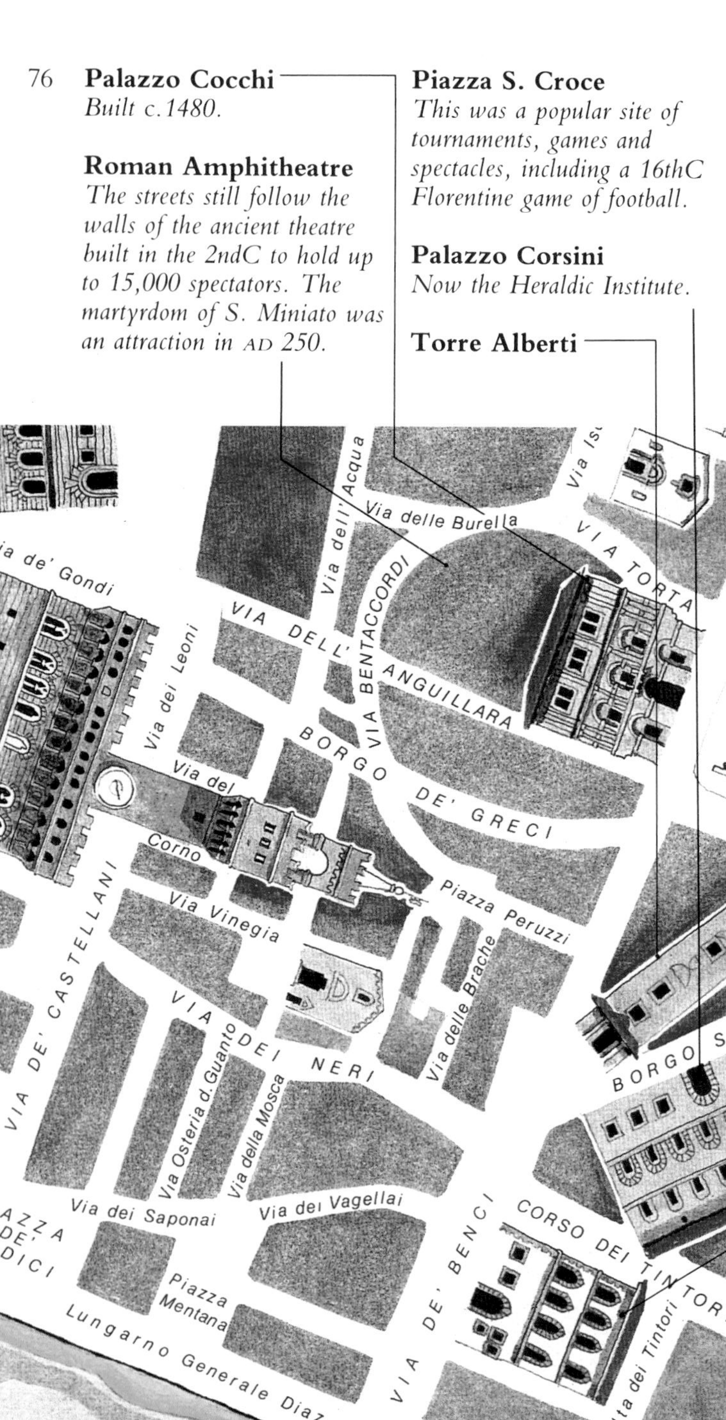

Museo Horne (Palazzo Corsi)
A collection of 14th–16thC painting and sculpture, housed in a 15thC building by Cronaca. Hours: 9.00–13.00; closed Saturday.

S. Croce
Floor plan on next page.

Pazzi Chapel and Museo dell'Opera di S. Croce
The chapel is one of Brunelleschi's most famous works; the interior is decorated with 12 roundels of the Apostles by Luca della Robbia. Hours: 10.00–12.30 and 15.00–17.00 (18.00 summer); closed Wednesday.

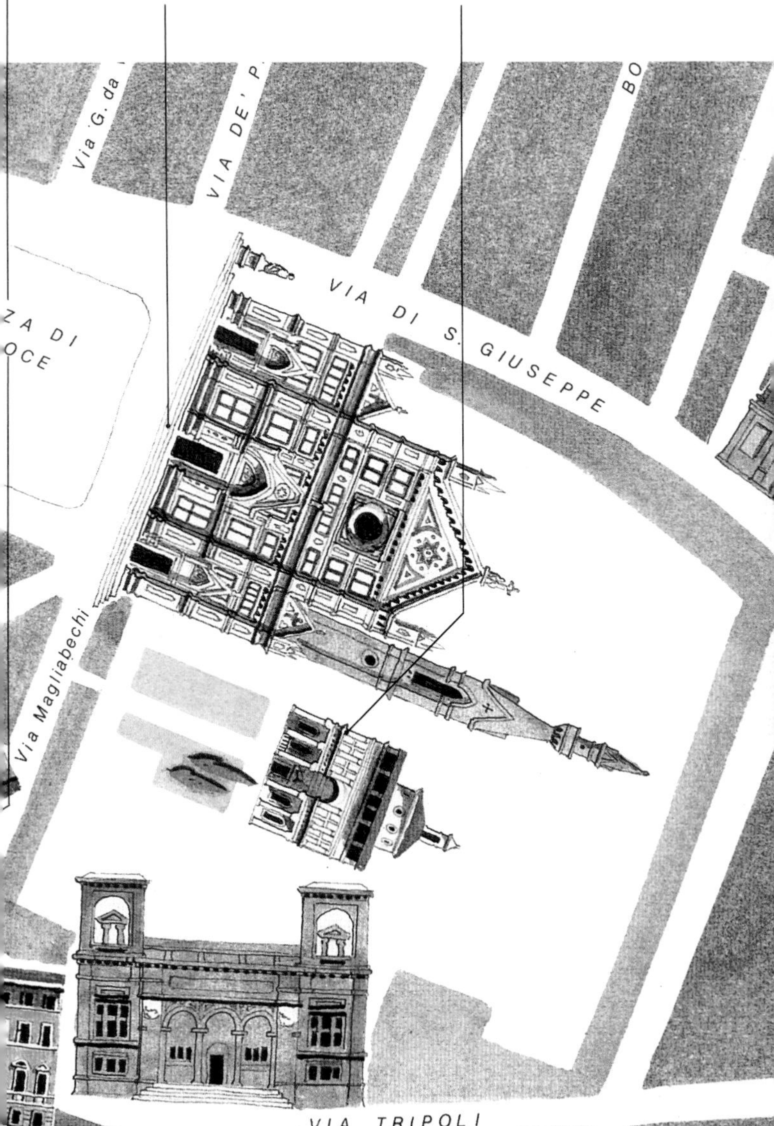

S. CROCE

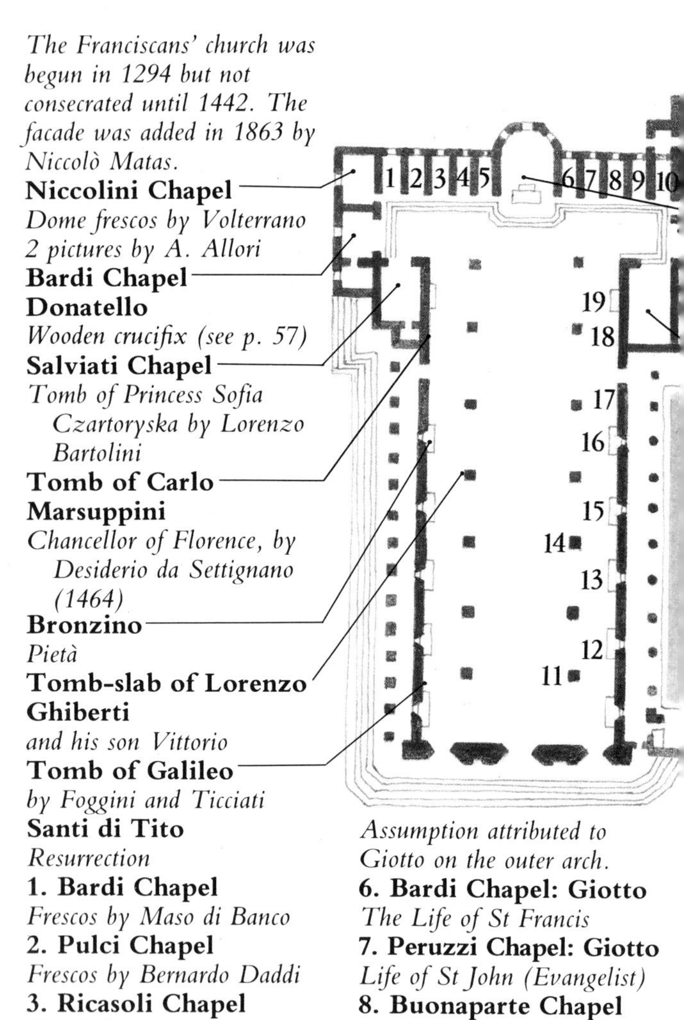

The Franciscans' church was begun in 1294 but not consecrated until 1442. The facade was added in 1863 by Niccolò Matas.

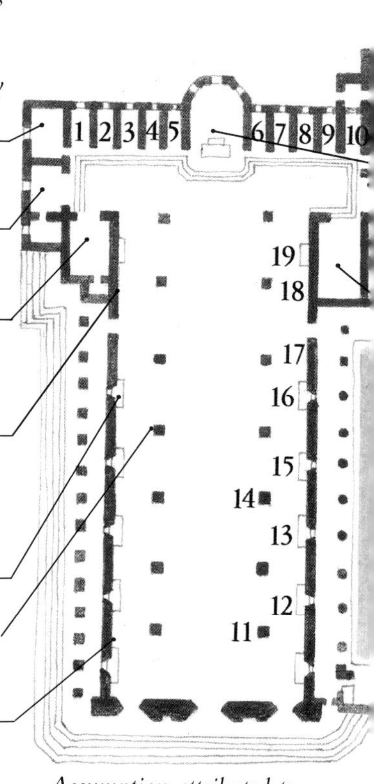

Niccolini Chapel
Dome frescos by Volterrano 2 pictures by A. Allori

Bardi Chapel

Donatello
Wooden crucifix (see p. 57)

Salviati Chapel
Tomb of Princess Sofia Czartoryska by Lorenzo Bartolini

Tomb of Carlo Marsuppini
Chancellor of Florence, by Desiderio da Settignano (1464)

Bronzino
Pietà

Tomb-slab of Lorenzo Ghiberti
and his son Vittorio

Tomb of Galileo
by Foggini and Ticciati

Santi di Tito
Resurrection

1. Bardi Chapel
Frescos by Maso di Banco

2. Pulci Chapel
Frescos by Bernardo Daddi

3. Ricasoli Chapel
19thC frescos

4. Capponi Chapel
Modern monument to Italian motherhood by Andreotti

5. Tosinghi Chapel
Assumption attributed to Giotto on the outer arch.

6. Bardi Chapel: Giotto
The Life of St Francis

7. Peruzzi Chapel: Giotto
Life of St John (Evangelist)

8. Buonaparte Chapel

9. Calderini Chapel
Frescoed by Taddeo Gaddi

10. Velluti Chapel
Faded frescos of St Michael

11. Madonna del Latte

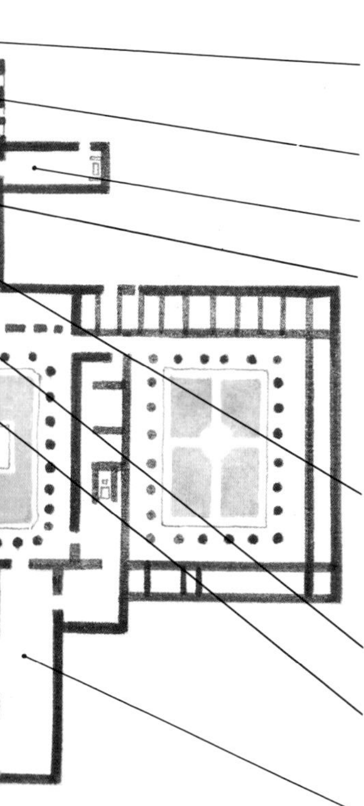

by Antonio Rossellino
12. Tomb of Michelangelo
by Vasari
13. Cenotaph of Dante
by Stefano Ricci (1829)
14. Pulpit
by Maiano
15. Canova
Tomb of Vittorio Alfieri
16. Tomb of Machiavelli
by Innocenzo Spinazzi (1787)

17. Donatello
Annunciation
Rinuccini Chapel
Frescoed by Giovanni da Milano and others (1366)
Sacristy
Crucifixion by Taddeo Gaddi
Novices' Chapel
Tabernacle by Mino da Fiesole
Sanctuary
Agnolo Gaddi
The Legend of the True Cross
Crucifix
School of Giotto
Altarpiece
Niccolò Gerini
Baroncelli Chapel
Frescos by Taddeo Gaddi
Giotto
Altarpiece of the Coronation of the Virgin
Pazzi Chapel
by Filippo Brunelleschi
Castellani Chapel
Frescos by Agnolo Gaddi and others
Museo dell 'Opera di S. Croce
Last Supper and Tree of the Cross, by Taddeo Gaddi
Cimabue's great crucifix
Traces of Hell by Orcagna
18. Tomb of Leonardo Bruno,
Chancellor of Florence, by Bernardo Rossellino
19. Tomb of Gioacchino Rossini,
the composer, by Cassioli

Forte di Belvedere

It was built to house a Spanish garrison enlisted to protect the duke from his republican-minded subjects. It has only been open to the public since 1958 and is now used for exhibitions. Well named, Belvedere means good views; it was designed in 1590 by the equally well-named Buontalenti. His 'good talents' are said to have even included the invention of the basic recipe for ice-cream.

Porta S. Giorgio

Part of walls built in 1258. The relief of St George is a copy.

Casa Galileo
To Galileo, the moons of Jupiter must have looked like the balls on the Medici arms, for he named them Medicea Sidera. *He was the first physicist to refuse to accept theology as a science. This refusal brought him before the Inquisition.*

Palazzo Torrigiani
A 16thC building.

Museo Bardini
An eclectic art collection, Hours: 9.00–14.00 (13.00 Sunday); closed Wednesday.

Palazzo dei Mozzi
Built between 1260–73.

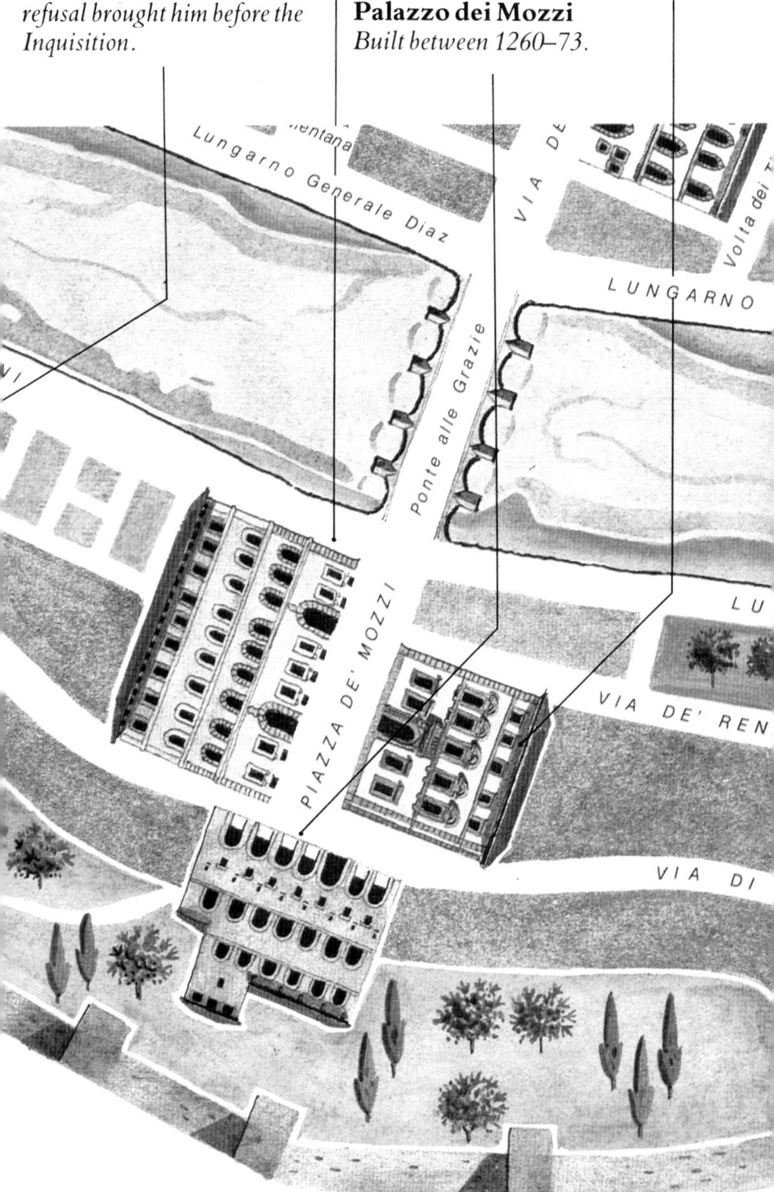

A Room with a View

This modest hotel, now the Jennings Riccioli, provided E. M. Forster with the model of the 'Pension Bertolini' in his novel A Room with a View. *In Forster's day there was a good view of the Duomo. This has since been blocked by the Biblioteca Nazionale.*

Biblioteca Nazionale

Formed from the old grand-ducal library of illuminated manuscripts and early books, the collection has letters of Machiavelli, Michelangelo, Poliziano and Tasso, and some 300 volumes of Galileo's papers. Hours: 9.00–19.00, weekdays.

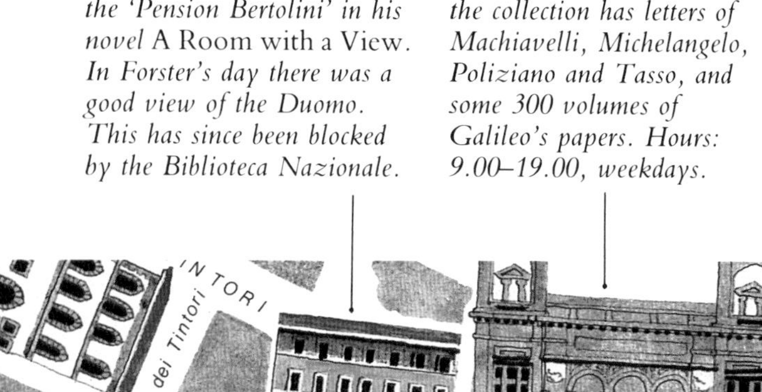

S. Niccolò
Michelangelo is said to have hidden in the bell tower to avoid being rounded up with other political activists at the fall of the Republic in 1529. He had been in charge of the southern defences against the armies of the Pope and the Emperor. Inside the church there are frescos of S. Ansano, and in the Sacristy, the Madonna della Cintola. (Late 15thC.)

Porta S. Miniato

Porta S. Niccolò
The tallest of the old gates.

S. MINIATO AL MONTE

The martyr Minias was beheaded in the amphitheatre of Florentia during the persecutions of Christians by the Emperor Decius in 250. He is said to have miraculously replaced his head and marched across the river and up the hill to this spot, where he expired. The church, the finest in Florence, was built over his tomb by Bishop Hildebrand in 1013. The facade was completed in 1270.

Chapel of the Cardinal of Portugal
He died in Florence in 1459 and his memorial was built in 1460 by Antonio Manetti. The tomb was carved by Antonio Rossellino, the altarpiece is by the Pollaiuolo brothers.

Raised Choir
The only one in Florence.

Apse Mosaic
Christ blessing Mary and S. Miniato, 1297 (light fee).

Sacristy
Frescos by Spinello Aretino.

Crypt
Frescos by Taddeo Gaddi.

Cappella del Crocifisso
Commissioned by Piero de' Medici in 1448, the panels were painted by Agnolo Gaddi; the terracotta roof is by Luca della Robbia.

I LUNGARNI

THE RIVERBANKS

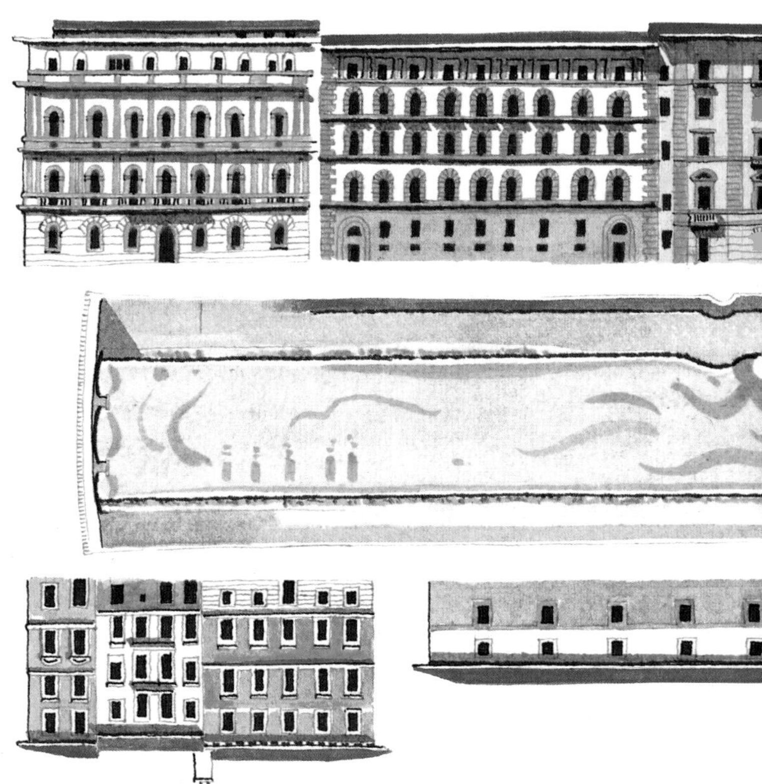

The Arno was a source of both wealth and pestilence in the 15thC. The river was used in washing, dyeing and curing of the cloth and leather which produced wealth but, together with the city's sewerage, created what Dante called 'a cursed and unlucky ditch'. It was not until the 16thC that it came to be a place of pleasure walks, appreciated for its views.

Grand Hotel
This was a favourite of Queen Victoria who stayed three times. It is built on the site of a Brunelleschi palace built for the Giustini family.

Ognissanti
The wealth of Florence was founded here in 1239 when the commune leased this land to the Order of the Umiliati, which began the wool industry. It employed, at its

S. Frediano in Cestello
The Cestelli (Cistercians) arrived in 1628 and rebuilt the church to the design of the Roman architect, Cerutti. The cupola was added by Antonio Ferri in 1698.

Granaio di Cosimo III
The granary (1695) is now a barracks.

peak c. 1425, a quarter of the city's population. The church and convent passed to the Franciscans in 1561, and they commissioned the facade from Nigetti 1637. In the convent next door (No. 42) is a St Augustine by Botticelli, who is buried in the church, and a Last Supper and a St Jerome by Domenico Ghirlandaio.

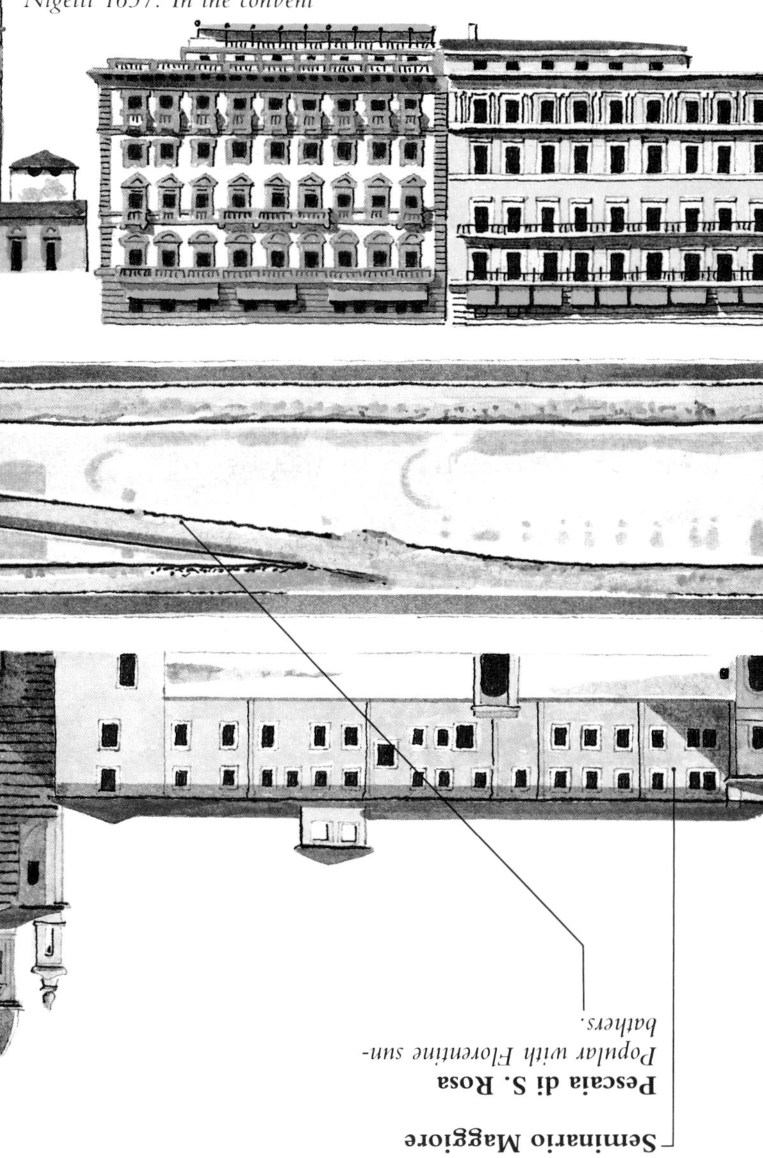

Lungarno Vespucci

Columbus died never knowing that he had discovered a new world. The Florentine, Amerigo Vespucci, an agent of the Medici bank in Seville, suspected the truth and he confirmed it on two voyages down the full length of the coast of South America. His reports to the bank caused great excitement when they

priceless books and works of art. At least the bridges held. In the flood of 1333, three were swept away and the water submerged the altar in the Baptistery. The chronicler Villani records that the streets and houses were filled with a foul-smelling mud that took six months to clear.

were published in 1504 under the title Novus Mundus, *leading Martin Wadseemuller to suggest, when he published his world map in 1507, that the land be named America.*

Piazza Goldoni
Named after the playwright.

Via de' Fossi
The street marks a ditch which ran along 12thC city walls that stood here.

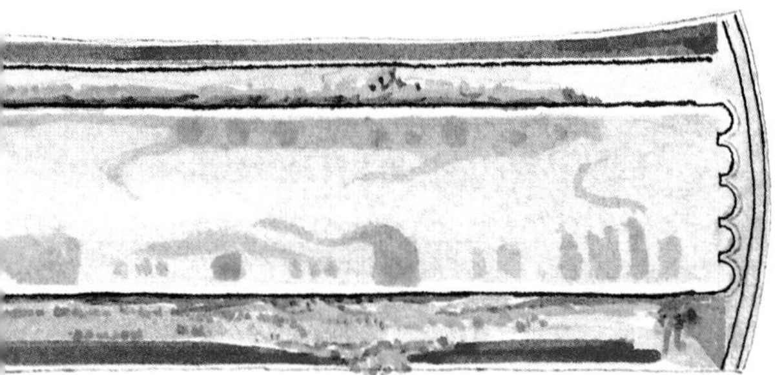

The Arno
'It would be a very plausible river,' said Mark Twain, 'if they would pump some water into it.' He never saw it in flood. In 1966 the river rose some 14 feet above the banks, putting 3,000 acres of the city under water. When it receded it disclosed ripped-up pavements, broken pipes, the wreckage of hundreds of cars and the ruin of thousands of

Palazzo Ricasoli

The Iron Baron, Bettino Ricasoli, was so angry at seeing his newly married wife being courted by another man at a ball one evening that he said, 'We must leave, my dear,' and escorted her to their carriage, where he ordered the coachman to drive, not home to the palazzo but 'To Brolio', his country estate, at

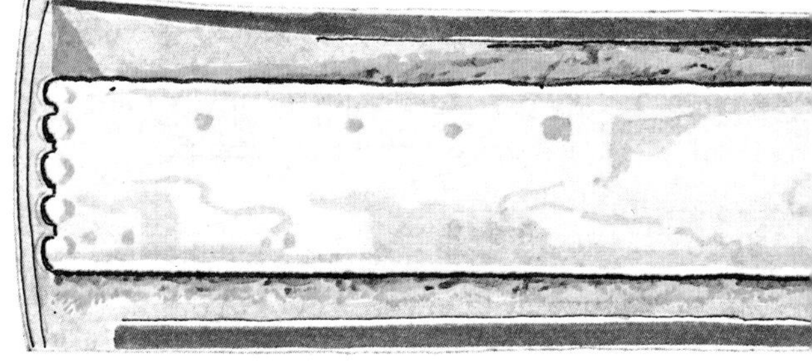

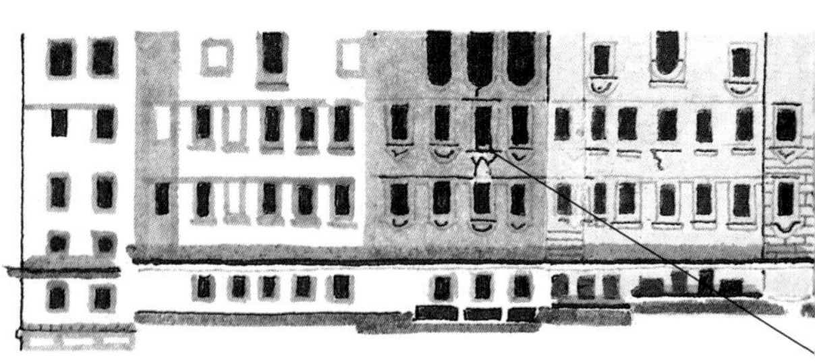

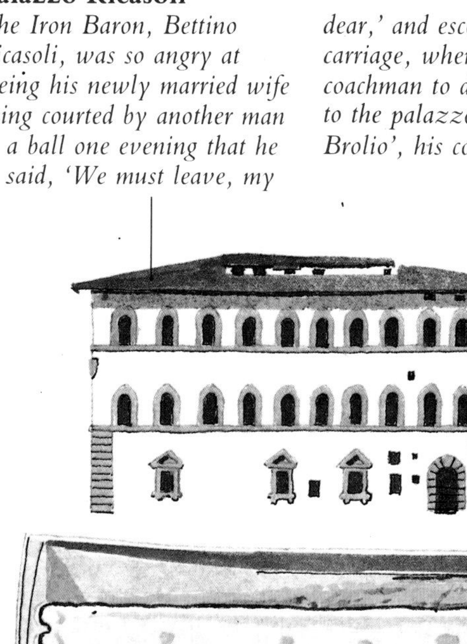

Ponte alla Carraia

First built in 1220, it is named after the carri (carts) that were used for the wool trade. On May Day 1304 a stage was set upon boats on the river for a performance of the Inferno with bonfires and men dressed as demons. It attracted so many people that the bridge collapsed under their weight and it was said that many died in their desire to learn of the next world.

which balls were never held and from which they never returned. He spent the rest of his years perfecting the blend of grapes that became the modern Chianti.

Palazzo Corsini
It houses the largest private art collection in the city (works by Filippino Lippi, Giovanni Bellini and others). For an appointment phone 283044 at No. 11 Via Parione.

Palazzo Lanfredini
The decoration is known as graffiti.

Presbyterian Church

Palazzo Medici

Palazzo Masetti

The Pretender, Charles Stuart (Bonnie Prince Charlie) was styled the Count of Albany, but his young wife preferred to be called Queen Louise, even after she left him to live here with the poet Vittorio Alfieri. Her 'Royal Palace' is now the British Consulate.

Palazzo Gianfigliazzi

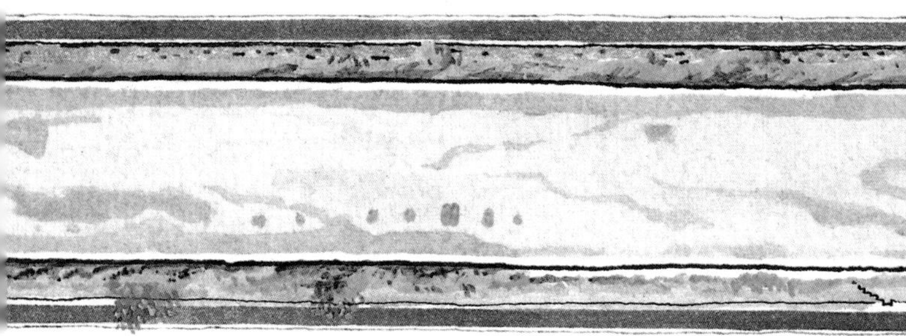

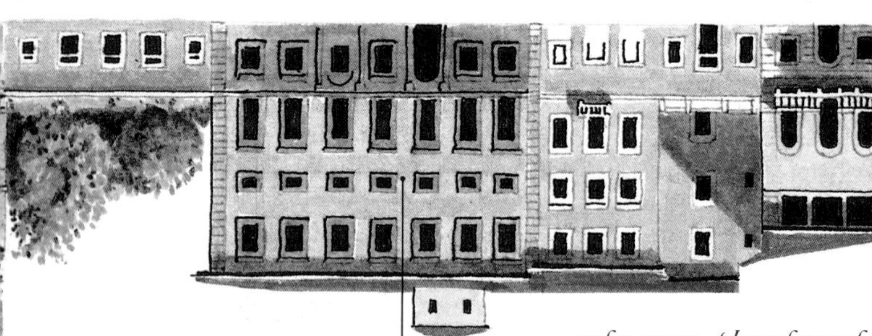

shouted 'If you sound your trumpets, we will ring our bells!' Realizing his danger in a call to arms, the king's thoughts turned to chickens. 'Capponi, Capponi,' he joked feebly, 'what a fine capon you are,' and gave in.

Palazzo Guicciardini

A 17thC palazzo with a private garden.

Ponte S. Trinita

A replica of the bridge, destroyed in 1944, which was built by Ammannati in 1567–9, based, it is thought, on a sketch by Michelangelo. The curve of the arches was a mystery to modern builders until it was noticed that they matched the curve on the sarcophagus supporting Michelangelo's Night and Day in the Medici tombs.

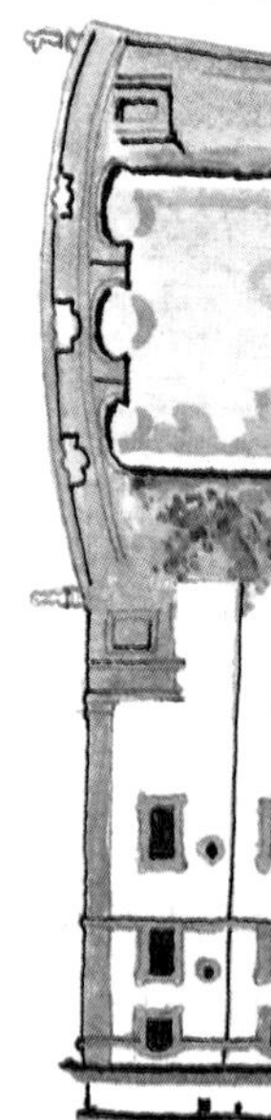

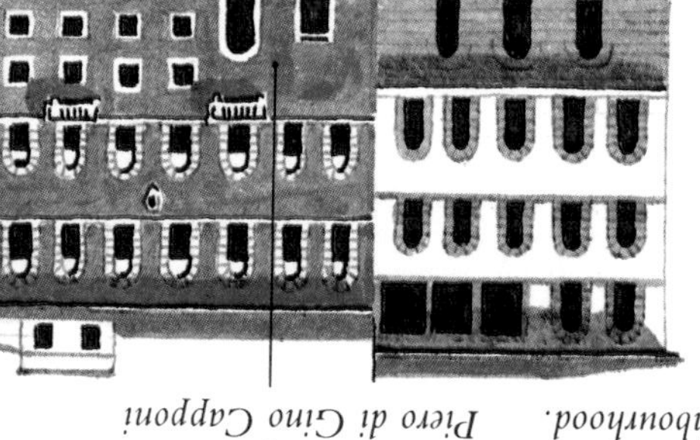

Palazzo Capponi

In a dispute over money with the city in 1494, the French king, Charles VIII, threatened to sound the trumpets to call his army which was camped outside the city walls. At this Piero di Gino Capponi

Oltrarno

It simply means 'over the Arno', the south bank. It was traditionally a working-class area until the dukes moved into the Pitti Palace and opened up the Via Maggio as a fashionable neighbourhood.

Palazzo Spini-Ferroni

When the famous but bankrupt shoemaker, Salvatore Ferragamo, rented a shop here in 1937, the owner inisisted that he buy this 13thC palazzo in nine instalments. Ferragamo's lawyers advised against it. The terms were such that should he miss a payment, he would lose everything.

of Burgundy and the King of Naples deemed it profitable to follow suit. In disgust the Frescobaldi family turned to land, in which there is less risk. Today they are amongst the largest landowners in Europe with many fine vine-yards that they have tended for six centuries. Their 13thC palazzo-fortress was elegantly remodelled in the 17thC.

Ferragamo went ahead, much encouraged by the owner. 'I knew you could do it,' he said at each payment. But at the eighth payment he was less happy and at the last was horrified. 'My God,' he said, 'You've got the building.' 'But what did you expect?' asked the surprised Ferragamo. 'I wagered that you would fail,' wailed the previous owner.

S. Jacopo sopr'Arno

Now used for exhibitions, the entrance is on Borgo S. Jacopo. The 17thC campanile was built by Gherardo Silvani.

Palazzo Frescobaldi

The Florentine banking system crashed in 1345 when King Edward III of England defaulted on vast loans. On hearing the news, the Duke

SS. Apostoli

One of the oldest churches in the city, the present building dates from the 10thC. Inside is the tomb of Prior Oddo Altoviti by Benedetto da Rovezzano (1507); a tabernacle by the Della Robbia; a Madonna and

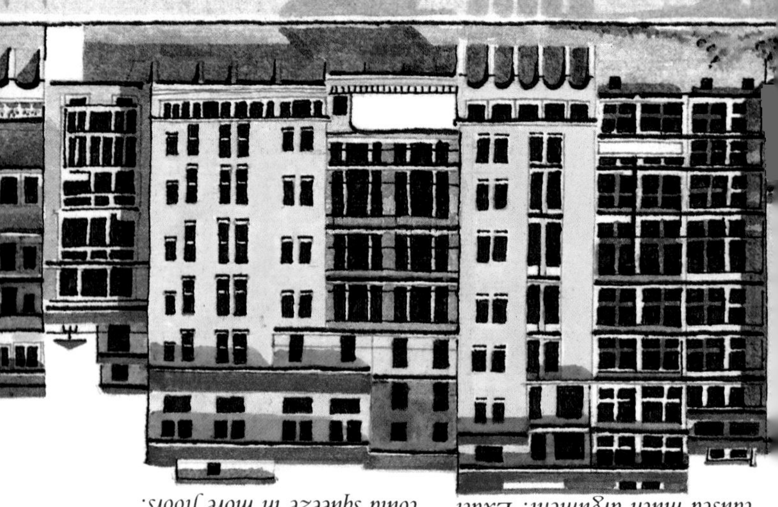

military traffic and the Allies' use of Bailey bridges ensured their advance. The rebuilding caused much argument. Exact replicas were rejected in favour of buildings 'in the style' of the old quarter, so that owners could squeeze in more floors.

Child by Jacopo di Cione c. 1375; and over the high altar hangs a Madonna and Child and Saints (c. 1384).

The first two green columns were removed from the Roman baths that were once near by.

War Damage

In August 1944, Hitler ordered all the bridges on the Arno to be blown up except 'the artistic one'. So the Ponte Vecchio was saved

but the ancient houses that stood here were reduced to rubble to block its approach. It was a pointless exercise. The old bridge couldn't take

PONTE VECCHIO

Bridges have been built and then swept away from this, the narrowest point of the river, since Roman times. The last to go was in the flood of 1333, caused, as are all floods on the Arno, by a sudden surge from a mountain tributary called the Sieve. This stone bridge was completed in 1345. Its shops were originally let by the commune to tanners and purse-makers, but by the 16thC, butchers had installed themselves, and the Archduke Ferdinand ruled that their *arte* was 'vile' and, more importantly, yielded him low rents. He threw them out in 1593 and opened the shops to 41 goldsmiths

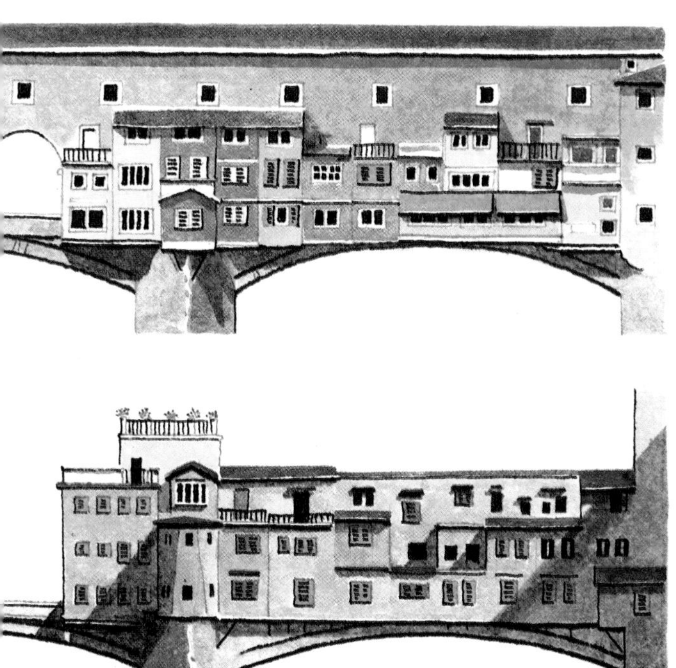

West side

and 8 jewellers who were prepared to double his income. Goldsmiths and jewellers still occupy the shops today.

Bust of Cellini

In honour of the greatest goldsmith of the Renaissance, this work was sculpted by Raffaele Romanelli in 1900.

Murder on the Bridge

On Easter Sunday, 1216, Buondelmonte dei Buondelmonti, dressed in white and mounted on a white charger, was struck down by assassins from the Amidei clan as he rode to his wedding, for he had broken a vow to wed one of their daughters in favour of a more beautiful girl from the rival Donati family. The murder was seized upon as an excuse for the eruption of war between the Guelph (papal) and the Ghibelline (imperial) factions in the city.

Vasari Corridor

It was built, in five months and with five deaths, to link the Palazzo Vecchio to the Pitti Palace on the occasion of the wedding of Cosimo I's son Francesco, to Joanna of Austria in 1565. About a quarter of a mile long, it crosses the river above the Ponte Vecchio and ends in the Boboli Gardens by the Buontalenti Grotto. The corridor remained for the private use of the reigning

family until 1868. The walls, now covered with artists' portraits, include one by Vasari. A guided tour can be arranged at the Uffizi ticket office.

Palazzo degli Uffizi

*In 1560 Cosimo I commissioned Vasari to build these offices (*uffici*) so that the various government departments could be brought under one roof. His son Francesco set aside the top floor as a picture gallery and began collecting the nucleus of the present collection, the finest in Italy. Arrive early to avoid the queues. Hours: 9.00–19.00; Sunday 9.00–13.00; closed Monday.*

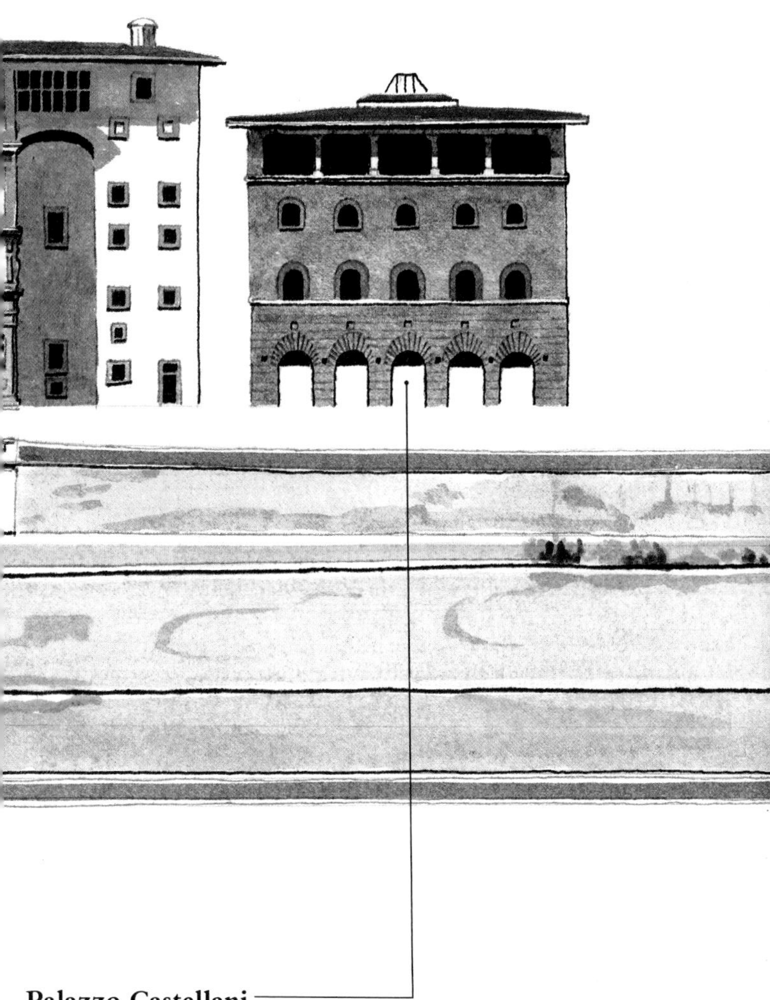

Palazzo Castellani
Museo di Storia della Scienza

The science museum is based on the collection of the Medici grand-dukes and includes the telescopes of Galileo, his compass, lode-stones and other instruments. On the second floor is a scientific library. Hours: 10.00–13.00 and 14.00–16.00; Sunday 10.00–13.00; closed on the last Sunday of the month.

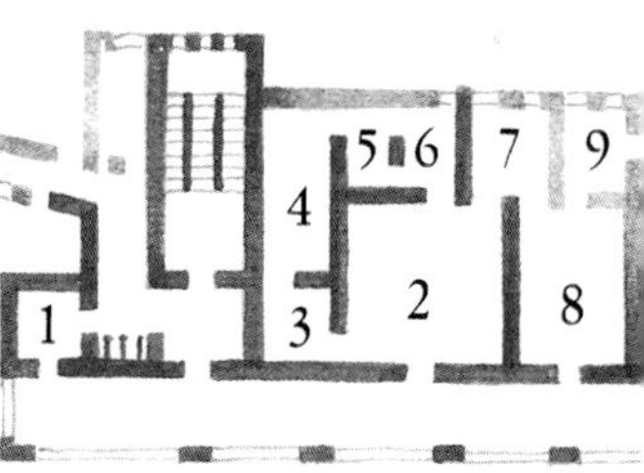

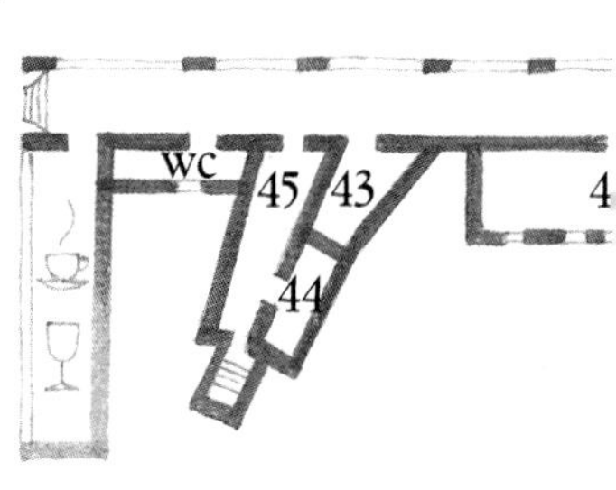

ROOM 2

TUSCAN PAINTING 12–14THC

Tuscan School
Crucifix with Stories of the Passion (12thC)
Berlinghieri School
Diptych: Madonna and Child with Saints (c.1228)
St Francis Receiving the Stigmata
School of Lucca
Crucifixion with Stories of the Passion (13thC)
Meliore di Jacopo
Altarpiece of the Redeemer and Saints (1271)
Magdalen Master
St Luke the Evangelist
Cimabue
Maestà (c.1285)
Duccio di Buoninsegna
Maestà (1285)
Giotto
Madonna in Glory
Madonna and Child

ROOM 3

SIENESE SCHOOL OF THE 14THC

Simone Martini
Annunciation and Saints, dated 1333
Ambrogio Lorenzetti
Four stories of St Nicholas on two panels
Presentation in the Temple
Pietro Lorenzetti
Madonna and Child
Madonna and Child with Saints
Polyptych: Stories of the Life of the Umilità
Three spires: Saints John, Mark and Luke
Niccolò di Ser Sozzo
Madonna and Child
Niccolò Bonaccorsi
Presentation of the Virgin in the Temple
Simone de' Crocifissi
Nativity

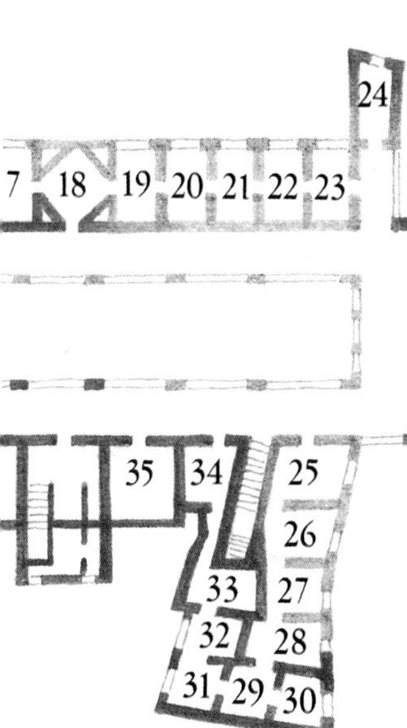

ROOM 4

14THC FLORENTINE PAINTING

Master of S. Cecilia
S. Cecilia and her life
Taddeo Gaddi
Madonna in Glory
Bernardo Daddi
Madonna and Child Enthroned with Sts Peter and Paul
Madonna and Child with Sts Matthew and Nicholas
Polyptych: Madonna and Child with Saints
Andrea Orcagna and Jacopo di Cione
The Life of St Matthew
Jacopo del Casentino
Madonna Enthroned
Nardo di Cione
Crucifixion
Giovanni da Milano
Polyptych with Saints
Giottino (?)
Pietà with Saints

ROOMS 5 & 6

GOTHIC PAINTING OF THE 14THC–15THC

Agnolo Gaddi
Crucifixion
Lorenzo Monaco
Coronation of the Virgin
Adoration of the Magi
North Italian Painter
St Benedict Exorcizing a Monk
St Benedict Blessing Poisoned Wine
St Benedict Performing a Miracle
Gherardo Starnina
Thebaid
Gentile da Fabriano
Adoration of the Magi
Quaratesi polyptych of four saints
Giovanni di Paolo
Madonna and Child (1445)
Jacopo Bellini
Madonna and Child

ROOM 7

EARLY RENAISSANCE

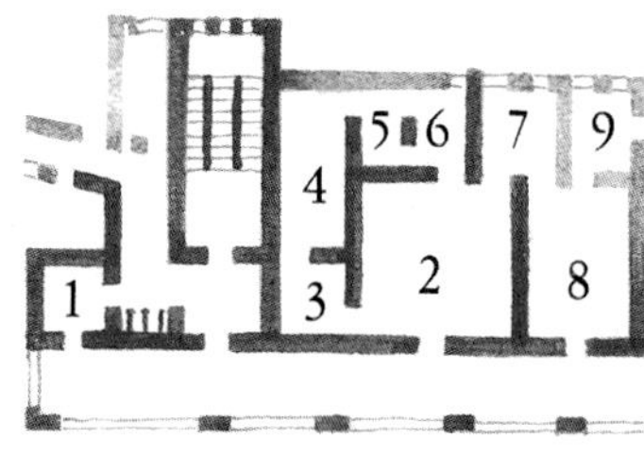

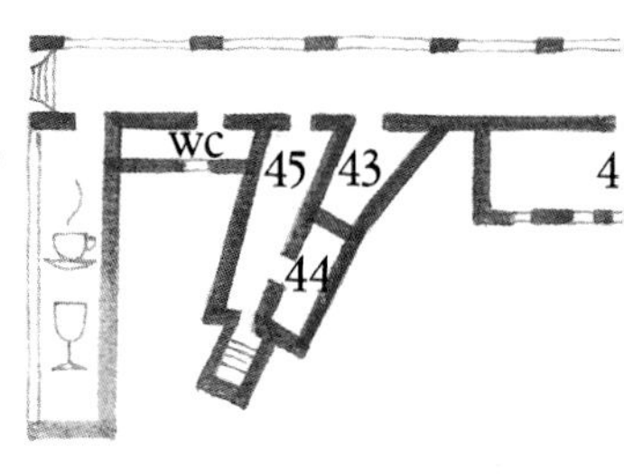

Masaccio and Masolino
Madonna and Child with St Anne and Angels
Fra Angelico
Coronation of the Virgin
Domenico Veneziano
Madonna and Child
Piero della Francesca
Portrait of Battista Sforza
Duke Federico di Montefeltro
Triumph of Duke Federico
Triumph of Battista Sforza
Paolo Uccello
Battle of San Romano

ROOM 8

15THC FLORENTINE

Filippo Lippi
Madonna and Child Enthroned with Saints
Francesco Pesellino
Miracle of St Anthony
Martyrdom of Sts Cosmas and Damian
Nativity
Filippo Lippi
Predella panel
Annunciation: Virgin and Angel, St Anthony Abbot and St John the Baptist
Adoration of the Child with Saints and Angels
Adoration of the Child with Two Saints
Coronation of the Virgin
Madonna and Child with Two Angels
Alesso Baldovinetti
Madonna and Child
Annunciation
Lorenzo di Pietro (Vecchietta)
Madonna and Child Enthroned
Matteo di Giovanni
Madonna and Child
Benozzo Gozzoli
Marriage of St Catherine
Pietà with Saints
Two Saints

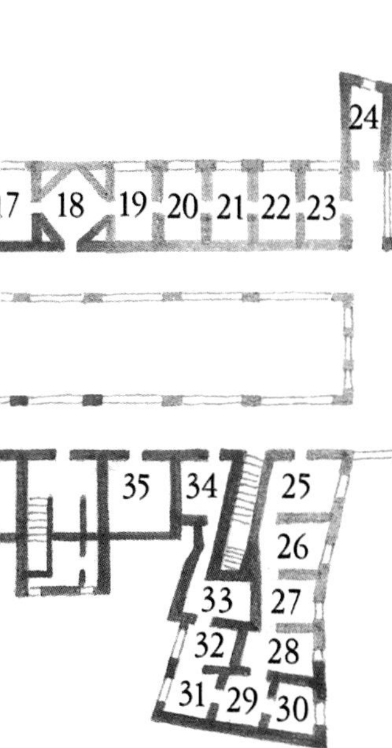

Botticelli
Madonna of the Rosegarden
Neroccio dei Landi with Francesco Giorgio
Three Stories of St Benedict

ROOM 9

POLLAIUOLO

Antonio and Piero del Pollaiuolo
Sts Vincent, James and Eustache
Portrait of Galeazzo Maria Sforza
Antonio del Pollaiuolo
Portrait of a Young Woman
Hercules and Anteus
Hercules and the Hydra
Sandro Botticelli
Strength
The Return of Judith
The Discovery of the Body of Holofernes
Piero del Pollaiuolo
Six panels of the Virtues

ROOMS 10–14

BOTTICELLI

Sandro Botticelli
Portrait of an Unknown Man
Madonna of the Loggia
Madonna and Child in Glory
Adoration of the Magi
Madonna and Child Enthroned with Saints
Salome with the Head of St John the Baptist
Removing the Heart of St Ignatius
Pietà
St Augustine and Youth
Madonna of the Magnificat
Madonna of the Pomegranate
Pallas and the Centaur
Primavera
Birth of Venus
St Augustine in his Study
Annunciation
Calumny
S. Marco Annunciation
St John of Patmos
St Augustine in his Study – both of these paintings are from S. Marco
Miracle of St Eligius

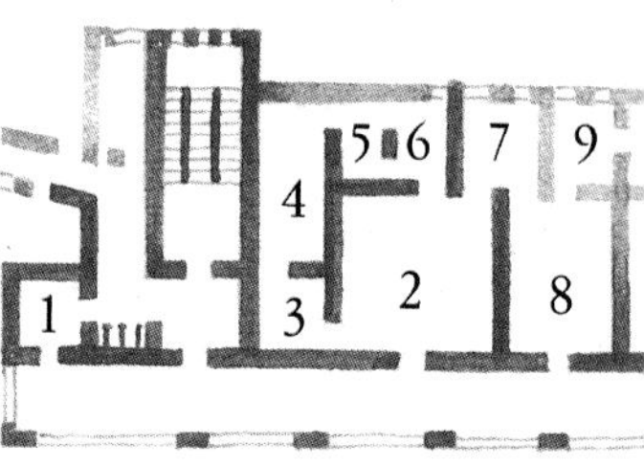

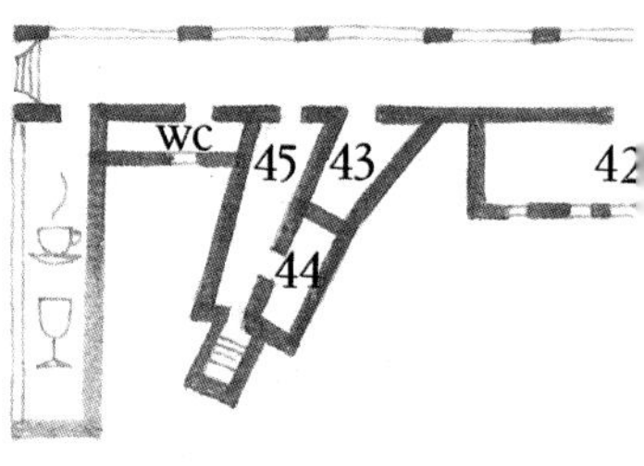

15THC FLEMISH PAINTING

Rogier van der Weyden
Deposition

Baroncelli Master
Pierantonio Baroncelli
His wife, Maria Bonciani

Nicholas Froment
Triptych:
Centre: Resurrection of Lazarus
Left: Martha at the Feet of Christ
Right: Mary Magdalen Washes the Feet of Christ
Outside: The Madonna and Child and the Donors

Hugo van der Goes
Portinari Altarpiece:
Outside: Annunciation and the Annunciation Angel
Inside centre: Adoration of the Shepherds
Left: Tommaso Portinari and Sons; right: Maria Portinari and Daughter

FLORENTINE PAINTING 1450–1500

Filippino Lippi
Self-portrait
Adoration of the Child
Madonna and Child (1486)
St Jerome
Adoration of the Magi
Portrait of an Old Man
Allegory

Bartolomeo di Giovanni
Two Miracles of St Benedict

Jacopo del Sellaio
The Triumph of Mordecai
The Banquet of Ahasueras
The Banquet of Queen Vashti

ROOM 15

15TH–16THC FLORENTINE

Francesco Botticini
Tobias and the Angel

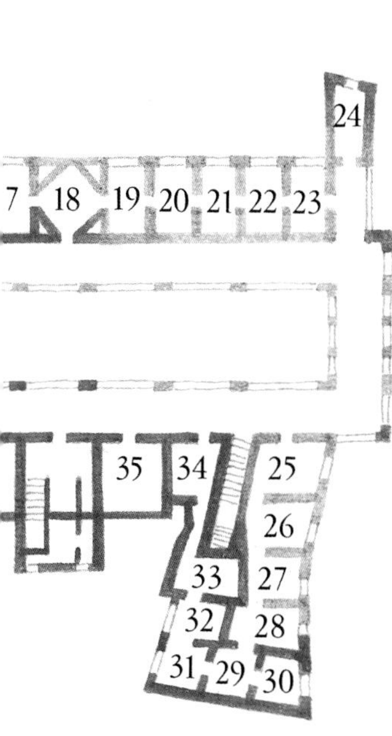

Andrea Verrocchio
Baptism of Christ
Leonardo da Vinci
Annunciation
Adoration of the Magi
Domenico Ghirlandaio
Adoration of the Magi
Two paintings of the Madonna and Child Enthroned with Saints
Lorenzo di Credi
Adoration of the Shepherds
Annunciation
Young Man with a Red Cap
Madonna and Child with Saints
Piero di Cosimo
Immaculate Conception
Madonna and Child with Musical Angel
Sacrifice for the Liberation of Andromeda
Perseus Liberates Andromeda

ROOM 16

Painted maps of Tuscany
Hans Memling
Portrait of a Man
Madonna and Child
Portrait of an Unknown Man
St Benedict
Portrait of Benedetto di Tommaso Portinari

ROOM 17

Sleeping Hermaphrodite, a copy of a Greek sculpture
Mantegna
Triptych

ROOM 18

THE TRIBUNE OF BUONTALENTI
Contains some fine sculpture, including the Medici Venus.
Alessandro Allori
Portrait of Bianca Cappello
Andrea del Sarto
Portrait of a Young Woman
Giovanni Bizzelli
Annunciation

Agnolo Bronzino
Maria de' Medici
Francesco de' Medici
Girl with a Book
Isabella de' Medici
Eleonora of Toledo with her Son Giovanni de' Medici
Young Man in Black
Portrait of Cosimo I
Bartolomeo Panciatichi
Lucrezia Panciatichi
Daniele da Volterra
Slaughter of the Innocents
Franciabigio
Madonna of the Well
Giulio Romano
Madonna and Child
Cecchino Salviati
Charity
Christ Carrying the Cross
Pontormo
Cosimo il Vecchio
Expulsion from Paradise
Leda and the Swan
Charity
Raffaello Sanzio
Young St John the Baptist
Ridolfo del Ghirlandaio
Portrait of a Man
Rosso Fiorentino
Musical Angel
Giorgio Vasari
Lorenzo il Magnifico
Immaculate Conception
The Miracle of the Prophet Elijah

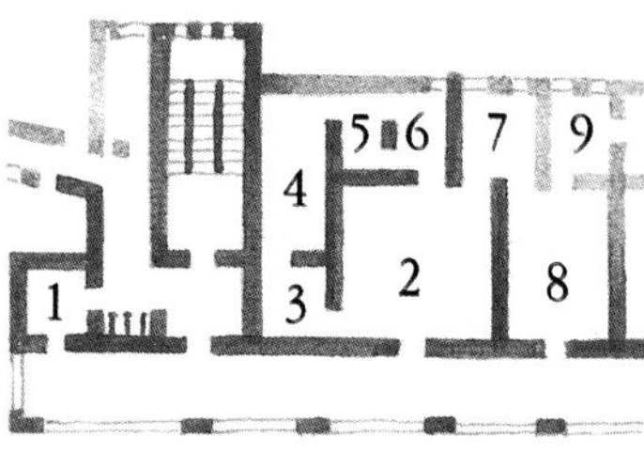

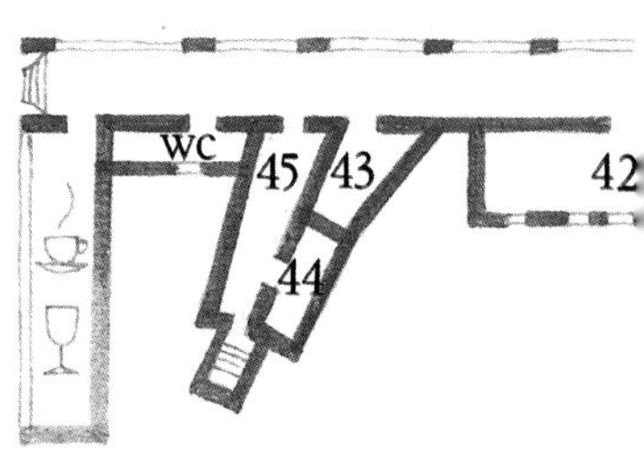

ROOM 19

CENTRAL ITALY

Melozzo da Forlì
Angel of the Annunciation
Virgin of the Annunciation
Pietro Perugino
Madonna and Child
Pietà
Francesco delle Opere
Don Biago Milanesi
Baldassare Vallombrosano
Portrait of a Young Man
Lorenzo Costa
Giovanni Bentivoglio
St Sebastian

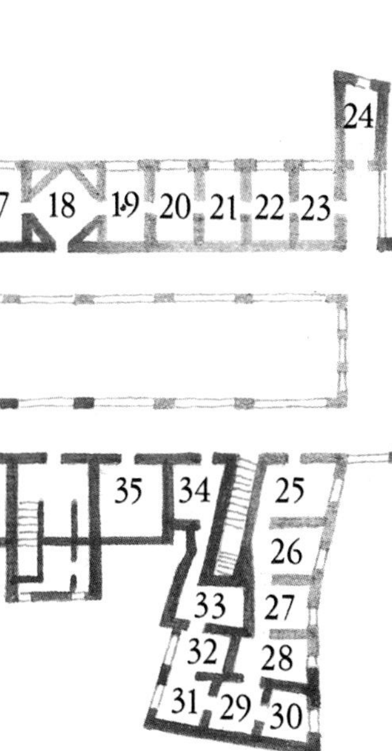

Francesco Francia
Portrait of Evangelista Scappi
Alessandro Araldi
Barbara Pallavicino
Giovanni Boccati
Madonna and Child with Four Angels
Bartolomeo Caporali
Madonna and Child with Four Angels
Antoniazzo Romano
Madonna and Child
Triptych: Madonna and Child

ROOM 20

GERMAN SCHOOL

Albrecht Dürer
The Artist's Father
Adoration of the Magi
Calvary
Madonna and Child
St Philip the Apostle
St James the Apostle
Lucas Cranach
Adam, Eve
Self-portrait
St George and the Princess
Luther and his Wife
Jan Bruegel (Elder)
Calvary

ROOM 21

VENETIAN SCHOOL

Mantegna
Madonna and Child
Ascension
Adoration of the Magi
Portrait of a Cardinal
Cosmè Tura
St Dominic
Giovanni Bellini
Allegory
Lamentation over the Body of Christ
Portrait of a Gentleman
Giorgione
Warrior with Equerry
Judgement of Solomon
Test of Fire before Pharaoh
Carpaccio
Warriors and Old Men
Fragment of Crucifixion

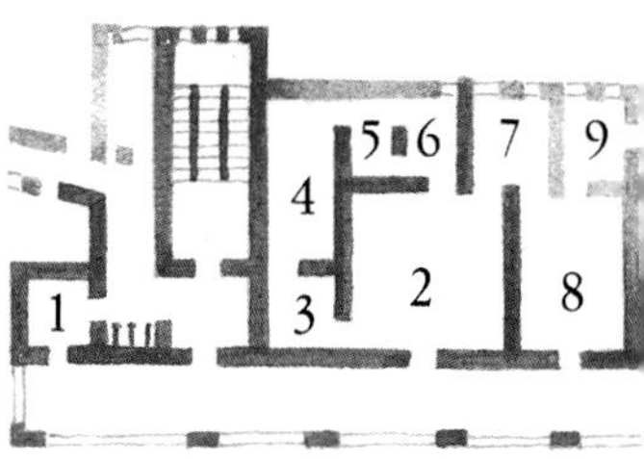

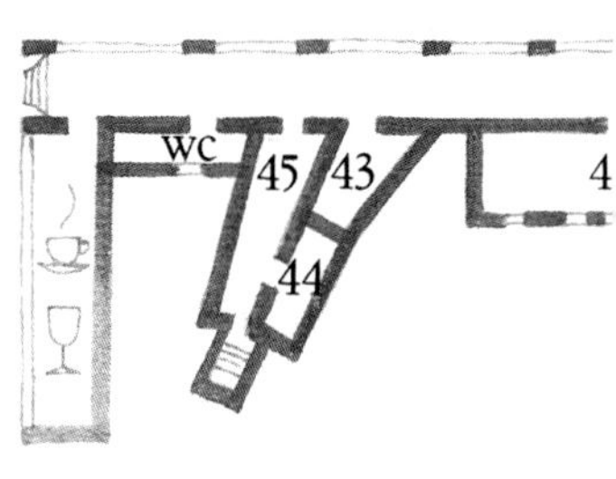

ROOM 22

GERMAN AND FLEMISH

Hans Holbein
Sir Richard Southwell
Self-portrait
Albrecht Altdorfer
The Departure and the Martyrdom of St Florian
Joos van Cleve
Three Portraits
Mater Dolorosa
Gerard David
Descent from the Cross
Adoration of the Magi
Bernaert van Orley
A Man and his Wife
Hoogstraeten Master
Madonna and Sts Barbara and Catherine

ROOM 23

CORREGGIO

Correggio
Rest on the Flight to Egypt
Madonna and Child
Sodoma
Christ Captured
Boccaccio Boccacino
Gypsy
Giovanni Ambrogio de Predis
Portrait of a Man
Giovanni Francesco Mainieri
Christ Carrying the Cross

ROOM 24

15th–18thC miniatures

ROOM 25

EARLY 16THC FLORENTINE

Michelangelo
The Doni Tondo of the Holy Family, painted in 1505
Mariotto Albertinelli
Visitation
Raphael
Portrait of Perugino
Rosso Fiorentino
Moses Defending the Daughters of Jethro
Giuliano Bugiardini
Portrait of a Woman

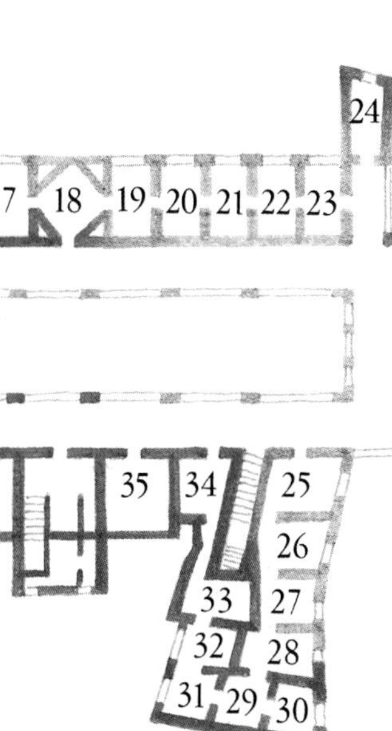

ROOM 26

RAPHAEL

Raphael

Madonna of the Goldfinch
Pope Leo X and Cardinals Giulio de' Medici and Luigi de' Rossi
Julius II (a replica)
Portrait of Francesco Maria della Rovere

Pontormo

Martyrdom of St Maurice and the Eleven Martyrs

Andrea del Sarto

St James and Two Children
Madonna of the Harpies

ROOM 27

PONTORMO

Pontormo

Supper at Emmaus
Portrait of Maria Salviati
Portrait of a Musician

Bronzino

Pietà
Holy Family

ROOM 28

TITIAN

Titian

Flora
Venus of Urbino
A Knight of Malta
Portrait of Francesco della Rovere, Duke of Urbino
Portrait of Eleonora Gonzaga della Rovere
Venus and Cupid

Palma Vecchio

Judith
Resurrection of Lazarus
Sacred Conversation

ROOMS 29 & 30

EMILIAN SCHOOL

Parmigianino

Madonna of the Long Neck
Madonna and Child with Saints

ROOM 31

16THC VENETIAN

Lorenzo Lotto

Head of a Young Man

Sebastiano del Piombo

La Fornarina

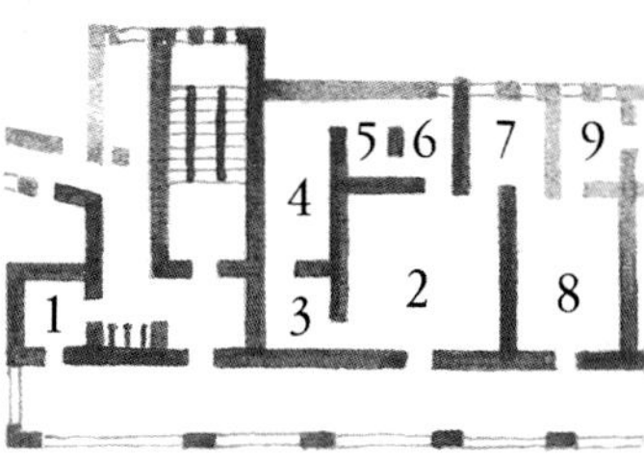

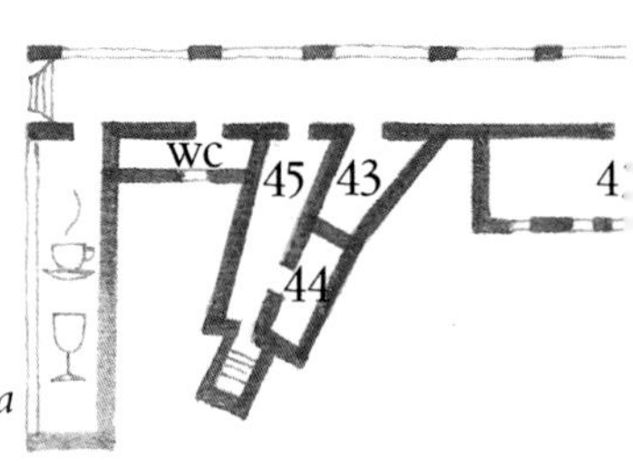

ROOM 32

Sebastiano del Piombo
Death of Adonis
Lorenzo Lotto
Holy Family

ROOM 33

16THC PAINTINGS
Clouet
Portrait of Francis I

ROOM 34

VERONESE
Paolo Veronese
Crowning of St Agatha
Annunciation
Holy Family with St Barbara
G. B. Moroni
Count Pietro Secco Suardi
Man with a Book
Giulio Campi
Portrait of his Father
Man with a Mandolin

ROOM 35

TINTORETTO
Tintoretto
Man with Red Hair
Portrait of an Admiral
Portrait of Sansovino
Old Man in a Fur
Leda and the Swan
Portrait of a Gentleman
Federico Barocci
Portrait of a Girl
Noli Me Tangere
Francesco Maria II della Rovere

ROOM 41

RUBENS AND VAN DYCK
Rubens
The Entry of Ferdinand of Austria into Antwerp
Triumphal Entry of Henry IV into Paris
Henry IV at the Battle of Ivry
Isabella Brandt
Equestrian Portrait of Philip IV of Spain
Hercules between Vice and Virtue
Van Dyck
Margaret of Lorraine

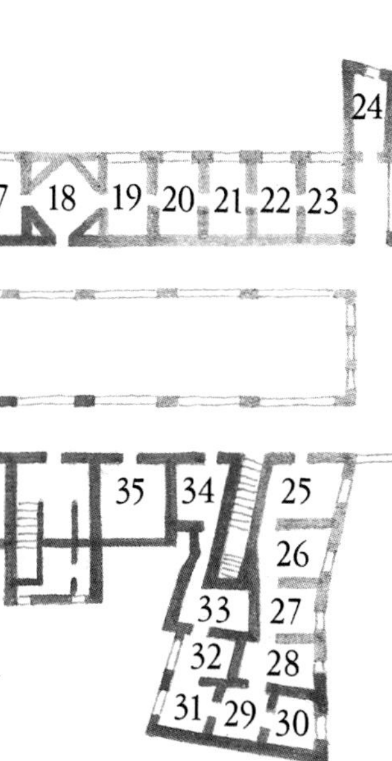

Equestrian Portrait of the Emperor Charles V
Sustermans's Mother
John of Montfort
Jacob Jordaens
Portrait of an Old Lady
Sustermans
Galileo Galilei

ROOM 42

SALA DI NIOBE
Roman copies of Greek statues of Niobe and her children
Canaletto
The Palazzo Ducale, Venice
The Turn in the Grand Canal

ROOM 43

Caravaggio
Sacrifice of Isaac
The Young Bacchus
Head of the Medusa (a shield)

ROOM 44

Rembrandt
Self-portrait
Portrait of an Old Man
Self-portrait as an Old Man
Jan Steen
Lunch Party
Jacob Ruysdael
Two Landscapes

ROOM 45

18THC PAINTINGS
Piazzetta
Susannah and the Elders
G. B. Tiepolo
Ceiling: The Erection of an Imperial Statue
Goya
Two portraits of Maria Theresa
Alessandro Longhi
Portrait of a Lady
Chardin
Two portraits of children
Jean Marc Nattier
Maria Adelaide of France as Diana
Étienne Liotard
Princess Maria Adelaide of France in Turkish Costume

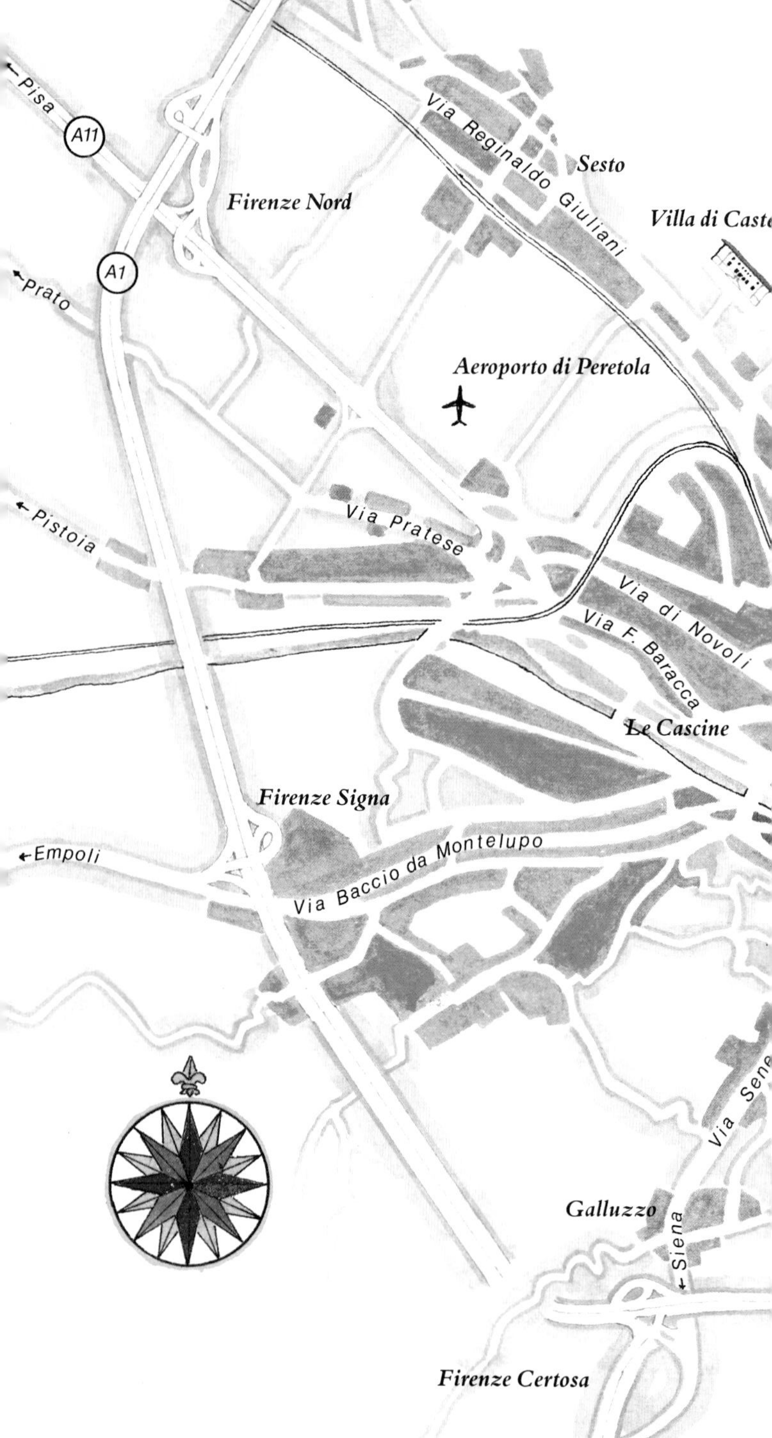

Pisa
A11
A1
Prato
Pistoia
Empoli
Firenze Nord
Via Reginaldo Giuliani
Sesto
Villa di Caste
Aeroporto di Peretola
Via Pratese
Via di Novoli
Via F. Baracca
Le Cascine
Firenze Signa
Via Baccio da Montelupo
Via Sene
Galluzzo
Siena
Firenze Certosa

ENVIRONS

Trespiano
della Petraia
Fiesole
Via Bolognese
Via Faentina
San Domenico
Viale Alessandro Volta
Maiano
Settignano
Villa i Tatti
Campo di Marte
Via Aretina
Arezzo →
Firenze Sud
Greve →
Roma →

FIESOLE

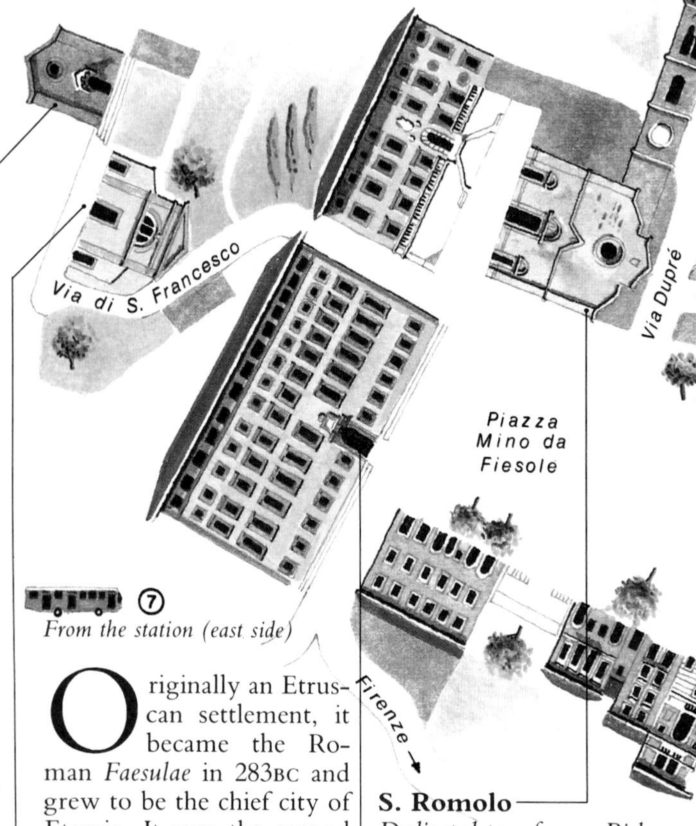

Originally an Etruscan settlement, it became the Roman *Faesulae* in 283BC and grew to be the chief city of Etruria. It was the second town to fall to Florence in the middle ages (1125) and never recovered its freedom.

S. Alessandro
Site of a temple to Bacchus.

S. Francesco
Built c. 1330. Over the high altar hangs an Annunciation by Raffaellino dei Carli.

Seminary

S. Romolo
Dedicated to a former Bishop of Fiesole, the cathedral was founded in 1028 and rebuilt in the 13–14thC. The campanile dates from 1213. Inside:

Mino da Fiesole
Tomb of Bishop Salutati

Bicci di Lorenzo
Altarpiece triptych

Giovanni della Robbia
Polychrome S. Romolo

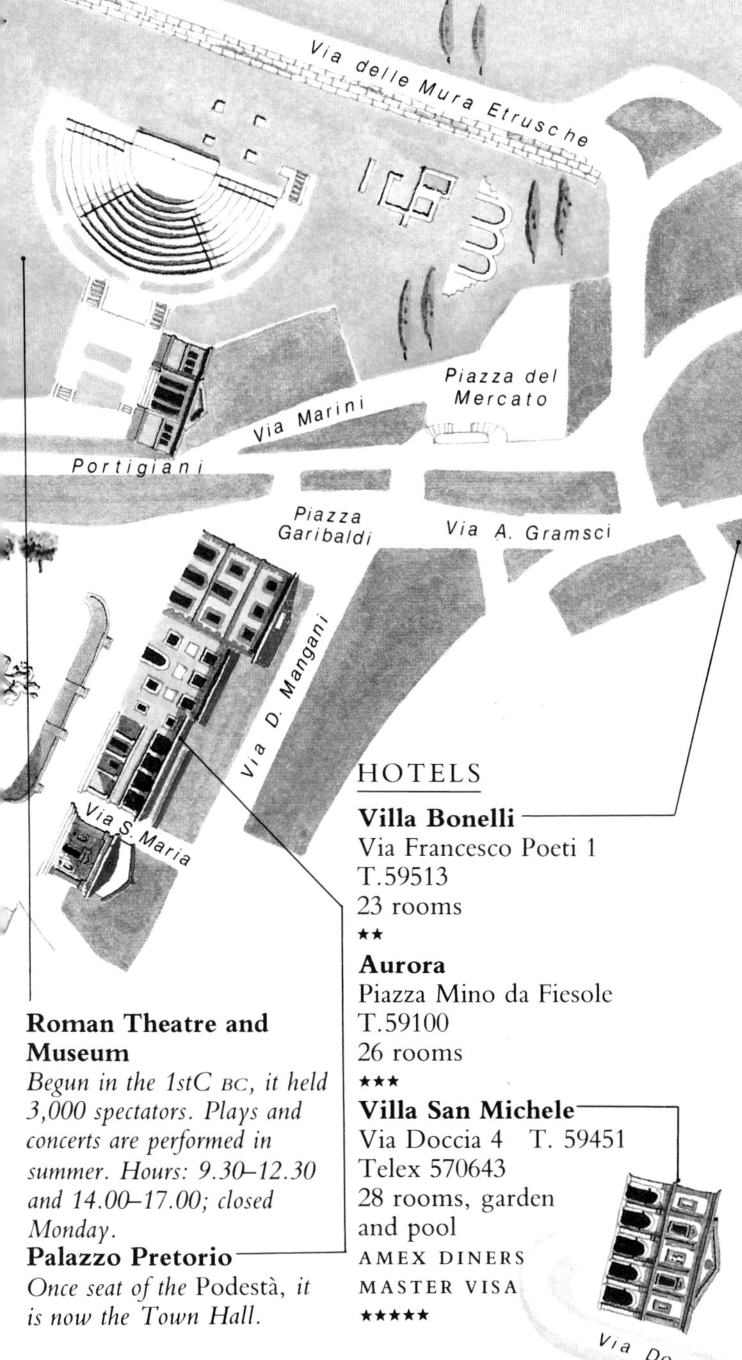

HOTELS

Villa Bonelli
Via Francesco Poeti 1
T.59513
23 rooms
★★

Aurora
Piazza Mino da Fiesole
T.59100
26 rooms
★★★

Villa San Michele
Via Doccia 4 T. 59451
Telex 570643
28 rooms, garden and pool
AMEX DINERS
MASTER VISA
★★★★★

Roman Theatre and Museum
Begun in the 1stC BC, *it held 3,000 spectators. Plays and concerts are performed in summer. Hours: 9.30–12.30 and 14.00–17.00; closed Monday.*

Palazzo Pretorio
Once seat of the Podestà, *it is now the Town Hall.*

TUSCANY

The birthplace of Italian culture, it takes its name from the ancient Etruscans who already dominated its wooded hills in the 7th–6thC BC. They founded the twelve city states of *Etruria*, some of the remains of which can be seen at Fiesole and Volterra. Their alphabet was the forerunner of the Latin one and some 10,000 of their inscriptions have survived. Alas, as of 1988, no one can read them. Their language is a mystery. *Toscana* is also the birthplace of the Italian language. Dante and Boccaccio both wrote in Tuscan, making it the language of literature. Today the local dialect is considered to be the purest spoken Italian.

The island of Elba became famous as the place of exile for Napoleon in 1814–15. Sailing south from it in 1841, Alexandre Dumas saw a 'large sugarloaf, lifting itself some two or three hundred metres above the sea', and was instantly inspired to write *The Count of Monte Cristo*.

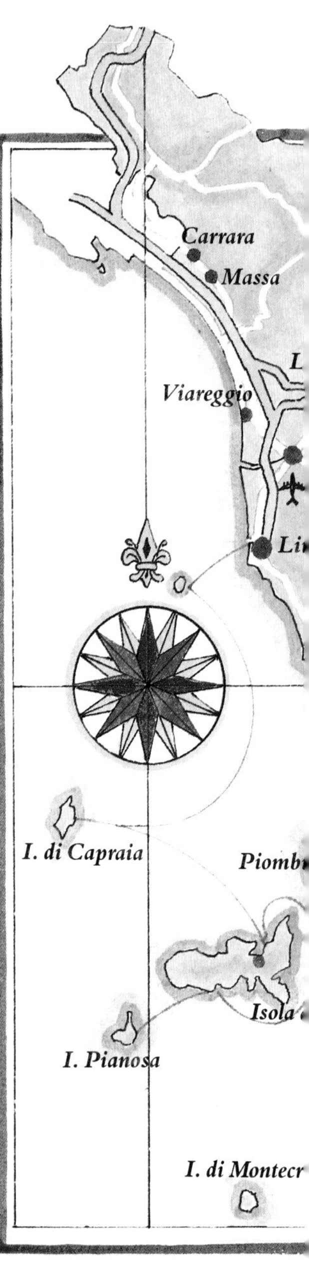

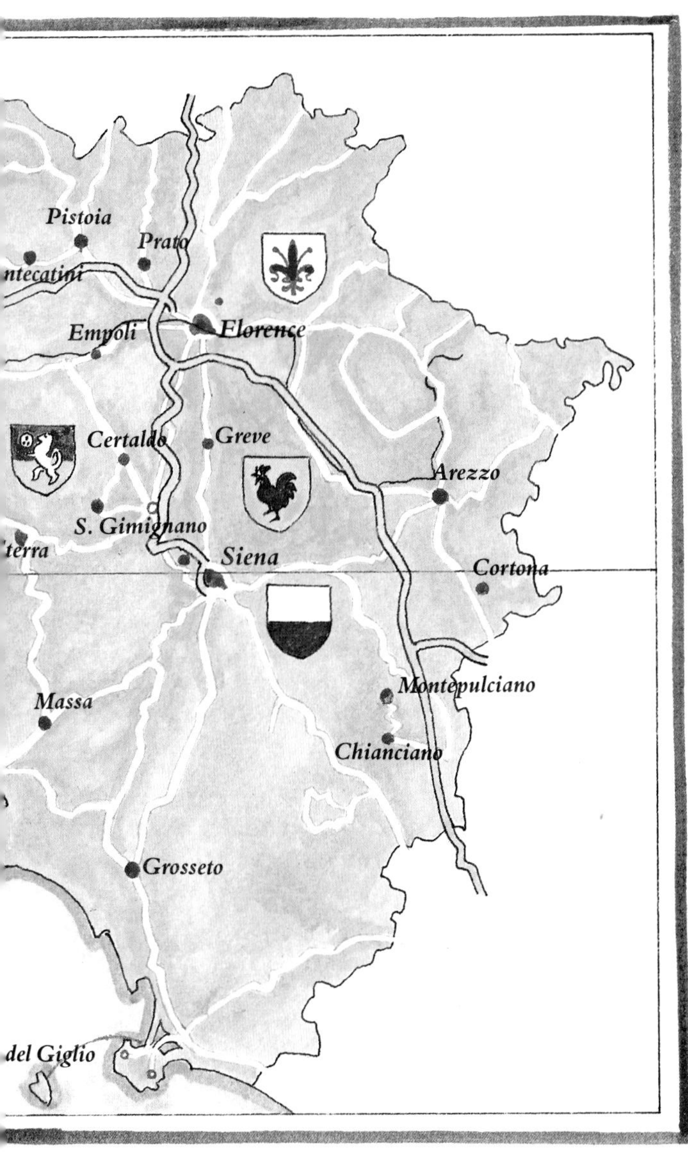
Pistoia
Prato
ntecatini
Empoli
Florence
Certaldo
Greve
Arezzo
S. Gimignano
'terra
Siena
Cortona
Massa
Montepulciano
Chianciano
Grosseto
del Giglio

SAN GIMIGNANO

Viewed from a distance, its 13 towers loom like a mini-Manhattan, but would have been more impressive in the middle ages, when there were 72. Built on Etruscan ruins and named after a 4thC Bishop of Modena, it is first mentioned in 991, when it was donated to the Bishops of Volterra by Hugo of Provence. The citizens were not consulted and it took them 150 years to establish their freedom and elect their own consuls. The town then fell victim to the civil strife common to other Italian cities and in 1199 it became necessary to elect a *Podestà*, an impartial foreigner, as chief executive. The arrival of the international Guelph–Ghibelline conflict aggravated matters. The city was alternatively Ghibelline under the Salvucci family or Guelph under the Ardinghelli. Dante arrived on embassy from Florence in 1300 to beg the citizens to remain in the Guelph league, but the bloody seesaw continued until 1353, when the city voted, by a majority of one, to renounce its freedom and submit to Florence.

Torre Ardinghelli
The twin towers of the arch-enemies of the Salvucci.

La Cisterna
Built in 1237.

S. Francesco
Now a Romanesque wine shop.

Porta S. Giovanni
Begun in the 13thC.

S. Maria Assunta
The cathedral was consecrated in 1148 by Eugene III.

INTERIOR, LEFT WALL:
Frescos by Bartolo di Fredi
Scenes from the Creation to the Story of Job

RIGHT WALL:
Frescos by Barna da Siena
Scenes from the Annunciation to the Crucifixion

INSIDE FACADE:
The Last Judgement
by Taddeo di Bartolo

S. FINA CHAPEL
The Life of S. Fina
by Domenico Ghirlandaio

The Devil's Tower
It is believed to be haunted.

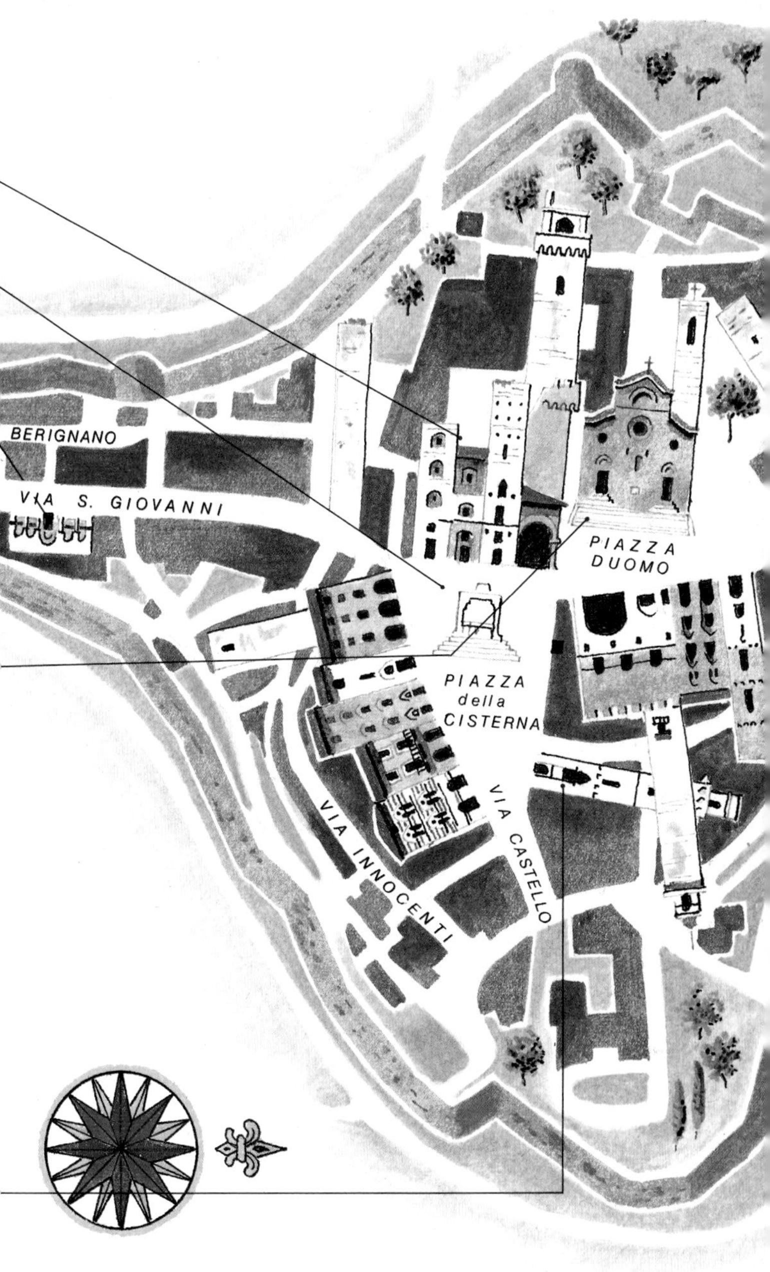
BERIGNANO
VIA S. GIOVANNI
PIAZZA DUOMO
PIAZZA della CISTERNA
VIA INNOCENTI
VIA CASTELLO

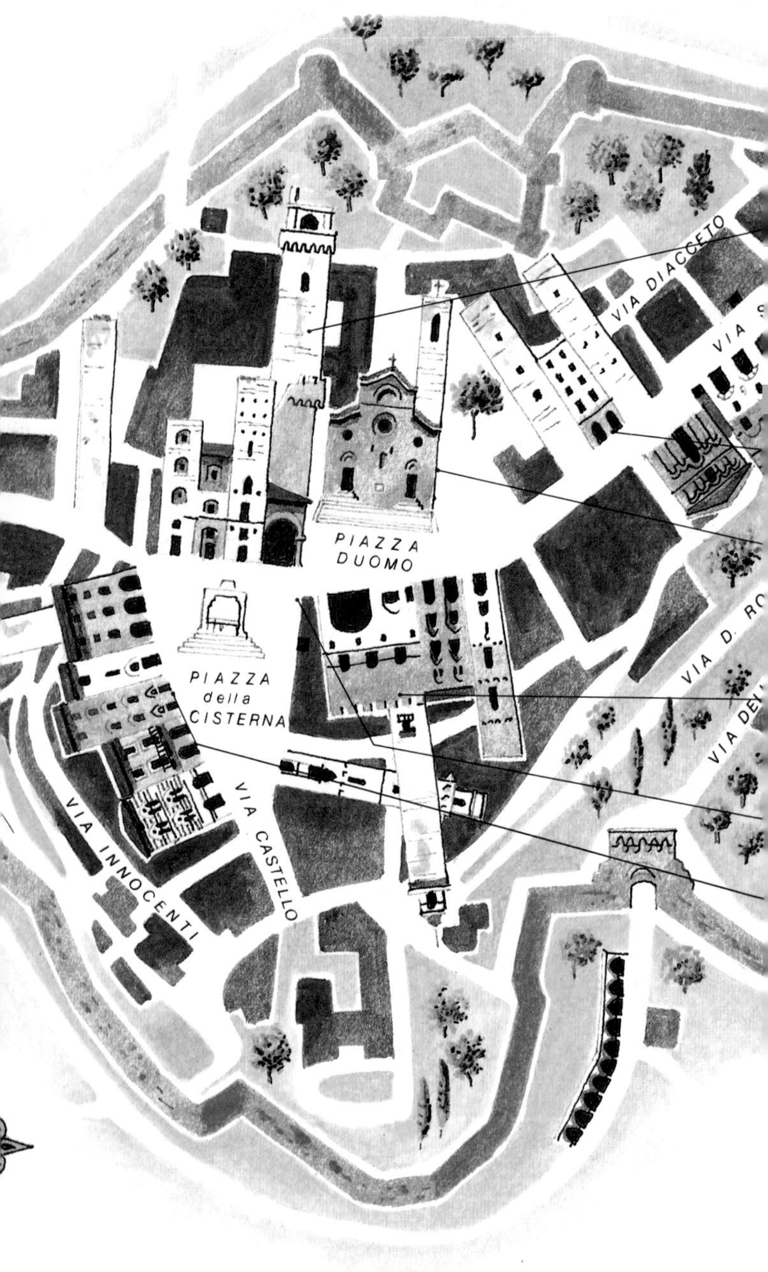
VIA DIACCETO
VIA S
PIAZZA
DUOMO
PIAZZA
della
CISTERNA
VIA D. RO
VIA DEL
VIA CASTELLO
VIA INNOCENTI

SAN GIMIGNANO

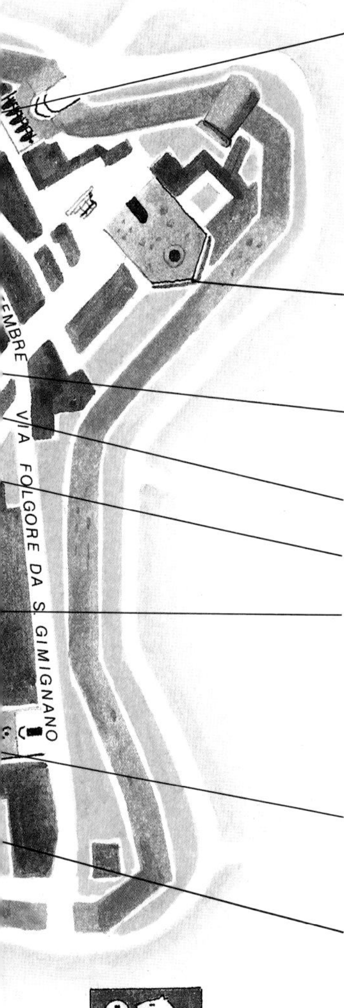

Palazzo del Popolo
Still the Town Hall, it was built in 1288. It is also the Museo Civico. In the council chamber visited by Dante is Lippo Memmi's Maestà. The gallery above has 13thC works of the Sienese and Florentine schools.

S. Agostino
Built 1280–98. The choir has frescos by Benozzo Gozzoli of the Life of S. Agostino.

Torre Salvucci
The twin towers are all that remain of the palace.

Torre Pesciolini
Built in the Florentine style.

Domenico Ghirlandaio
Fresco of the Annunciation

Palazzo del Podestà
A decree in 1255 set the height of this tower (51m) as the legal limit for all others in the city.

HOTELS

Hotel Leon Bianco
T.941294 21 rooms
AMEX MASTER VISA
★★

Hotel La Cisterna
T.940328 Telex 575152
46 rooms
Restaurant closed Tuesday and midday Wednesday.
AMEX DINERS MASTER VISA
★★★

Florence–Siena

There is a rail connection, but the Siena station is deep in a valley. The Florentine SITA bus terminus is on p. 54. See endpaper for Siena.

TIMETABLE

Departing **Florence**		*Arriving* **Siena**	*Departing* **Siena**		*Arriving* **Florence**
6.45	Daily	8.00	6.15	Daily	7.50
7.10	Daily	8.45	6.30	Mon–Fri	8.15
7.15	Mon–Fri	8.30	6.45	Mon–Sat	8.00
7.45	Mon–Fri	9.00	7.00	Mon–Sat	8.15
8.05	Mon–Sat	9.20	8.00	Mon–Sat	9.15
8.30	Mon–Fri	9.45	8.15	Daily	9.30
9.15	Mon–Sat	10.30	9.20	Daily	10.55
10.10	Daily	11.25	9.20	Mon–Sat	10.35
11.20	Mon–Sat	12.35	10.45	Mon–Fri	12.00
12.00	Daily	13.15	11.45	Mon–Sat	13.00
12.45	Mon–Sat	14.00	11.45	Holidays	13.15
13.30	Mon–Fri	15.05	13.00	Mon–Sat	14.15
14.10	Mon–Sat	15.25	13.45	Daily	15.20
14.30	Daily	15.45	14.00	Daily	15.15
15.30	Daily	17.05	15.20	Mon–Sat	16.55
17.10	Mon–Fri	18.25	17.00	Mon–Fri	18.15
17.20	Daily	18.35	17.25	Daily	19.00
17.50	Mon–Fri	19.25	17.35	Daily	18.50
18.25	Mon–Sat	20.00	18.45	Mon–Fri	20.00
18.35	Mon–Fri	19.50	19.10	Daily	20.25
19.00	Daily	20.15	20.15	Daily	21.50
18.35	Holidays	20.05	20.15	Mon–Fri	21.30

SIENA

'Cor magis tibi Sena pandit'
(Siena opens her heart to you)

An inscription on the Porta Camollia

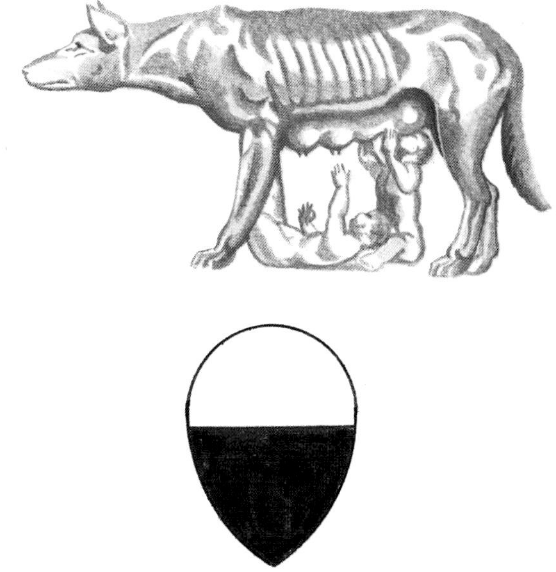

The *Balzana*
the emblem of Siena

The Sienese of the middle ages were unaware that *Sena Julia* had been founded by Augustus, on the site of an Etruscan settlement. So they invented their own founders, Senius and Ascius, the sons of Remus, which explains the many statues to the she-wolf and her twins in the city. Its importance grew in the medieval period from its position on the Francigena, the main road from Rome to northern Europe. Like other Tuscan cities, it declared its independence after the death of the last Margrave of Tuscany in 1115 and in 1186 won the right from the Emperor Barbarossa to mint coins and elect consuls. Without water for industry, the Sienese turned to banking and commerce. This soon brought them into conflict with Florence. As it was a Guelph city, the Sienese declared themselves for the Ghibelline cause, which prompted the Florentines to field an army in 1260 to teach them a lesson. The ensuing battle of Montaperti was a disaster for Florence and the greatest victory in the history of Siena, an event that neither side has ever forgotten. The victory was short-lived. Within ten years the Ghibelline nobles were defeated, allowing the Guelph middle class, the *popolo grosso*, to seize power. Their government, the Nine, lasted longer than any other in the republic. It brought 76 years of peace with Florence, an unprecedented period of public building and the flowering of Sienese art with Duccio, Simone Martini and the brothers Lorenzetti. The aftermath of the Great Plague of 1348 provided the nobles with the opportunity to overthrow the Nine and there followed a long series of unstable governments. In 1526, there was another great victory over the Florentines outside the Porta Camollia, but the end was in sight. Siena was too small to maintain its independence. In 1555, after a 16-month siege, which reduced the population from 40,000 to 8,000, Siena was absorbed, by Spanish arms, into the Grand Duchy of Tuscany. It was joined by plebiscite to the kingdom of Italy in 1859, which became a Republic in 1946.

It was a mortal sin to charge for the lending of money in the middle ages. Usurers could be denied Christian burial, so various devices were invented to get over the problem. The loan became a temporary gift, for which the interest could be a 'thankyou' present, or a penalty for late repayment, the late repayment having previously been agreed. To prevent forgery, each pious usurer would head his documents with a cross, so that anyone altering it would be guilty of blasphemy.

From 1260 to the 16thC, the Florentine gold florin was Europe's 'hard' currency and Florentine and Sienese bankers dominated European trade. They had branches all over the continent, issuing bills of exchange, changing currencies, insuring cargoes and making loans. The commercial rates could be as high as 25 per cent. On loans to monarchs, where the risk was greater, it could be 100 per cent. The Florentine banking system almost collapsed in the 1340s when Edward III of England defaulted. The richest prize for

any bank was the papal accounts. Here the profits of usury were enormous. When Giovanni di Bicci de' Medici won it in 1413, he was able to build the largest banking organization in the world.

For the common people, the *monti di pietà* were formed. These were pawn banks, inspired by the Franciscans, which lent money at little or no interest. In Siena, in 1472, the authorities took the unusual step of forming their own *monte* (the word means accumulation) and installed it in the vacant Castellare Salimbeni, the home of cut-throat bankers who had been exiled. Later, to fund its working capital, it was granted the income from rich *paschi* (pastures). Thus it became the Monte dei Paschi di Siena. Under the terms of its charter it paid 50 per cent of its profits to Siena. Now the world's oldest bank, it still does.

THE CONTRADE

Every person born within the city walls is born into a *contrada*. Membership is for life. It is said that if a woman is obliged to give birth outside her territory, pots of earth will be rushed from the *contrada* to support her bed, so that the new *contradaiolo* will be born on home soil. He, or she, will have two baptisms, one for Christ and one for the *contrada*, the second being at the *contrada* fountain on the *contrada*'s saint's day. Its sons are married in the *contrada* church and may be buried in the *contrada* flag. Loyalty is intense. There were once 59 parishes of urban militia which were the origin of the *contrade*. At the fall of the republic these numbered 23 and were permitted to provide some local government. Six were suppressed by the authorities after riots in 1675 and their territories were swallowed by the remaining seventeen. Other Tuscan cities also had *contrade* but they withered away. Only Siena had the institution that bred the rivalry that was necessary to keep them alive – the Palio.

Aquila

Chiocciola

Onda

Pantera

Selva

Tartuca Civetta Leocorno

Nicchio Torre Valdimontone

Bruco Drago Giraffa

Istrice Lupa Oca

THE PALIO

The Palio is the painted prize for which ten riders gallop bareback around the great Campo of Siena twice a year. It's all over in 90 seconds, but the outcome has been plotted and planned for months before. Lots decide which of the 17 *contrade* will race, which horse they will get and its position on the starting line. To counter luck, secret deals and cunning alliances are formed to impede the chances of traditional enemies. The best horse usually attracts the best jockeys. These are highly paid mercenaries, who are not above being bribed. Once the horses are allocated, grooms are selected to sleep with the animal which is closely guarded at all times, drugs being forbidden, but not unknown. On the day of the race the horse is taken into the church of the *contrada* where it is blessed and sprinkled with holy water. If it should chance to defecate, this is considered a good omen. After a grand parade of all 17 *contrade* whips are distributed to the riders, which they use more against each other than the horse (the only rule forbids taking an opponent's reins). The race begins and ends around 6.30 in the evening, the winner being the first horse, with or without its rider, to complete three laps.

The July 2nd Palio celebrates the miracle of the death of the Spanish soldier whose arquebus blew up as he took a shot at Our Lady

of Provenzano in 1594. The 16th August race is held for the feast of the Assumption.

Contrada Form

Over the past 300 years, the number of victories scored by each *contrada* is:

Oca	*55*
Chiocciola	*49*
Torre	*43*
Valdimontone	*42*
Nicchio	*41*
Tartuca	*40*
Istrice	*38*
Onda	*36*
Bruco	*33*
Lupa	*33*
Selva	*33*
Civetta	*31*
Drago	*31*
Giraffa	*29*
Leocorno	*24*
Aquila	*23*
Pantera	*22*

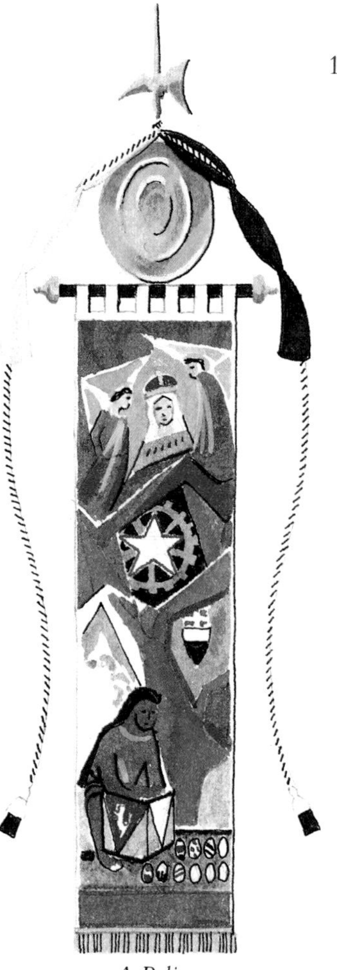

A Palio

Porta Camollia
Outside these gates a vast Florentine army was put to flight in 1526, by prayers to the Virgin and a surprise Sienese sortie. A friend wrote to Machiavelli, telling him of his normal disbelief in the supernatural, 'but this', he said, 'has been like a story from the Bible'.

Chiesa di Fontegiusta
Completed in 1484.

S. Bartolomeo
The church of the contrada *Istrice (porcupine), formerly SS. Vincenzo and Anastasio.*

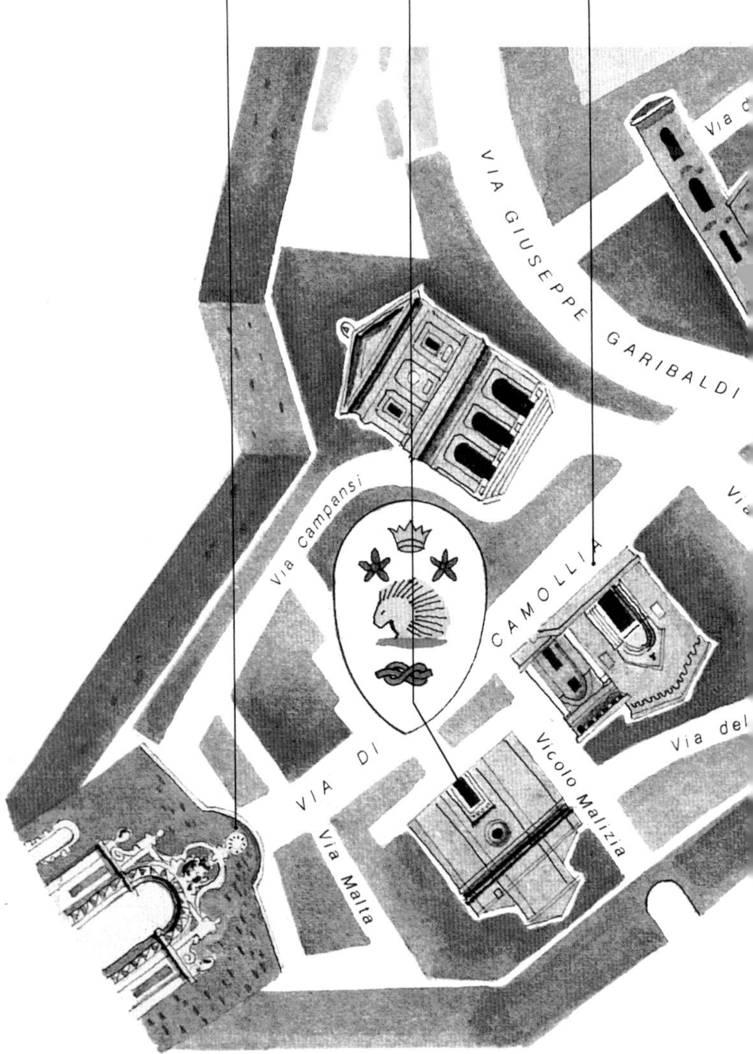

S. Stefano
A 12thC church rebuilt in 1641. It contains a Madonna and Child with Saints by Andrea Vanni (1400).

Post and Telegraph Office

S. Maria delle Nevi
The altarpiece of Our Lady of the Snows was painted in 1477 by Matteo di Giovanni.

S. Caterina
The contrada *Drago (dragon) made this their church in 1789.*

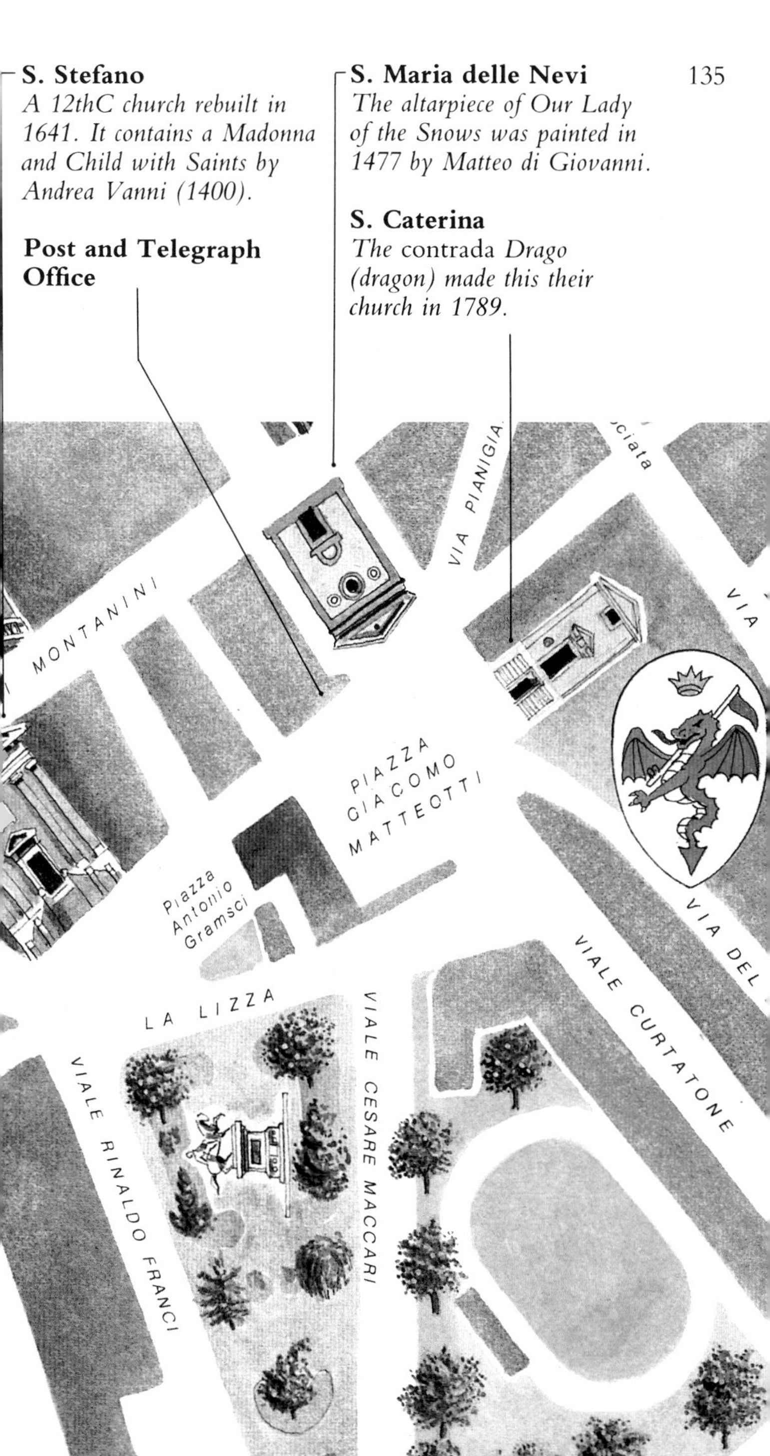

S. Domenico
Begun in 1226, the church has the only authentic portrait of St Catherine, painted by her friend Andrea Vanni. It hangs in the chapel where she took the veil and where some of her miracles occurred. Sodoma's frescos are considered to be masterpieces.

S. Caterina in Fontebranda
The church of the contrada *Oca (goose), also called the 'infamous ones' for their record Palio victories.*

Fonte Branda
One of the oldest fountains in the city.

St Catherine of Siena

The mystic Caterina Benincasa was born in this house, the daughter of a wealthy dyer, in 1347. She had visions from the age of 5 and became a lay sister of the Dominicans in 1363. Her social views, her conversions and her work with victims of the plague and leprosy earned her a following. In 1376 she went to Avignon where she persuaded Pope Gregory XI to return to Rome. Her Dialogue *is an Italian classic and she is a patron saint of Italy. Hours: 9.00–12.30 and 14.00–17.30.*

Fonte Nuova
It was new in the 14thC.

S. Rocco
The 16thC church of the Lupa (she-wolf) contrada.

Castellare Salimbeni
The home of the world's oldest bank, the Monte dei Paschi di Siena, founded here in 1472. The bank now owns the other two buildings on the square, left, Palazzo Tantucci (1548) and right, Palazzo Spannocchi (1473). It also houses the Economics and Banking faculties of the University of Siena.

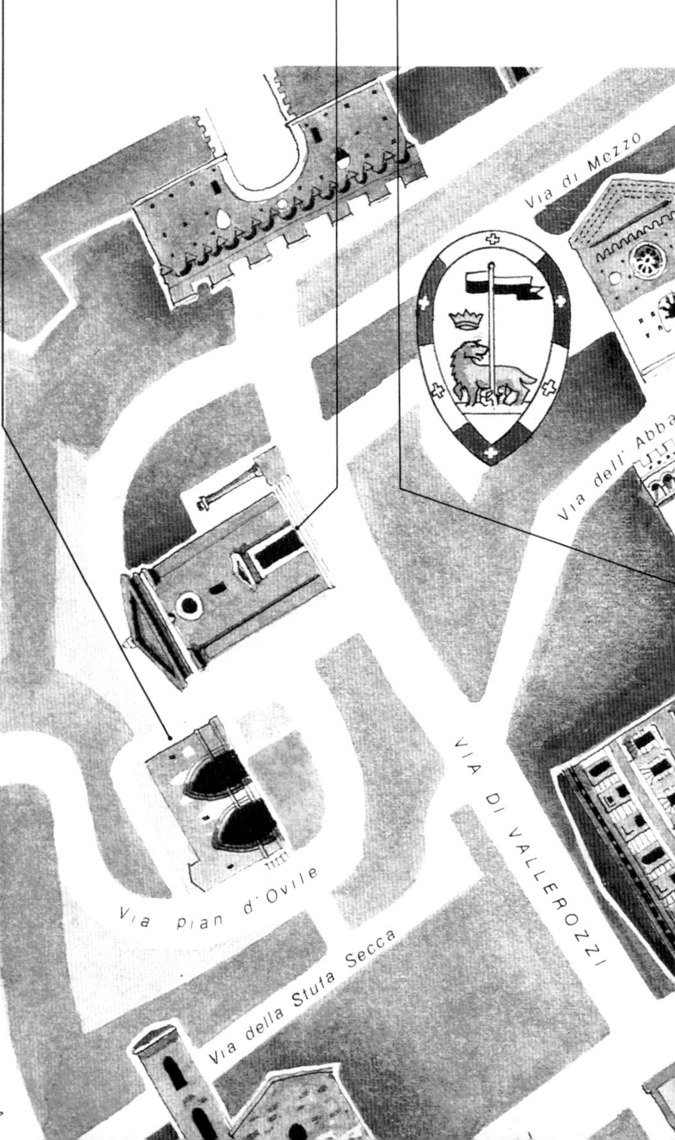

S. Donato
Begun about 1119.

Palazzo Tolomei
After pitched battles between the Salimbeni and the Tolomei clans in 1341, the Salimbeni chose to end the vendetta by inviting their rivals to a reconciliation lunch at which a Tolomei and a Salimbeni sat alternately. As the eldest Salimbeni rose, saying 'Now my children, to each his own,' each Salimbeni produced a knife, and turned and murdered his guest. The tombs of the victims line a staircase in S. Francesco.

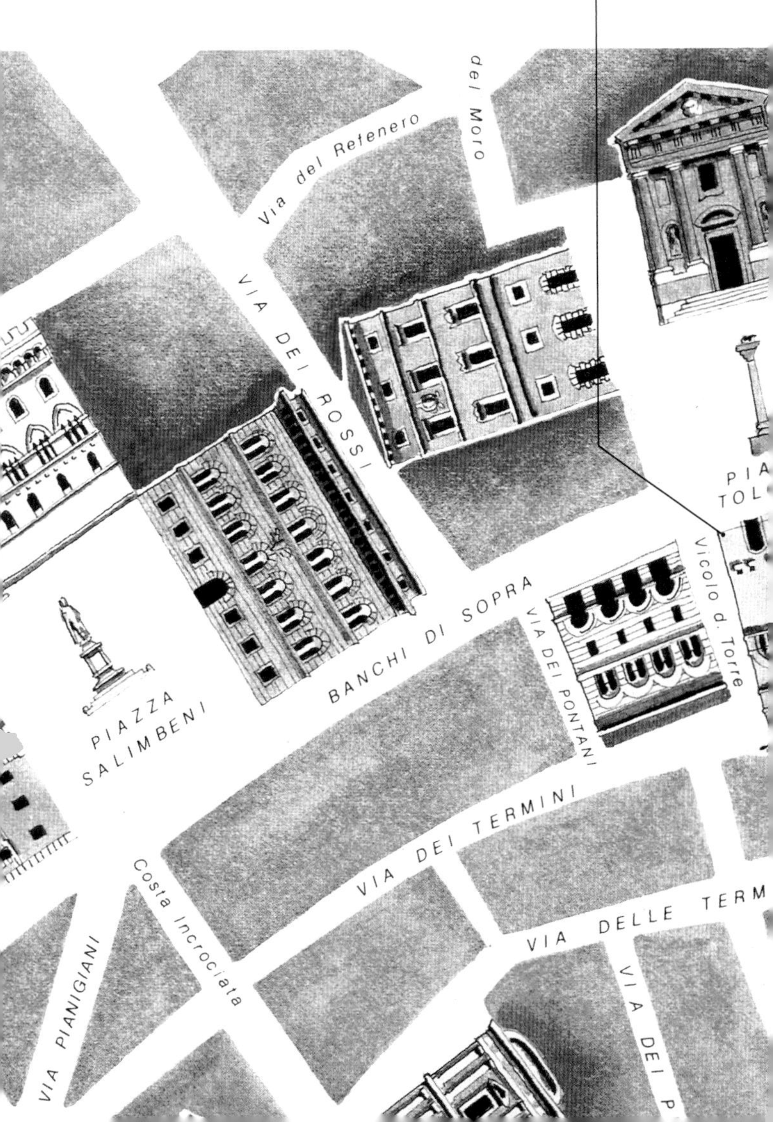

S. Cristoforo
(1720) The church of the contrada *Civetta (owl).*

Palazzo Sansedoni
1216, extended in 1339.

Il Campo
The 'field', lying between the three terzi *has always been the heart of Siena. Its present shape was formalized under the rule of the Nine who divided the Campo into nine strips to remind us of their good government. It has been the scene of battles, riots, bullfights and, of course, the Palio.*

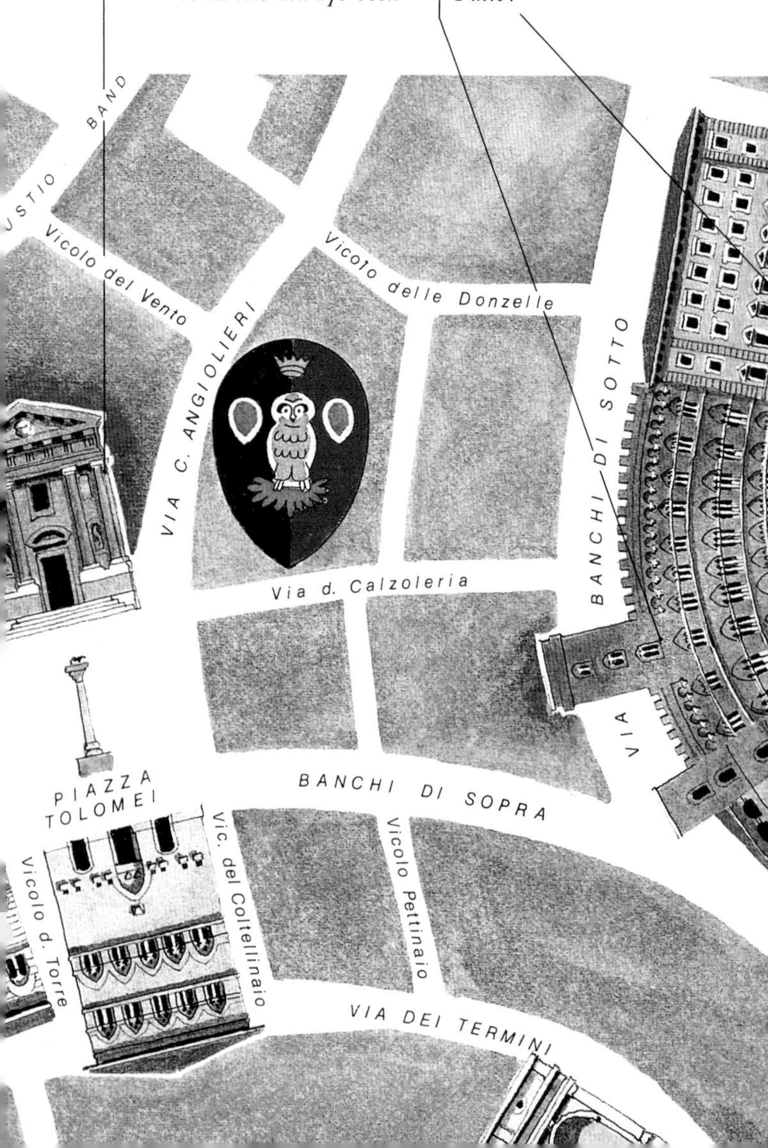

Fonte Gaia
The Gay Fountain is a 19thC copy of Jacopo della Quercia's creation of 1409–19, one of the first works of the Renaissance.

Palazzo Pubblico
Built by the Nine (from 1297) the Torre del Mangia rises 86 metres and is named after an early ringer of the bell Sunto (S. Maria Assunta). The chapel at the foot of the tower was built in 1334.

LANDING

Sienese ceramics dating from the 16–18thC

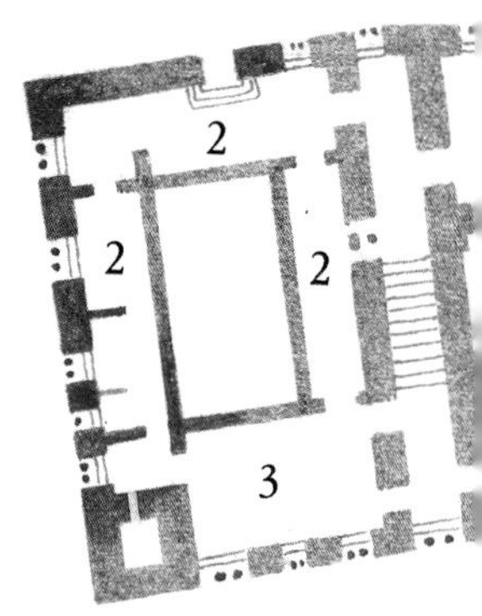

ROOM 2

PICTURE GALLERY
Dutch, German, Italian and Sienese works of the 16–18thC

ROOM 3

SALA DEL RISORGIMENTO
Six frescos of the Birth of Modern Italy by the Sienese artists Amos Cassioli and Cesare Maccari (1886–91)

ROOM 4

SALA DI BALIA
Spinello Aretino
Frescos (1407) of the life of the Sienese Pope Alexander III and his conflict with the Emperor Federico Barbarossa

ROOM 5

ANTECHAMBER
Wooden sculpture, caskets, etc.
Matteo di Giovanni
Madonna and Child with Angels

ROOM 6

SALA DEL CONCISTORO
Bernardo Rossellino
Sculpted doorway
Beccafumi
Frescos of Civil Virtues
Three Gobelin tapestries: Earth, Air and Fire

ROOM 7

Carved she-wolf with twins

ROOM 8

Taddeo di Bartolo
Frescos (1414) of virtues, ancient Romans, and a huge St Christopher

ROOM 9

CHAPEL OF THE NINE
Taddeo di Bartolo
Frescos of the life of the Virgin (1408)
Sodoma
Holy Family with St Leonard

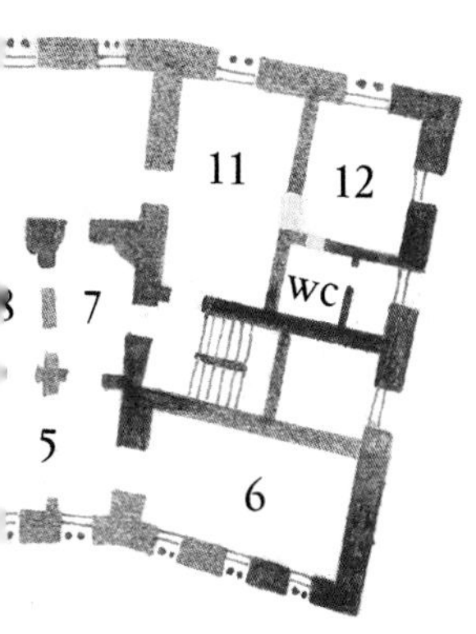

Domenico di Niccolò
21 choir stalls with carved panels illustrating articles of the Creed

ROOM 10

SALA DEL MAPPAMONDO

It is named after a map of the world by Lorenzetti which no longer exists.

LEFT WALL:
Simone Martini
Maestà
Simone painted it in 1315 but had to restore it six years later because of damp.

RIGHT WALL:
Simone Martini(?)
The work is dated 1328 and was believed to represent Guidoriccio da Fogliano riding to the siege of Montemassi, but some experts think it was painted much later. Controversy rages.

BELOW CENTRE:
Duccio
The Submission of a Castle to Siena

EITHER SIDE:
Sodoma
St Ansano and St Victor

FACING WINDOW:
Lippo Vanni
Battle of Val di Chiana
Francesco d'Andrea and Giovanni di Cristoforo Ghini
Battle of Poggio Imperiale

BELOW:
Sts Bernardino and Catherine

ROOM 11

THE SALA DELLA PACE

Ambrogio Lorenzetti
Allegory of Good Government
Effects in Town
Effects in the Country
Allegory of Bad Government
Painted in 1339 for the Nine.

ROOM 12

SALA DEI PILASTRI

Neroccio di Bartolomeo
S. Bernardino in the Campo
Guido da Siena
Maestà

Hours: 9.00–19.00; winter 9.00–18.00.

144 **Baptistery**

This was built under the Duomo in 1316–25. Lorenzo di Pietro, called Vecchietta, frescoed the vaults and the walls of the apse. The hexagonal font, still in use for baptisms, is by Jacopo della Quercia and is decorated with 6 bronze bas-reliefs. Two, the Baptism of Christ and the Capture of the Baptist, are by Lorenzo Ghiberti; Herod's Banquet is by Donatello; the Birth of the Baptist and the Baptist Preaching are by Giovanni di Torino and Zacharias by della Quercia (all c. 1427).

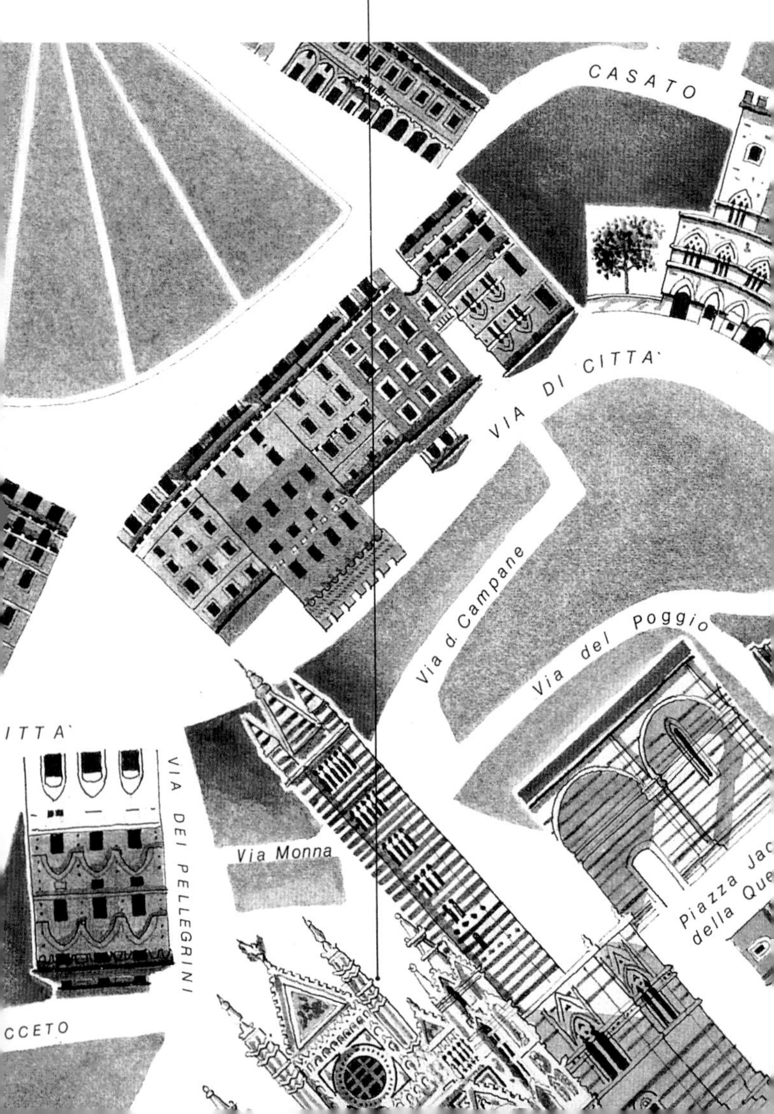

Palazzo Chigi-Saracini
This is the home of the renowned Accademia Musicale Chigiana whose master classes each July to September have attracted musicians such as Segovia, Pablo Casals and others who enjoy playing amongst the artworks of the Chigi-Saracini collection.

Pinacoteca Nazionale
The last descendant of the Buonsignori family donated this building (built c. 1440) to the city to be used as the National Picture Gallery of Siena. Over 700 works are housed in 28 rooms, the world's finest collection of Sienese painting.

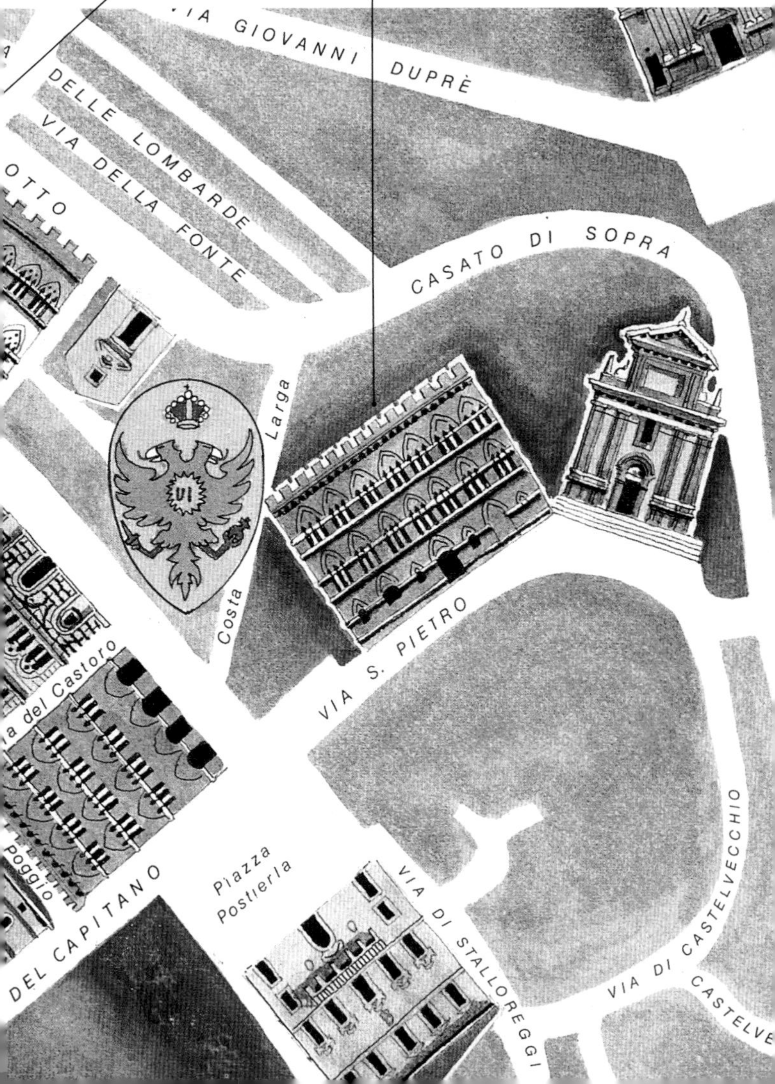

PINACOTECA

This is a selection of the finest examples from the 700 works of Sienese art on display. The exhibition is chronological, beginning on the second floor. Hours: 9.00–14.00 (13.00 holidays).

ROOM I

Altarcloth
Christ Blessing and 6 scenes (1215), one of the first Sienese paintings
Guido da Siena
Panel: Transfiguration, The Entry into Jerusalem, Resurrection of Lazarus

ROOM II

Guido da Siena
St Peter with 6 scenes
Madonna and Child (1262)
Sienese School
The Baptist with 12 scenes

ROOM III

Duccio
Madonna and Child with Saints
Niccolò di Segna
Madonna della Misericordia
Duccio
Madonna and Child with SS. Agostino, Paolo, Pietro and Domenico

ROOM IV

Duccio
Madonna dei Francescani

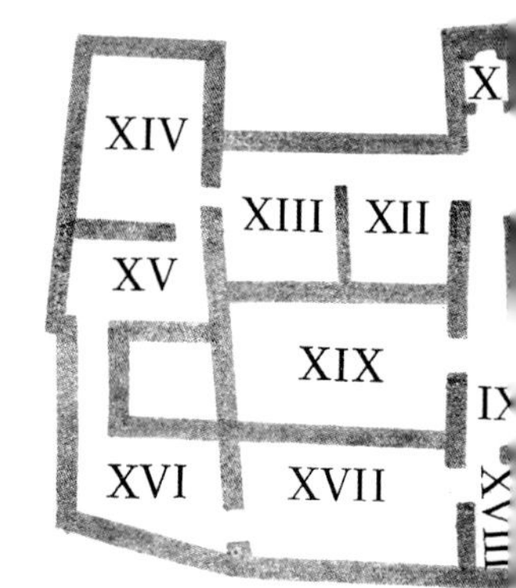

ROOM V

Bartolo di Fredi
Adoration of the Magi (c. 1375)

ROOM VI

Simone Martini
Madonna and Child
Lippo Memmi
Madonna and Child
Maestro di Palazzo Venezia
Mystical Marriage of St Catherine of Alexandria

ROOM VII

Ambrogio Lorenzetti
Triptych: Madonna and Child and Saints (c. 1330)
City by the Sea
A Castle by a Lake (two of the earliest known European landscapes)
Madonna and Child

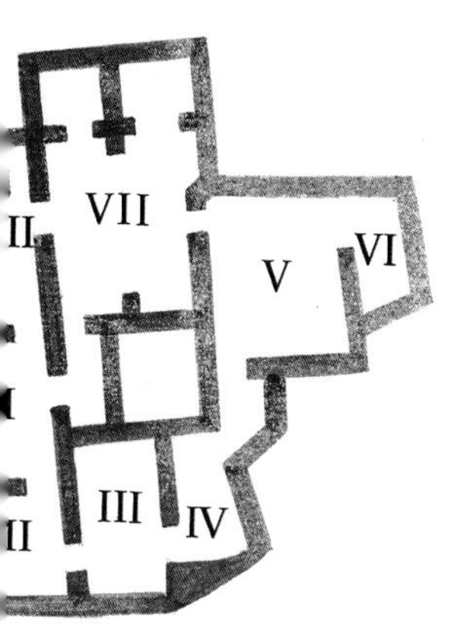

Maestà
Annunciation (signed 1344)
Pietro Lorenzetti
Madonna and Child with St Nicholas of Bari and the Prophet Elijah
Carmelite altarpiece
Sts Agnes and Catherine
Paolo di Giovanni Fei
Nativity with Saints

ROOM IX

Domenico di Bartolo
Madonna and Child with Angels (signed 1433)
Michelino da Besozzo
Marriage of St Catherine of Alexandria with the Baptist and St Anthony Abbot

ROOM XIII

Giovanni di Paolo
The Last Judgement, Paradise and the Inferno
Sassetta
The Last Supper
St Anthony Abbot beating the Devil
Giovanni di Paolo
Madonna of the Umiltà

ROOM XIV

Matteo di Giovanni
Madonna and Child with Angels
Neroccio
Madonna and Child with Saints (c. 1475)
Francesco di Giorgio Martini
Nativity with Saints Thomas Aquinas and Bernardino
Neroccio
Madonna and Child with Saints Michael Archangel and Bernardino (triptych)

ROOM XVIII

Sano di Pietro
The Madonna recommends Siena to Pope Callisto III
Madonna and Child with Saints (1444)

ROOM XIX

Francesco di Giorgio
Coronation of the Virgin

ROOMS XXX–XXXIII

Sodoma
Nativity, Deposition, Judith, Scourging of Christ

S. Sebastiano
This 16thC church belongs to the contrada *Selva (forest).*

Palazzo Arcivescovile
The archbishop's palace. Inside is the famous painting of the nursing Madonna, the Madonna del Latte, by Ambrogio Lorenzetti.

Spedale di S. Maria della Scala
The civic hospital is said to have been founded in the 9thC for pilgrims. The Hall of the Pilgrims has ten 15thC frescos illustrating aid to the poor. In the nearby church is a bronze Christ Risen by Vecchietta.

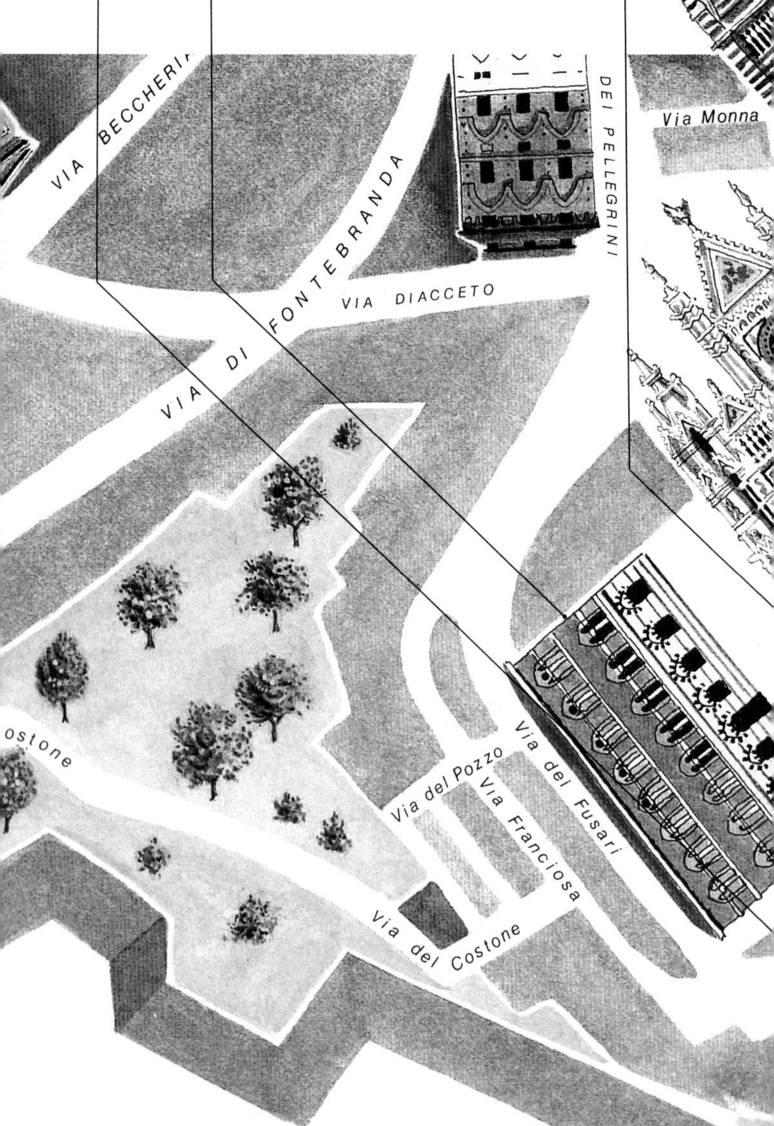

Museo dell'Opera Metropolitana
Built into the nave of the abandoned new cathedral, the museum is on three floors. Ground Floor: Sculptures from the Duomo facade by Giovanni Pisano and school. 1st Floor: Works by Duccio including the Maestà (1311). 2nd Floor: Reliquaries, A Crucifixion by Giovanni Pisano and the Madonna of the Large Eyes (c. 1220).

Palazzo della Prefettura
Built in the 15thC, it was altered for the Medici by Buontalenti in the 16thC.

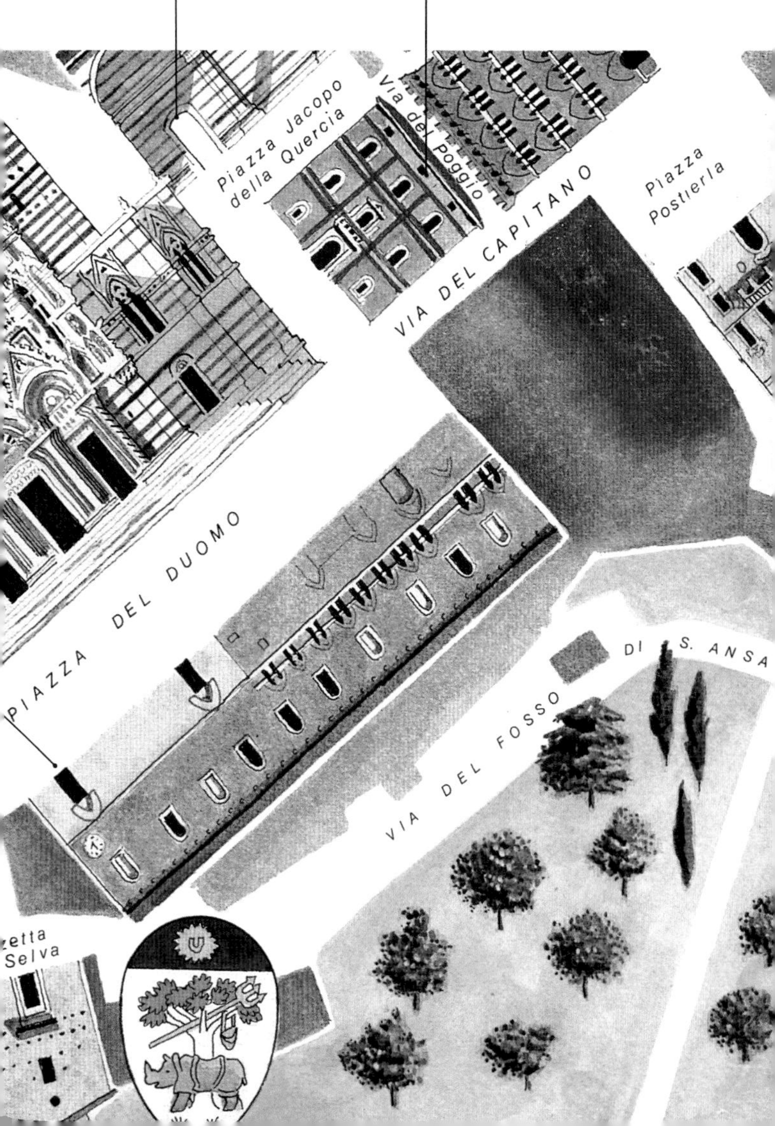

IL DUOMO

S. MARIA DELLA ASSUNTA

The Virgin Mary became Queen of Siena on Thursday 3 September 1260 as a Florentine army gathered to destroy the city. The Bishop led a procession of the populace to the Duomo, where he placed the keys of the city upon the altar of the Virgin and besought her protection. The next day the numerically fewer Sienese sallied forth and miraculously massacred the Florentines at the battle of Montaperti. The cathedral was begun in 1196 on the site of an earlier church (and possibly on the site of an even earlier temple to Minerva). It was almost complete in 1339, when it was found to be too small for the growing population and it was decided to build the grandest cathedral in Italy, using the present building as the transept of the new one. Work began, but the population problem was solved in 1348 with the disastrous appearance of the plague, the Black Death which halved the

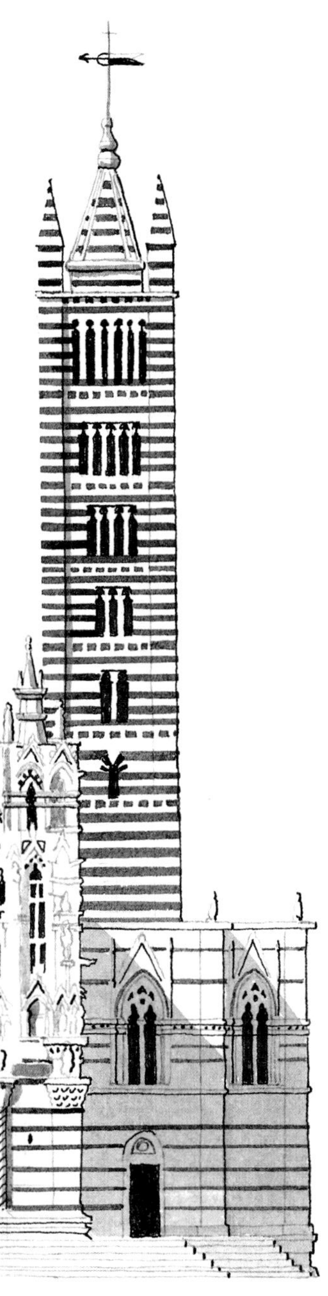

citizens' numbers. The survivors then found fatal flaws in the construction and the project was abandoned. The new nave is now used for outdoor concerts.

Campanile
Completed in 1313.
Central Angel
By Tommaso Redi (1639).
The Mosaics
Venetian works of 1887.
Upper Facade
This gothic work was created in the second half of the 14thC. Around the window are the four evangelists surrounded by prophets and patriarchs.
Lower Facade
By Giovanni Pisano and his students, who began in 1285. Many of the statues are copies, the originals having been removed to the cathedral museum.
Sts Joachim and Anne
The story of the parents of the Virgin were carved over the main door by Tino da Camaino in the early 14thC.
Bronze Door
A modern work by Enrico Manfrini (1958).

THE

Sacristy
Two paintings of S. Bernardino preaching in Siena

Pavement
This was laid down over six centuries beginning in 1373.
1. The Sacrifice of Isaac
2. Joshua and the Battle with the Amorite Kings (1426)
3. Moses on Mount Sinai

Pulpit
by Nicola Pisano (1267)
4. Moses Brings Forth Water from the Rock
5. The Story of Judith
6. Slaughter of the Innocents
7. Expulsion of Herod

Chapel of St John the Baptist
Frescos by Pinturicchio

Donatello
Bronze St John the Baptist
Tomb of Bishop Pecci

Piccolomini Library
Built by Pius III in memory of his uncle, Pius II, it has many illuminated choir books and 10 frescos of the Life of Enea Piccolomini (Pius II) by Pinturicchio.

The Sibyls
The Sibyls were supposed to have prophesied the coming of Christ to the classical world.
8. Albunean Sibyl
9. Samian Sibyl (1483)
10. Phrygian Sibyl
11. Hellespontian Sibyl
12. Libyan Sibyl

13. The Five Virtues, Fortitude, Justice, Mercy Prudence and Temperance
14. David with his Sling
15. David the Psalmist
16. Goliath (1423)
17. The Story of Samson
18. The Emperor Sigismund and his Ministers (1434)
19. The Death of Absalom

Central Hexagon
Seven scenes from the story of Elijah by Domenico Beccafumi (c. 1524)
20. The Story of Jephthah

Chapel of the Madonna del Voto
Six times the citizens have placed the keys to the city before this image and prayed for deliverance from crisis. The first was on the eve of the battle of Montaperti, the last in June 1944.
21. The Wheel of Fortune; the oldest work (1373)
22. The Persian Sibyl
23. Allegory of the Hill of Knowledge by Pinturicchio
24. The Cumaean Sibyl
25. The Imperial Eagle
26. The Delphic Sibyl
27. Sienese She-wolf with other named Tuscan Cities
28. The Cimmerian Sibyl
29. Hermes Trismegistus passes Wisdom to the Eastern and Western Worlds
30. The Erythraean Sibyl

Palazzo Piccolomini delle Papesse
Built for Caterina Piccolomini, the sister of Pope Pius II.

S. Giovanni Battista
This has been the church of the contrada *Aquila (eagle) since 1788. They adopted the imperial eagle as their symbol on the occasion of a friendly visit of the Emperor Charles V in 1536. Few survived the second visit of his troops in 1555.*

S. Pietro alle Scale
Inside is Rutilio Manetti's Repose in Egypt (1621).

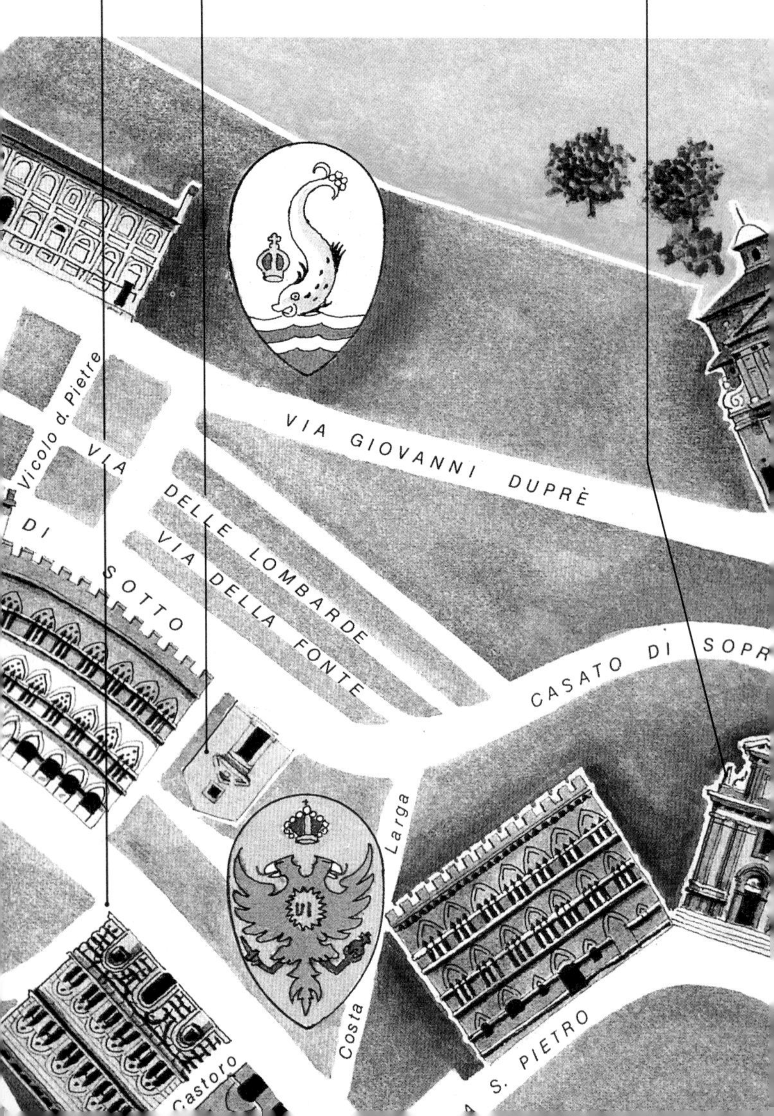

S. Giuseppe
The 16thC church of the contrada *Onda (wave).*

S. Agostino
Dedicated to the local saint Agostino Novello, who died in 1309. In the Piccolomini Chapel are the Slaughter of the Innocents by Matteo di Giovanni, a Madonna and Child and Saints by Ambrogio Lorenzetti, a triptych of S. Agostino by Simone Martini (1330) and the Adoration of the Magi, a masterpiece by Sodoma. The church also contains a Crucifixion by Perugino.

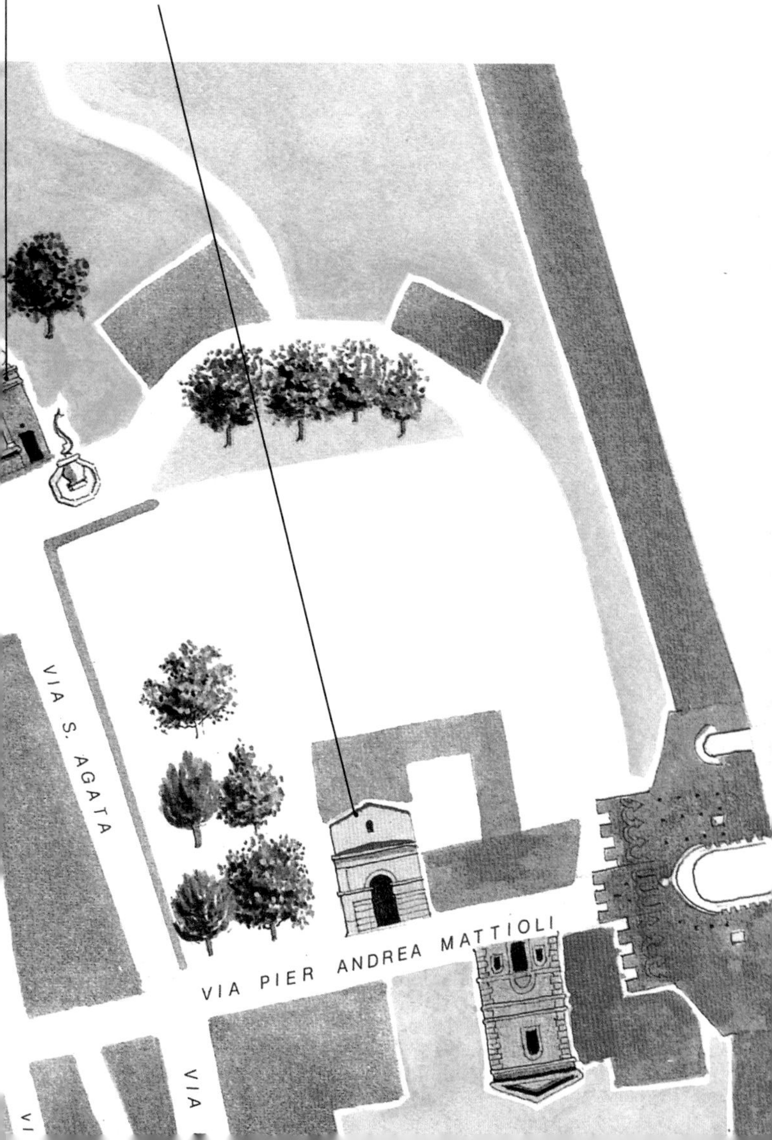

Via della Diana
Dante mocked the Sienese in the Purgatorio *(XIII, 153) for 'looking for Diana's bed'. They had dug a deep hole near by to tap the river Diana that was supposed to flow beneath the city, but like its namesake, the river was a myth.*

S. Antonio di Padova
The contrada *Tartuca (tortoise) built this church in 1684. Their fountain at the top of the street is a boon for thirsty travellers.*

S. Ansano

Palazzo Marsili

Oratorio della Madonna de Rosario
This 18thC building is the seat of the contrada *Chiocciola (snail). Running street battles between them and the Tartuca so inflamed the city in the 19thC that peace had to be arranged with a special service in the chapel on the Campo. The enmity persists and re-runs of the old skirmishes break out at Palio time.*

S. Lucia
The church of the contrada *Pantera (panther). Their oratorio is S. Ansano.*

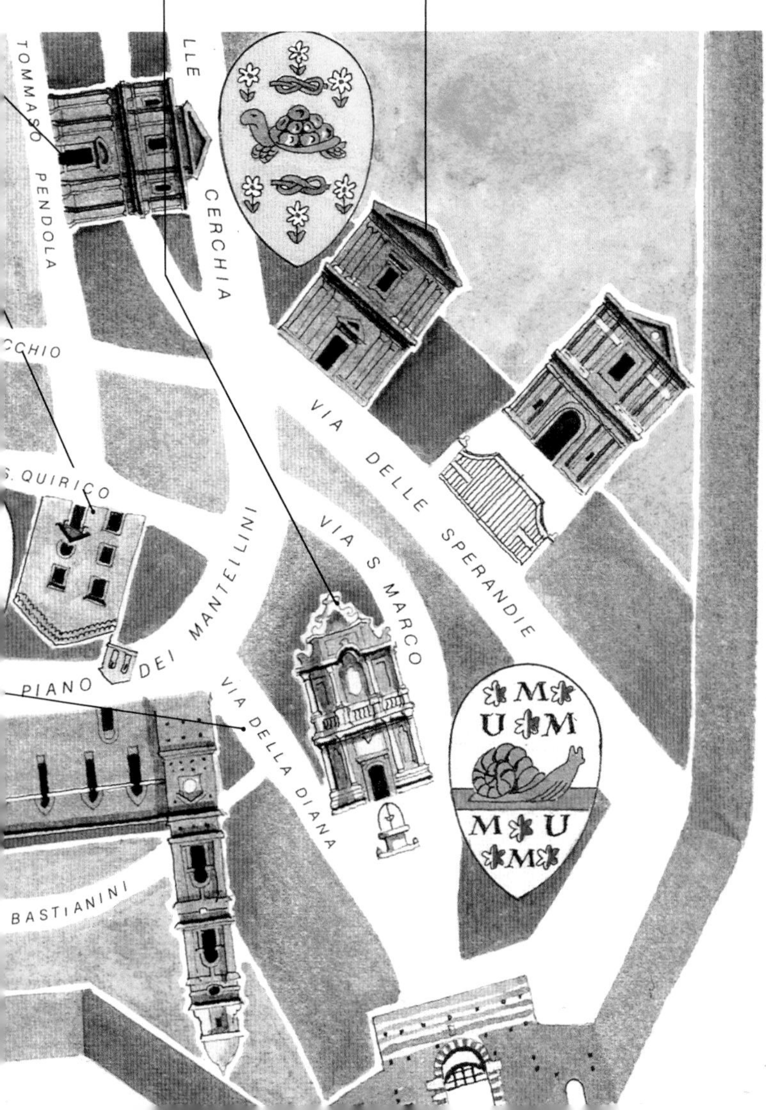

Oratorio della Visitazione
The seat of the contrada *Bruco (caterpillar), it was built in 1680.*

S. Francesco
The Franciscans arrived in 1326 and completed the basilica 150 years later. Inside it is decorated with frescos by Ambrogio and Pietro Lorenzetti.

Oratorio di S. Bernardino
S. Bernardino of Siena, known as the peoples' preacher, often taught here,

but his condemnation of usury cannot have been popular in a city of bankers. The upper Oratorio was frescoed by Sodoma.

S. Maria di Provenzano
A fallen woman with an incurable disease prayed to an outdoor icon of the Madonna in 1594 and was miraculously cured. To house so potent an image, this church was built within the year. It is the seat of the contrada *Giraffa.*

S. Vigilio
Rebuilt in the 18thC.

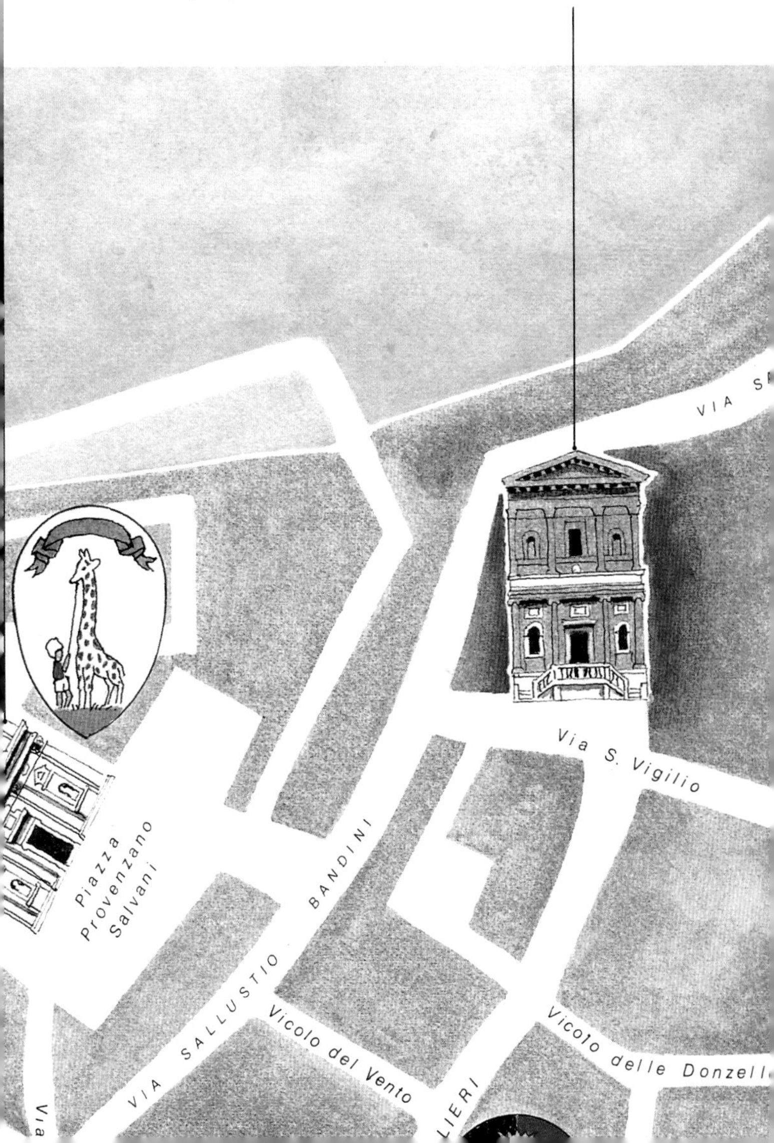

Archivo di Stato
Boccaccio's will and a unique series of painted bindings for the municipal account books can be seen. Hours: 9.00–14.00 (13.00 Saturday).

S. Giovanni Battista
The church of the contrada *Leocorno (unicorn), 1563.*

Loggia del Papa
It was built in 1462 to celebrate the election of the Sienese Pope, Pius II, born Enea Silvio Piccolomini. A former poet laureate of the Emperor Frederick III, he is the only pope to have left poems, a novella and an autobiography.

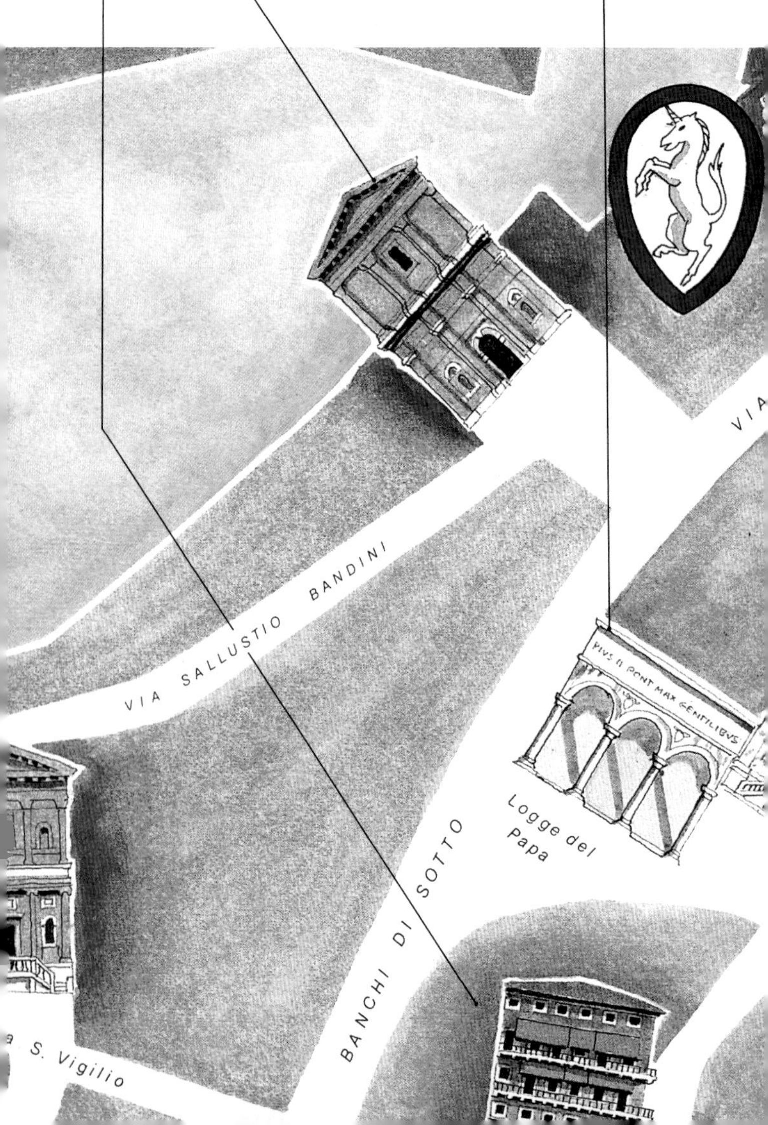

S. Giorgio
This was rebuilt on the site of an earlier church in 1741.

S. Martino
The church was built in 1537, the facade added in 1613. Within is Lorenzo Cini's painting of the victory at Camollia.

S. Giacomo
Built in 1531 to celebrate the victory over the Florentines outside the Porta Camollia, this is the church of the contrada *Torre. Next door is their museum of Palio trophies and Sodoma's The Way to Calvary. Admission on application to the* Priore.

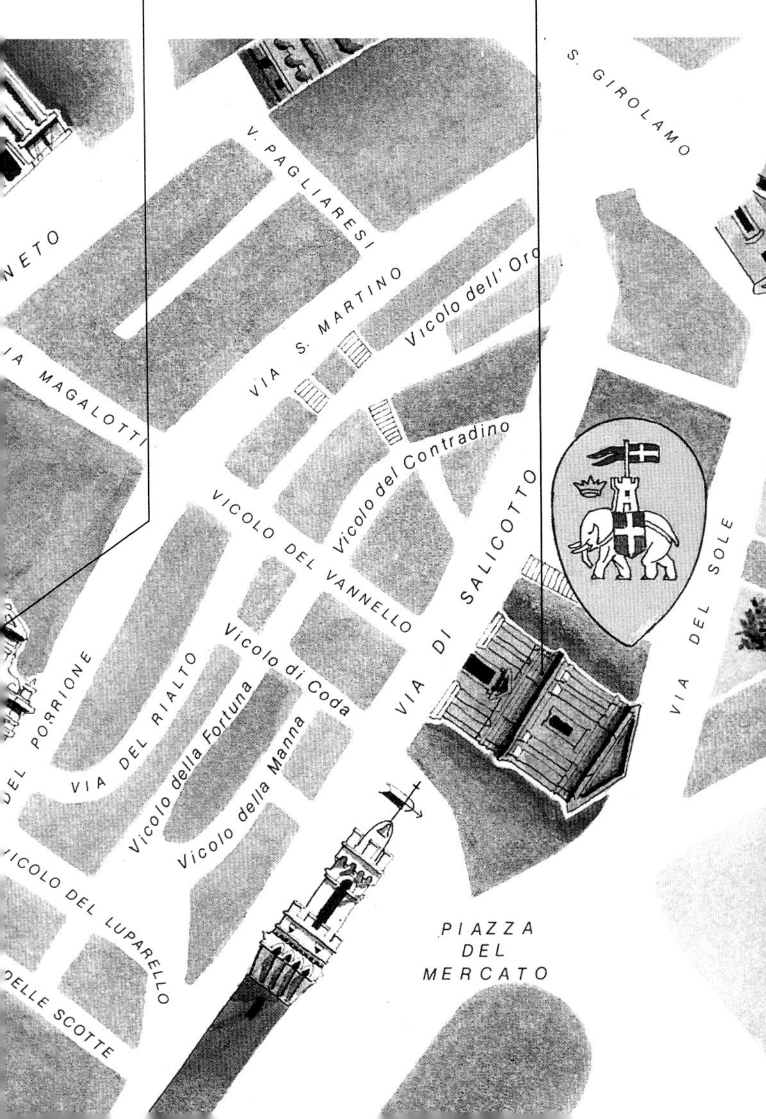

S. Spirito

Within its 1519 portal is a crucifix by Sano di Pietro and works by Vanni and Sodoma.

Sodoma

Giovanni Antonio Bazzi arrived in Siena in 1505 to become one of the city's most famous artists. Vasari says he was named for his homosexuality, but his tax return (c. 1531) tells another story: 'I have an ape and a talking raven which I keep in a cage so that he can't teach a theological ass to talk . . . I possess three beastly she animals, which are women,

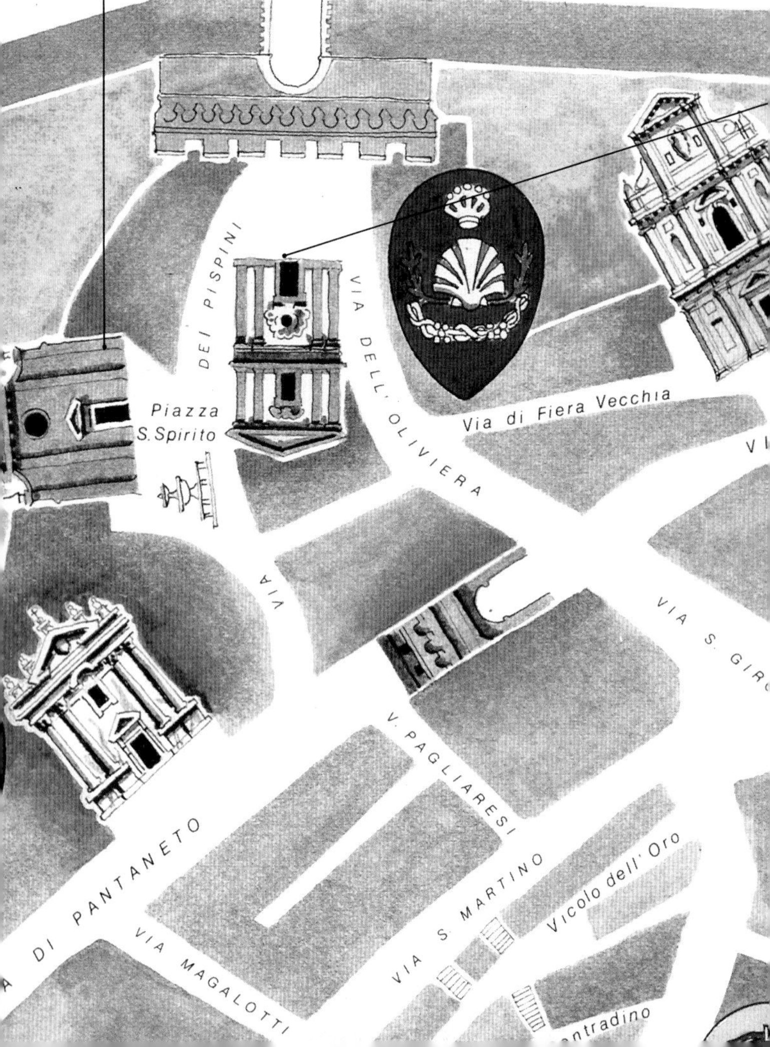

and I also have thirty grown-up children which is a real encumbrance . . . and as twelve children exempt a man from taxation, I recommend myself to you. Farewell.'

S. Gaetano
Built in the 17thC for the contrada *Nicchio (shell).*

S. Girolamo
Founded in the 14thC.

S. Maria dei Servi
This contains Marcovaldo's masterpiece of 1261, the Madonna del Bordone, the Madonna del Popolo by Lippo Memmi and the Massacre of the Innocents by Pietro Lorenzetti.

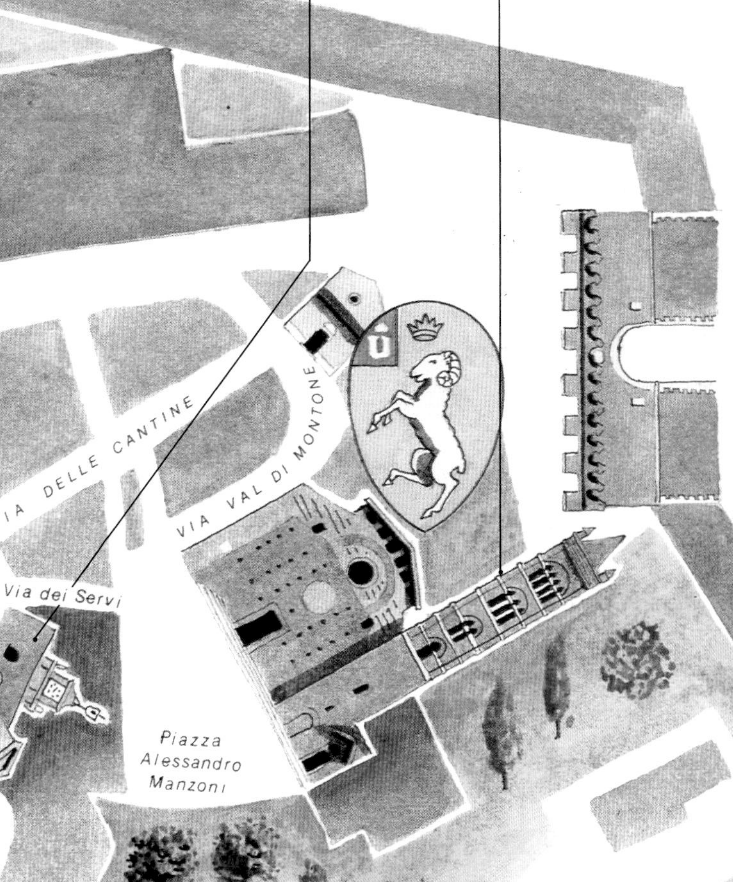

RESTAURANTS

Tullio ai Tre Cristi
Vicolo Provenzano 1
T.280608
Closed Mon.
AMEX
$$+14%

Guido
Vicolo Pettinaio
T.280042
Closed Mon.
AMEX
$$+15%

L'Angolo
Via Garibaldi 15
T.289251
Closed Sat.
AMEX DINERS MASTER VISA
$$+10%

Grotta S. Caterina–da Bagoga
Via della Galluzza
T.282208
Closed Mon.
$$

Mariotti–Da Mugolone
Via dei Pellegrini 8
T.283235
Closed Sun. evening and Thurs.
AMEX DINERS MASTER VISA $$

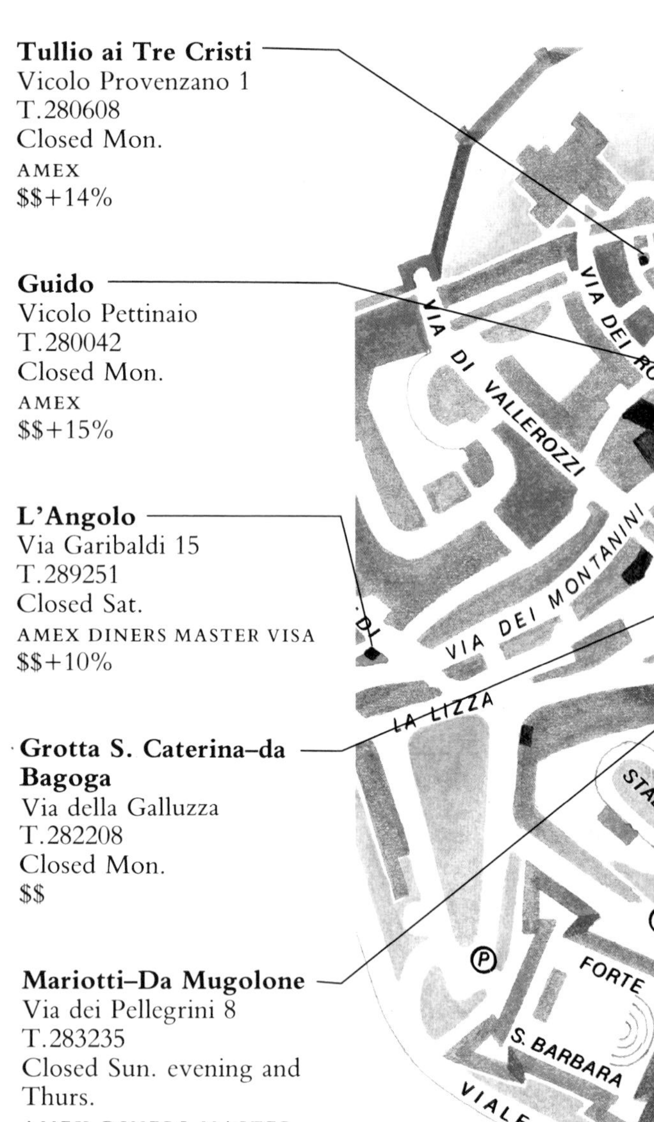

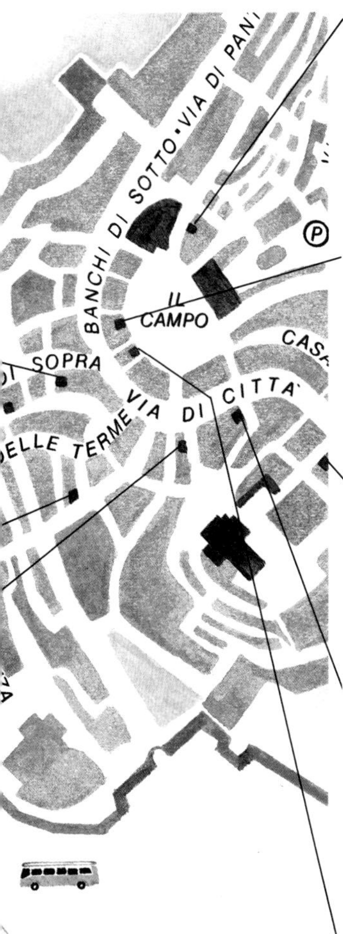

Nello la Taverna
Via del Porrione 28
T.289043
Closed Sun. evening and Mon.
AMEX DINERS MASTER VISA
$$+13%

Il Campo
Piazza del Campo 50
T.280725
Closed Tues.
AMEX DINERS MASTER VISA
$$+12%

Al Marsili
Via del Castoro 3
T.47154
Closed Mon.
AMEX DINERS MASTER
$$$+15%

La Campane
Via delle Campane 6
T.284035
Closed Sun. in Nov., July and Aug. Mon. other months
AMEX DINERS MASTER VISA
$$+12%

Al Mangia
Piazza del Campo 42
T.281121
Closed Mon.
AMEX DINERS MASTER VISA
$$$+12%

RESTAURANTS

Baldini
Via il Prato 96
T.287663
Closed Sat.
AMEX DINERS MASTER VISA
$$

Gourmet
Via il Prato 68
T.294766
Closed Sun.
AMEX DINERS
$$+15%

La Carrabaccia
Via Palazzuolo 190
T.214782, bookings only
Closed Sun. midday
Mon., and Aug.
AMEX DINERS MASTER VISA
$$

Del Carmine
Piazza del Carmine 18
T.218601
Closed Sun. (Sept.–April);
closed Sat. other months
AMEX DINERS MASTER VISA
$$

Drago Verde
Via del Leone 50
T.224002
Closed Sun. and midday
Sat.
AMEX DINERS VISA
$$$+12%

Il Profeta
Borgo Ognissanti 93
T.212265
Closed Sun., Mon., and Aug.
AMEX DINERS VISA
$$$+12%

Tredici Gobbi
Via Porcellana 9
T.298769
Closed Sun., Mon., and Aug.
AMEX DINERS VISA
$$$+10%

Buca Lapi
Via del Trebbio 1
T.213768
Closed Sun. and midday Mon.
AMEX DINERS VISA
$$$+12%

Buca Mario
Piazza Ottaviani 16
T.214179
Closed Wed. and midday Thurs.
AMEX VISA
$$$

Natale
Lungarno Acciaiuoli 80
T.213968
Closed Tues.
MASTER VISA
$$, service extra

RESTAURANTS

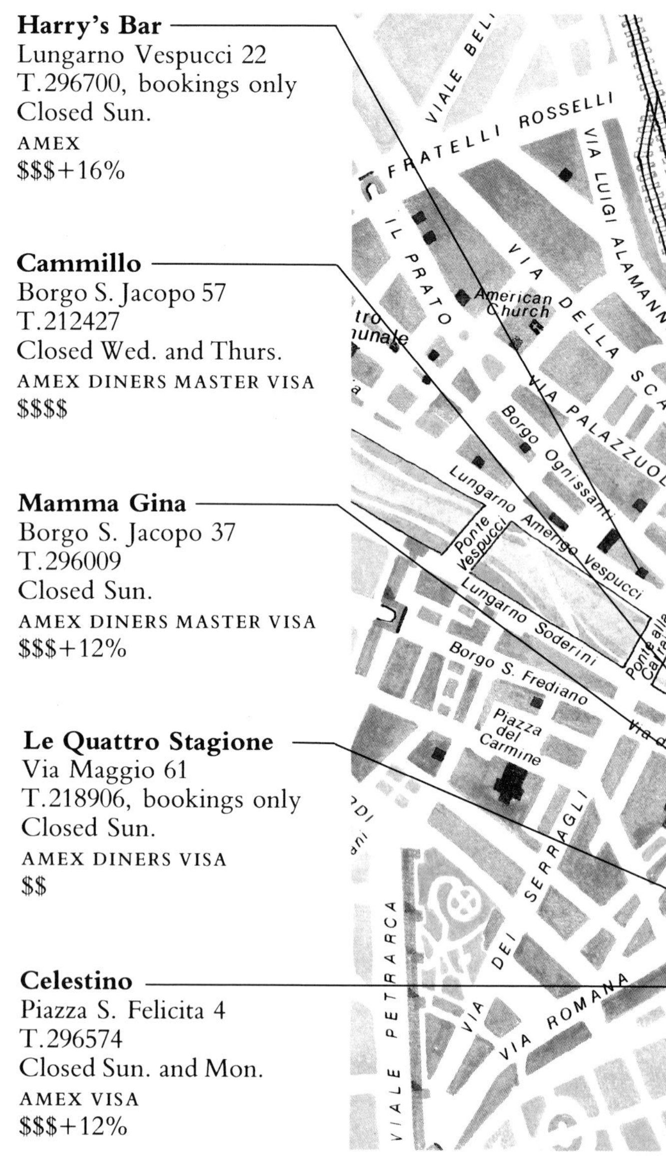

Harry's Bar
Lungarno Vespucci 22
T.296700, bookings only
Closed Sun.
AMEX
$$$+16%

Cammillo
Borgo S. Jacopo 57
T.212427
Closed Wed. and Thurs.
AMEX DINERS MASTER VISA
$$$$

Mamma Gina
Borgo S. Jacopo 37
T.296009
Closed Sun.
AMEX DINERS MASTER VISA
$$$+12%

Le Quattro Stagione
Via Maggio 61
T.218906, bookings only
Closed Sun.
AMEX DINERS VISA
$$

Celestino
Piazza S. Felicita 4
T.296574
Closed Sun. and Mon.
AMEX VISA
$$$+12%

IN FLORENCE

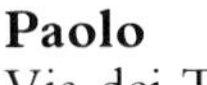

Paolo
Via dei Tavolini 12
T.216215
Closed Tues.
AMEX DINERS MASTER VISA
$$+12%

Il Cavallino
Via delle Farine 6
T.215818
Closed Tues. evening and Wed.
AMEX DINERS MASTER VISA
$$+12%

Da Dante
Via delle Terme 23
T.294566, bookings only
Closed Sun. and midday Mon.
AMEX DINERS MASTER VISA
$$$$

Antico Fattore
Via Lambertesca 1
T.261215
Closed Sun. and Mon.
AMEX
$$

Bordino
Via Stracciatella 9
T.213048
Closed Sun.
AMEX DINERS MASTER VISA
$$

RESTAURANTS

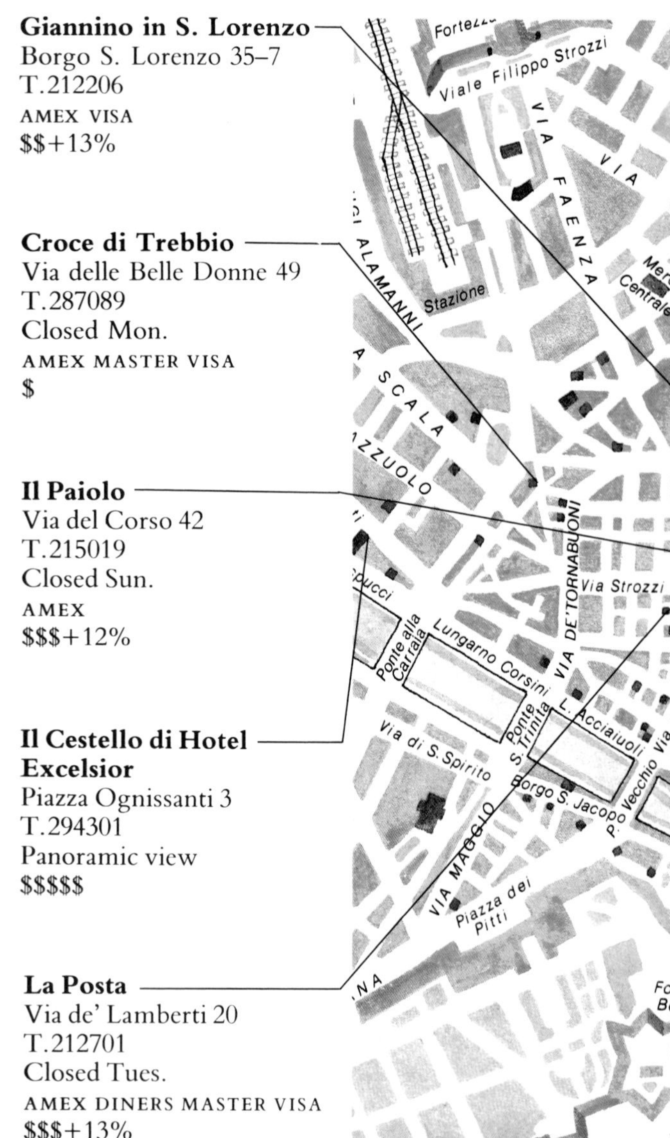

Giannino in S. Lorenzo
Borgo S. Lorenzo 35–7
T.212206
AMEX VISA
$$+13%

Croce di Trebbio
Via delle Belle Donne 49
T.287089
Closed Mon.
AMEX MASTER VISA
$

Il Paiolo
Via del Corso 42
T.215019
Closed Sun.
AMEX
$$$+12%

Il Cestello di Hotel Excelsior
Piazza Ognissanti 3
T.294301
Panoramic view
$$$$$

La Posta
Via de' Lamberti 20
T.212701
Closed Tues.
AMEX DINERS MASTER VISA
$$$+13%

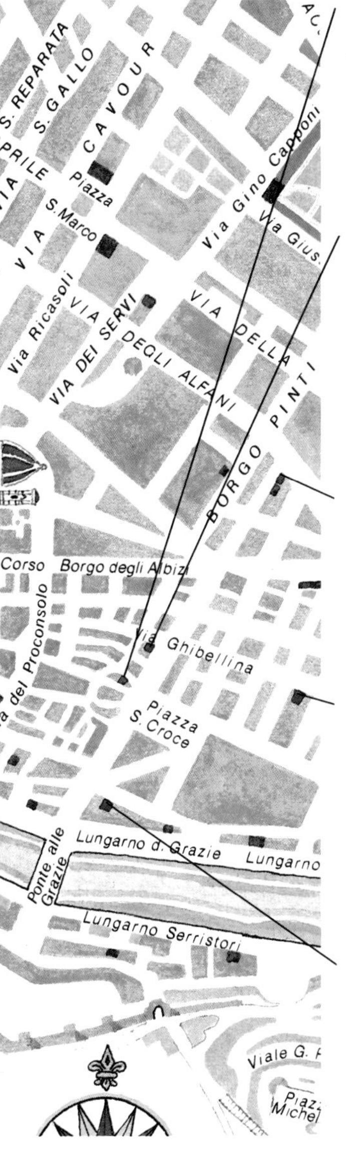

Leo in S. Croce
Via Torta 7
T.210829
Closed Mon.
AMEX DINERS MASTER VISA
$$+12%

***Enoteca Pinchiorri**
Via Ghibellina 87
T.242777, bookings required
Closed Sun. and midday Mon.
$$$$$+12%

***Da Noi**
Via Fiesolana 46
T.242917, bookings only
Closed Sun. and Mon.
$$$

Dino
Via Ghibellina 51
T.141452
Closed Sun. evening and Mon.
AMEX DINERS MASTER VISA
$$+12%

Il Fagioli
Corso Tintori 47
T.244285
Closed Sun. (also Sat. in summer) and Aug.
$$

HOTELS

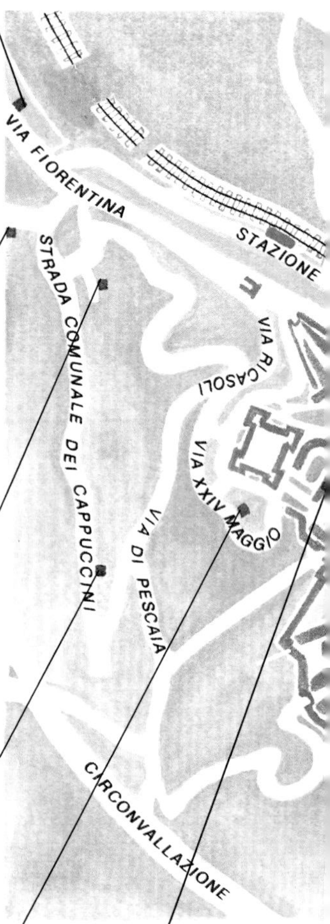

Grand Hotel Villa Patrizia
Via Fiorentina 58
T.50431; telex 574366
33 rooms
AMEX DINERS MASTER VISA
★★★

Park Hotel
Via di Marciano 18
T.44803; telex 571005
69 rooms; 15thC building in a park
AMEX DINERS MASTER VISA
★★★★

Garden
Via Custoza 2
T.47056; telex 574239
64 rooms; swimming-pool
AMEX DINERS VISA
★★★

Castagneto
Via dei Cappuccini 39
T.45103
11 rooms; no restaurant
★★★

Lea
Viale 24 Maggio 10
T.283207
13 rooms
★★

Chiusarelli
Viale Curtatone 9
T.280562
50 rooms
★★★

IN SIENA

Villa Scacciapensieri
Via di Scacciapensieri 10
T.41442; telex 573390
27 rooms; garden; swimming-pool
AMEX DINERS MASTER VISA
★★★★

Minerva
Via Garibaldi 72
T.284474
49 rooms
AMEX DINERS MASTER VISA
★★

Jolly Excelsior
La Lizza
T.288448; telex 573345
126 rooms
AMEX DINERS MASTER VISA
★★★★

Duomo
Via Stalloreggi 38
T.289088
14 rooms
AMEX VISA
★★

Palazzo Ravizza
Piano dei Mantellini 34
T.280462
28 rooms; 17thC, with garden
AMEX DINERS MASTER VISA
★★★

Certosa di Maggiano
Strada di Certosa 82
T.288180; telex 574221
14 rooms; 14thC monastery; garden; swimming-pool
AMEX DINERS MASTER VISA
★★★★

HOTELS IN

Villa Medici
Via il Prato 42
Post 50123; T.261331
Telex 570179
107 rooms; swimming-pool
AMEX DINERS MASTER VISA
★★★★★

Michelangelo
Via Fratelli Rossi 2
Post 50123; T.278711
Telex 571113
138 rooms
AMEX DINERS MASTER VISA
★★★★

Grand Hotel
Piazza Ognissanti 1
Post 50123; T.6813861
Telex 570055
Roof-garden restaurant
AMEX DINERS MASTER VISA
★★★★★

Excelsior
Piazza Ognissanti 3
Post 50123; T.264201
Telex 570022; 205 rooms
Top-floor restaurant
AMEX DINERS MASTER VISA
★★★★★

Grand Hotel Minerva
Piazza S. Maria Novella 16
Post 50123; T.284555
Telex 570414
107 rooms; swimming-pool
AMEX DINERS MASTER VISA
★★★★

Croce di Malta
Via della Scala 7
Post 50123; T.218351
Telex 570540
98 rooms; swimming-pool
AMEX DINERS MASTER VISA
★★★★

FLORENCE

Majestic
Via del Melarancia 1
Post 50123; T.264021
Telex 570628
104 rooms
AMEX DINERS MASTER VISA
★★★★

Pullman Astoria
Via del Giglio 9
Post 50123; T. 298095
Telex 571070
90 rooms
AMEX DINERS MASTER VISA
★★★★

De la Ville
Piazza Antinori 1
Post 50123; T.261805
Telex 570518
75 rooms
AMEX DINERS MASTER VISA
★★★★

Savoy
Piazza della Repubblica 7
Post 50123; T. 283313
Telex 570220
101 rooms
AMEX DINERS MASTER VISA
★★★★★

Baglioni
Piazza Unità Italiana 6
Post 50123; T.218441
Telex 570225; 195 rooms
Roof-garden restaurant
AMEX DINERS MASTER VISA
★★★★

Lungarno
Borgo S. Jacopo 14
Post 50125; T.264211
Telex 570129
71 rooms
AMEX DINERS MASTER VISA
★★★★

HOTELS IN

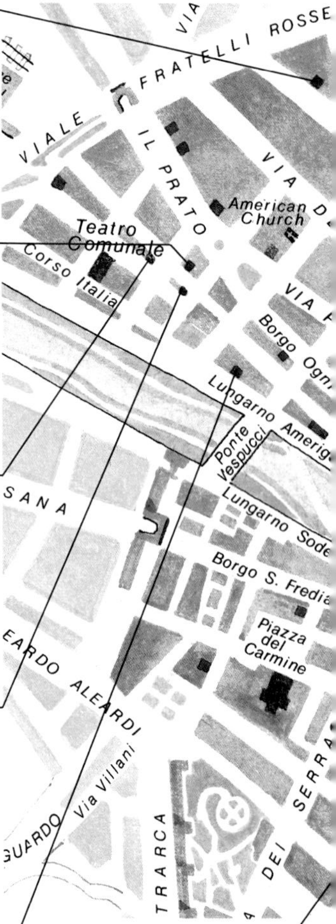

Londra
Via Jacopo da Diacceto 16
Post 50123; T.262791
Telex 571152
105 rooms
AMEX DINERS MASTER VISA
★★★★

Montebello Splendid
Via Montebello 60
Post 50123; T.298051
Telex 574009
37 rooms
AMEX DINERS MASTER VISA
★★★★

Anglo American
Via Garibaldi 9
Post 50123; T.282114
Telex 570289
107 rooms
AMEX MASTER VISA
★★★★

Kraft
Via Solferino 2
Post 50123; T.284273
Telex 571523; 66 rooms
Roof-garden restaurant
Swimming-pool
AMEX DINERS MASTER VISA
★★★★

Principe
Lungarno Vespucci 34
Post 50123; T.284848
Telex 571400
20 rooms
★★★★

Beacci Tornabuoni
Via Tornabuoni 3
Post 50123; T.268377
31 rooms
AMEX DINERS VISA
★★★

Aprile
Via della Scala 6
Post 50123; T.216237
29 rooms
AMEX MASTER VISA
★★★

Milano Terminus
Via de' Cerretani 10
Post 50123; T.283372
Telex 580515
82 rooms
AMEX DINERS MASTER VISA
★★★★

Calzaiuoli
Via Calzaiuoli 6
Post 50122; T.212456
Telex 580589
37 rooms
AMEX DINERS
★★★

Della Signoria
Via delle Terme 1
Post 50123; T.214530
Telex 571561
27 rooms
AMEX DINERS MASTER VISA
★★★★

Augustus
Piazzetta dell'Oro 5
Post 50123; T.283054
Telex 570110
67 rooms
AMEX MASTER VISA
★★★★

Pitti Palace
Via Barbadori 2
Post 50125; T.282257
40 rooms
AMEX VISA
★★

HOTELS IN

Pierre
Via de' Lamberti 5
Post 50123; T.217512
Telex 573175
39 rooms
AMEX DINERS VISA
★★★★

Hermitage
Vicolo Marzio
1 Piazza del Pesce;
Post 50122; T.287216
19 rooms
VISA
★★★

Continental
Lungarno Acciaiuoli 2
Post 50123; T.282392
Telex 580525
61 rooms; terrace view
AMEX DINERS MASTER VISA
★★★

Fiorino
Via Osteria del Guanto 6
Post 50122; T.210579
23 rooms
★★

Balestri
Piazza Mentana 7
Post 50122; T.214743
50 rooms
AMEX VISA
★★★

Silla
Via de' Renai 5
Post 50125; T.2342888
29 rooms
AMEX DINERS MASTER VISA
★★

FLORENCE

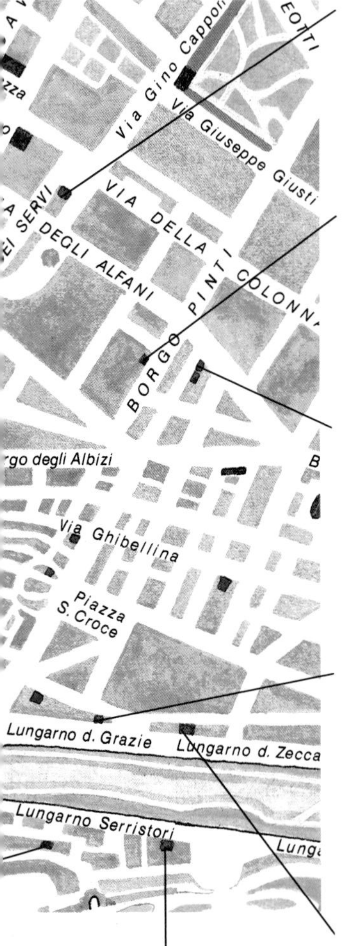

Loggiato dei Serviti
Piazza SS. Annunziata 3
Post 50122; T.219165
17 rooms
AMEX DINERS MASTER VISA
★★★

Monna Lisa
Borgo Pinti 27
Post 50123; T.2479751
20 rooms
AMEX DINERS VISA
★★★★

Ariston
Via Fiesolana 40
Post 50122; T.2476980
Telex 571603
26 rooms
AMEX MASTER VISA
★★

Plaza Hotel Lucchesi
Lungarno della Zecca Vecchia 38
Post 50122; T.264141
Telex 570302
97 rooms
AMEX DINERS MASTER VISA
★★★★

San Remo
Lungarno Serristori 13
Post 50125; T.2342823
19 rooms
AMEX MASTER VISA
★★

Jennings Riccioli
Lungarno delle Grazie 2
Post 50122; T. 244751
50 rooms; *pensione* of E. M. Forster's *Room with a View*
AMEX MASTER VISA
★★★

CALENDAR

JANUARY

Florence
The opera season continues at the Teatro Comunale until the middle of the month.

1–9°C 35–48°F

FEBRUARY

Florence
Carnival is celebrated the week before Lent.

2–11°C 36–52°F

MARCH

Florence
International fashion collections are shown in the Sala Bianca of the Pitti Palace (Room 15, p. 43) or at the Palazzo delle Esposizione inside the Fortezza da Basso (p. 58).

4–11°C 40–59°F 

CALENDAR

7–20°C 45–68°F

APRIL

Florence
On Easter Sunday, a cart laden with fireworks is ignited outside the Duomo at midday by a 'dove' flying down a wire from the high altar. Floral displays decorate the Piazza della Signoria. A crafts exhibition is held in the Fortezza da Basso.

11–23°C 53–74°F

MAY

Florence
An annual Iris Festival is held in Piazza Michelangelo to celebrate the city's symbol, the lily of Florence. The ***Maggio Musicale*** *of opera, ballet and concerts is held until the end of June. Singing crickets are sold on Ascension Day in the Cascine.*

14–28°C 58–83°F

JUNE

Fiesole
The ***Estate Fiesolana*** *– festival of concerts, ballet and theatre held in the Roman amphitheatre until September.*

Florence
St John the Baptist's day (24th) is marked by fireworks and a 16thC game of football in the Piazza della Signoria.

JULY

Siena
The first of the two Palios is held on the 2nd. It is preceded by rehearsals and a grand procession. The ***Accademia Musicale Chigiana*** *begins its summer festival, which continues until September.*

17–31°C 62–89°F

AUGUST

Siena
The second Palio is held on the 16th in honour of the Feast of the Assumption.

16–31°C 61–88°F

SEPTEMBER

Greve
The Chianti Classico wine fair is held in the first week.

Florence
On the eve of the Nativity (7th) children run through the streets with paper lanterns for the ***Festa delle Rificolone*** *(lanterns).*

14–27°C 58–81°F

CALENDAR

OCTOBER

Florence
The winter fashion collections are unveiled at the Pitti Palace. An antiques fair is held every odd year at the Palazzo Strozzi.

10–20°C 51–69°F

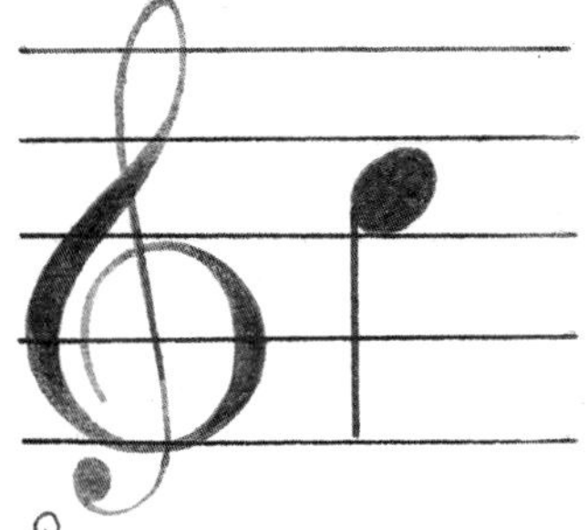

NOVEMBER

Florence
The main concert season opens in the Teatro Comunale and continues until the middle of December.

5–14°C 42–58°F

DECEMBER

Florence
The opera season opens at the Teatro Comunale until the middle of January.

2–10°C 37–50°F

EMERGENCY!

113

POLICE
FIRE
AMBULANCE
The number is free. You will be asked which service you need.

AMBULANCE
FIRST AID
21 22 22

NIGHT DOCTOR
47 78 91

POLICE
Carabinieri (emergency) 112
Vigili Urbani 29 20 12
Questura 49 771
Railway Police 21 22 96

AIRLINES
Alitalia 26 30 51
(Reservations) 27 88
10–12 Lungarno Acciaiuoli
British Airways 21 86 55
36–8 Via della Vigna Nuova
Pan Am 28 27 16
4 Lungarno Acciaiuoli
TWA 28 46 91
Piazza S. Trinita 1

ROAD SERVICE
Car breakdown 116

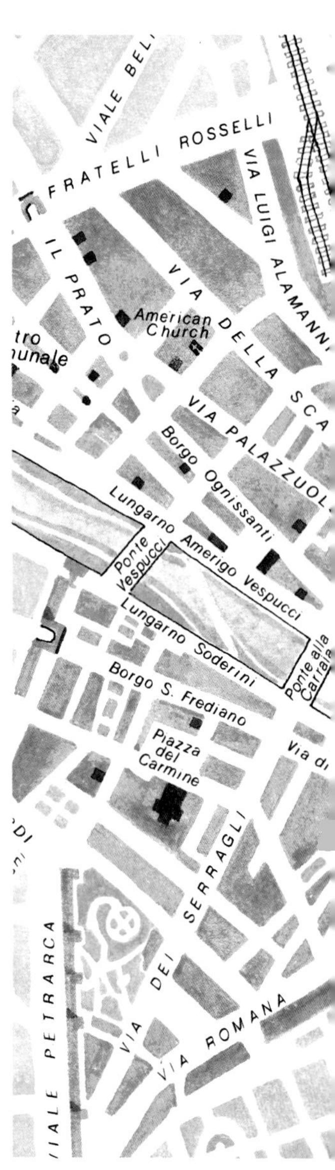

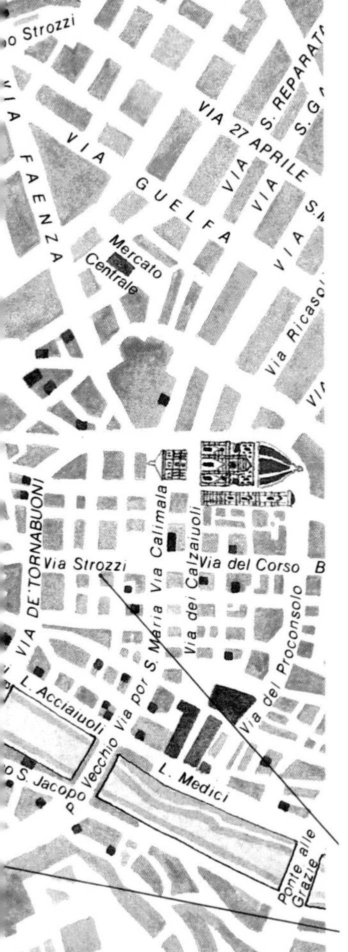

CONSULATES
Austria 21 53 52
Belgium 28 20 94
Denmark 21 10 07
France 21 35 09
Germany, West 29 47 22
Great Britain 28 41 33
Monaco 58 78 97
Netherlands 47 52 49
Norway 22 80 316
San Marino 21 08 64
Spain 21 21 73
Sweden 29 68 34
Switzerland 22 24 34
USA 29 82 76

LOST PROPERTY
Lost Property Office
19 Via Circondaria
36 79 43
For property lost in taxis report to the Vigili Urbani.

TRAVEL INFORMATION
Railway 27 87 85
Airport Pisa (050) 28 088
Road news 06 42 12

POST OFFICE
53–5 Via Pietrapiana

AMERICAN EXPRESS
49 Via de' Guicciardini

TOURIST OFFICE
15 Via Tornabuoni
21 65 44/5

BIBLIOGRAPHY

ACTON, HAROLD, AND CHANEY, EDWARD, eds., *Florence, a Traveller's Companion*, 1986

AVERY, CHARLES, *Florentine Renaissance Sculpture*, 1970

BENTLEY, JAMES, *A Guide to Tuscany*, 1987

BERENSON, BERNARD, *The Italian Painters of the Renaissance*, 1930

BORSOOK, EVE, *The Companion Guide to Florence*, 5th ed., 1988

BRUCKER, GENE ADAM, *Florence 1138–1737*, 1984

CAGLIARITANO, UBALDO, *The History of Siena*, Siena, 1986

CELLINI, BENVENUTO, *Autobiography* (1728)

CHAMBERLAIN, E. R., *The World of the Italian Renaissance*, 1982

CLARK, KENNETH, *The Florence Baptistery Doors*, 1980

DAVID, ELIZABETH, *Italian Food*, 1954; new ed., 1987

FERRAGAMO, SALVATORE, *Shoemaker of Dreams*, 1957

HALE, J. R., *Florence and the Medici*, 1977

HALE, J. R., ed., *Concise Encyclopedia of the Italian Renaissance*, 1981

HAY, DENYS, *The Italian Renaissance*, 2nd ed., 1977

HIBBERT, CHRISTOPHER, *The Rise and Fall of the House of the Medici*,1979

HIGSON, JOHN W., *A Historical Guide to Florence*, 1973

MACADAM, ALTA, *Blue Guide Florence*, 4th ed., 1988

MACADAM, ALTA, *Blue Guide Northern Italy*, 8th ed., 1984

MCCARTHY, MARY, *The Stones of Florence and Venice Observed*, 1972

MICHELIN, *Italy*

ORIGO, IRIS, *The Merchant of Prato*, new ed., 1963

PLUMB, J. H., *The Pelican Book of the Renaissance*, 1982

RAISON, LAURA, ed., *Tuscany: an Introduction*, 1986

RAY, CYRIL, *The Wines of Italy*, 1966

ROMER, ELIZABETH, *The Tuscan Year*, 1984

ROOT, WAVERLEY, *The Cooking of Italy*, 1969

ROSS, JANET, *The Lives of the Early Medici as Told in their Correspondence*, 1910

VASARI, GIORGIO, *Lives of the Artists* (1555)

WASSERMAN, SHELDON AND PAULINE, *Italy's Noble Red Wines*, 1986

INDEX

SELECTED STREET INDEX

FLORENCE

SIENA

EMERGENCY
S I E N A

113

POLICE
FIRE
AMBULANCE
The number is free. You will be asked which service you need.

POST OFFICE

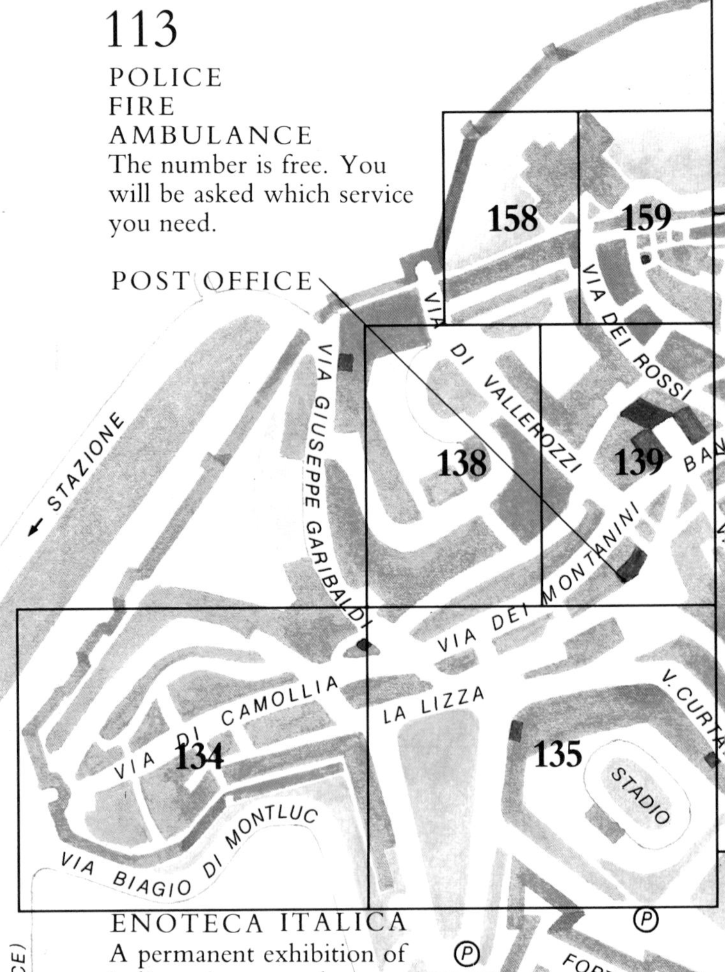

ENOTECA ITALICA
A permanent exhibition of Italian wines open by appointment only, but a bar is open daily.